An Irresistible Kiss

"It is getting late, sir. I think I will go to my room now . . . if you will please excuse me."

Lord Pelham extended a hand to assist her. After a second of mute protest, she put her hand in his, and the instant he gripped it his duty to a guest and his honor as a gentleman were forgotten, submerged in the tide of desire that had been swelling in him from his first glimpse of her. One quick pull and his arms encircled her before she could regain her balance. He kissed her then, savoring the sweetness of that trembling mouth. All too soon she began to struggle, twisting in his arms and attempting to turn away. He closed his eyes and released her.

He half expected her to bolt for the door, but she did not bolt, nor did she cower. When she spoke there was only the tiniest tremor discernible.

"That was a dastardly thing to do."

The Gamester's Daughter

by

Dorothy Mack

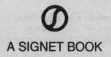

A SIGNET BOOK

SIGNET
Published by the Penguin Group
Penguin Putnam Inc., 375 Hudson Street,
New York, New York 10014, U.S.A.
Penguin Books Ltd, 27 Wrights Lane,
London W8 5TZ, England
Penguin Books Australia Ltd, Ringwood,
Victoria, Australia
Penguin Books Canada Ltd, 10 Alcorn Avenue,
Toronto, Ontario, Canada M4V 3B2
Penguin Books (N.Z.) Ltd, 182–190 Wairau Road,
Auckland 10, New Zealand

Penguin Books Ltd, Registered Offices:
Harmondsworth, Middlesex, England

First published by Signet, an imprint of Dutton Signet,
a member of Penguin Putnam Inc.

First Printing, March, 1998
10 9 8 7 6 5 4 3 2 1

Copyright © Dorothy McKittrick, 1998
All rights reserved

 REGISTERED TRADEMARK—MARCA REGISTRADA

Printed in the United States of America

Chapter One

Paris, 1816

Muted footfalls on the stone provided a rhythmic accompaniment to the men's quiet conversation as they strolled across the Pont Marie to the Île Saint-Louis. They paused midway in unspoken accord, their eyes irrestistibly drawn to the neighboring Ile de la Cité, where the magnificent bulk of Nôtre Dame stood out against a night sky whose mantle was spattered with the pinpricks of a myriad stars.

After a moment of silent appreciation, the taller man sighed and turned back to his companion. "My last night in Paris," he said, obvious regret in his voice. "I'm glad we decided to walk, Louis. It would have been a crime to waste any time cooped up in a carriage with that glorious sky overhead."

"Very true, my friend, but to my mind it is a much greater crime to contemplate leaving Paris after a paltry three-or-four-day stay. Surely I can persuade you to remain longer? My services as guide are totally at your disposal," declared the other man with an expansive gesture of one hand. "You have only to say what you would like to do, and all will be arranged. Could anyone but a Philistine refuse such an offer?" Dark eyes full of mischief reflected the challenge in the invitation.

The larger man laughed, but shook his head as he turned left along the Quai d'Anjou in response to another eloquent hand signal from his companion. "You may believe I would seize upon your magnificent offer had I only my own wishes to consult, Louis, but that is, unhappily, not the case."

The conversation was being conducted in French, but the speaker, though fluent, revealed his origins by a decided English accent as he continued. "I could not refuse to support my cousin Henri at his nuptials, but I really cannot prolong my absence from England at present. My elder sister, who has been in India with her husband for many years, shipped her children back home recently in the charge of a governess who absconded almost as soon as the boat docked. When I received my sister's letter announcing what she proposed to do, I invited a widowed aunt to Beechwood to play propriety, but it has not answered. My aunt never had any children of her own and, what is worse, fancies herself a martyr to ailments too numerous to catalogue; in short, she shows no signs of ever being able to cope with Celeste's brood and greeted the news of this trip to France with sustained hysterics. My mind is not at all easy about being away even for a sennight.

"I assure you it is no laughing matter," he protested when the man called Louis reacted not with the ready sympathy to be expected from a friend of long standing, but with a rude burst of laughter.

"Oh, but it is, my friend. To think that I should live to see the disengaged Miles Pelham, who always valued his freedom from emotional ties above all things, saddled with a . . . a brood of children! By the way, of how many does a brood—delicious word—consist?"

"In this case, five. Damn your eyes, Louis," the Englishman went on as the other chortled anew, "and that Gallic memory that dredges up the ridiculous and ancient posturings of schoolboys."

"Ah, but in this instance memory was assisted by painful recollections of the drubbing I took at your hands and Henri's that summer after the Peace of Amiens simply because, unlike you two sports-minded barbarians, I was respectfully appreciative of the multiple charms of your fair English misses."

"That carefree summer before the fighting resumed seems a lifetime ago. And despite your susceptibility to English girls and, I suspect, those of all other countries," Miles Pelham retorted, the gleam of his teeth visible in the moonlight, "you remain unwed at thirty—"

"While you find your precious independence curbed by five

children. Life is amusing, is it not? We must endeavor to make your last night in Paris memorable."

"Is that why you have brought me to this bustling quarter?" asked the Englishman, peering at the dignified and dimly lighted edifices lining the quiet street.

"Do not be deceived by the rather staid facades of the *hôtel particulières* on the Île, my friend. The interiors are often more luxurious than you might expect, and in any case they are no longer inhabited solely by the sober financiers of the ancien régime who built them so long ago. Our destination this evening is such a house, though not nearly so grand. I thought you would appreciate the majesty of the Hôtel de Le Vau, which we are passing now, and the Hôtel Lambert up ahead, which has a magnificent entrance on Rue Saint Louis-en-l'Isle."

"Just where are we heading, Louis?" the Englishman inquired, pausing to admire the stately proportions of the building his friend indicated, "To a soirée?"

"No, I thought it might be amusing to visit a gaming house run by fellow countrymen of yours."

"A gaming house on the Île and an English one to boot? I am amazed that this quiet area would seem propitious for such an endeavor or that the residents would allow it in the first place. I heard nothing about such an enterprise when I visited Henri in Paris last autumn."

"However it was accomplished, it has been in existence for over six months. For a while it was all the crack, as you would say, but I believe it is not quite so popular lately. Such places eventually go out of fashion, of course, eclipsed by newer establishments where the play is deeper or the suppers more elaborate—who knows? It never reached the popularity that the Salon des Étrangers enjoyed before Bonaparte's escape from Elba, but that was a period of utter madness, when it was not uncommon for enormous fortunes to be gambled away in an evening."

"Do I apprehend that you are bringing me to this place to witness its decline? What a refreshingly novel idea for entertaining visitors."

Beyond a quick grin, the Frenchman ignored the other's delicate irony, declaiming soulfully, "We have come because I also have not changed over the years. I am still susceptible to the incomparable charms of your countrywomen." His friend's puzzled look prompted a fuller explanation. "Mlle. Herbert is the prime reason for the success of the house where we shall play tonight."

"Are you saying an Englishwoman is the proprietor of a gaming house in Paris?"

"No, no, Miles, you misunderstand. Mlle. Herbert is the *daughter* of the proprietor—one of the proprietors, I should say. There are two partners, both former officers in Wellington's army who sold out after Waterloo and stayed on in Paris. Mlle. Herbert came over from England to join her father about six months ago. I must confess that until her arrival I had almost forgotten that particular brilliance of complexion that is seen in many young English girls."

"I take it Miss Herbert shares in this particular English characteristic?"

"She does indeed. If that were all, it would be sufficient to bestow distinction upon her, but it is just the beginning. She has incredible eyes that sometimes appear green, sometimes brown or gray, according to her mood or the color of her gown. The eyes alone could make a man lose his heart and his discretion without even taking into account a delightful profile and a figure to make the heart stop." In his enthusiasm the Frenchman tucked his walking stick under his arm in order to use both hands to sketch an impression of feminine curves in the air.

"You may scoff," he said, interpreting the little smile on his friend's lips.

"Not at all," the Englishman replied. "You see me all eagerness to make the acquaintance of your charmer."

"Alas, it pains me to admit that she is not my *chère amie*, though not from lack of trying. All of Paris is at her feet."

"Out for bigger game is she?"

"No, you have mistaken her character. Mlle. Herbert is *toute à fait* respectable. When she goes about socially, it is with her father or in the company of married friends. She accepts no invitations from the patrons of the gaming house."

"Then you must make her an offer she cannot refuse if you are perishing for love of the lady," Miles Pelham said carelessly.

"Pardon? I do not understand."

"An offer of marriage."

"Marriage? Mais, c'est impossible!" In his eagerness to make his friend understand, the Frenchman switched to English. "One has one's duty to one's name, you comprehend, Miles, and there is no fortune. Oh, I see. You are making a game of me as you were used to do."

"Cheer up, Louis. Water will eventually wear away stone. Miss Herbert may yet fall into your arms if you persist in your attentions and employ that brand of Gallic charm that you perfected in England all those years ago."

"It is clear that you do not believe that she is respectable, but you will change your mind when you meet her. Everything about her is most elegant, her air, address, manners—"

"When, by the way, am I going to be granted the pleasure? We are nearly back to the rue des Deux Ponts."

The Frenchman stopped in his tracks and looked around, slapping his forehead with his palm in chagrin. "What an idiot I am. We have walked past the building while I—declaimed, would you say?—about Mlle. Herbert's charms. I beg your pardon."

"Not at all," Miles said amiably, allowing himself to be steered back the way they had come. "I have enjoyed the mild air and your eloquent description of Miss Herbert. I gather her eyes are the indeterminate color we call hazel. Is she blond or brunet?"

"Neither. Her hair is somewhere between honey and caramel in color and has the sheen of smoothest silk."

"It sounds delectable."

The irony in the gentle murmur escaped his friend, who once again waxed eloquent in praise of his goddess. "Yes, it is very lovely, but I believe I forgot to mention the most appealing feature of all. She has two intriguing . . . *fossettes*—"

"Two *what*?" The Englishman looked blank.

"You know, those little dents from smiling. I do not know

what they are called in English, but she has one in her cheek, like so, and another in her chin."

Enlightenment dawned on Miles Pelham as his friend jabbed his right cheek with a finger. "Oh, you mean *dimples*, a feature one associates with children somehow."

"I assure you there is nothing childish about Mlle. Herbert. Ah, here we are. We go through the doorway where that couple are entering and up the stairs."

The Parisian gaming house into which Louis ushered him a few moments later was not unlike its many counterparts in London, Miles Pelham decided after a cursory look around. It seemed to consist of two rooms set up to accommodate all the games of chance currently popular. He noted that the first room contained an alcove that could be curtained off for those desiring to engage in a private contest. Closer inspection revealed that no attempt had been made to introduce an element of elegance, unlike some of the private clubs he'd visited in the past. Here the furnishings were strictly functional, if not actually shabby, leading to the speculation that the proprietors had embarked on their enterprise with limited financial resources.

If there had been some falling off of attendance recently as Louis had intimated, it was not evident on this occasion. There was a well-patronized faro table at one end of the first room. At another small table two young bloods were engaged in a game of *écarte*, while several spectators placed bets on the outcome. Serious games of whist were under way at two other tables.

While Miles Pelham gazed about the room, a tall man in his mid-forties with light brown hair and cold blue eyes came up to greet the new arrivals. Louis introduced him as Captain Marple, one of the owners of the establishment, and the men shook hands. After a brief exchange of civilities during which Captain Marple ascertained that the newcomer was leaving Paris on the morrow, he lost interest in them, wished the visitor a safe journey, and withdrew.

Even so short a conversation had been unable to engage Louis's attention beyond a surface politeness that failed to disguise his impatience to go in search of his paragon.

Miles's lips twitched in sympathy as he allowed himself to be led into the second and, he saw at once, larger room. Here, too, the decor was minimal with the walls painted a rather bilious shade of green that was unlikely to inspire patrons with a desire to linger on the premises. Fortunately, that thought had barely framed itself in the back of his mind when he noted the presence of several ladies attired in the soft pastels that were all the rage that Season. Cheered by this grace note, Miles began a slow visual sweep of the room, trying to discover which of the ladies was the notable Miss Herbert.

His gaze was immediately caught by an impressive diamond parure blazing about the neck of a woman seated at the crowded roulette table. A quick inspection of the girth of the lady's pink gown, however, settled the question of whether she might be the proprietor's daughter.

Seeing the direction of his friend's glance, Louis whispered, "That is Lady Selkirk, another of your countrywomen currently residing in Paris."

"Ah, yes, the Selkirk diamonds are famous in London for their sheer ostentation."

"Lord and Lady Selkirk live in great style in the area around the Tuileries."

"The merchants and suppliers who enjoy their custom would be well advised not to extend credit for too long, however, if there is any truth to the rumors circulating in London following their rather hasty departure this spring."

When his friend did not comment on this *on dit*, Miles glanced across the room to the group that had stolen Louis's attention and his own gaze became rapt. There was no smallest doubt in his mind that the girl in the honey-colored gown who was chatting animatedly with five or six gentlemen was the celebrated Miss Herbert. Nor had Louis exaggerated the young woman's attractions, which were as described, only more so. From the shine of the burnished curls falling from a topknot in artless profusion over her ears to the dainty slippers on her slender feet, everything about Miss Herbert's appearance made an instantaneous appeal to the beholder, bypassing the critical faculties that might eventually assess the actual degree

of beauty she possessed. He could not determine the color of
her eyes at this distance, but there was no denying that they
were large and expressive, and her delightful smile was further
enhanced by the deep dimple playing in one cheek with each
movement of her mouth.

In the midst of his fascinated appraisal, Miles felt a tug on
his elbow as Louis urged him forward. The sudden movement
drew Miss Herbert's notice, and she glanced their way.

Miles's feet continued to carry him forward in contradiction
to his impression that time had come to a halt while their eyes
locked together in a tenuous, wordless, but vital communication, at least so it seemed at that instant. Miss Herbert had
turned away from the group of which she'd been the center,
and she must have taken a step toward the approaching men.
Miles distinctly saw her eyes widen before her lashes veiled
her expression. He could feel a pulse beating madly in his
throat and consciously steeled himself to preserve a calm demeanor during the coming introduction.

An introduction that never took place.

Louis had cleared his throat prior to launching into a greeting when a preemptory masculine voice said in French, "Here
you are, my lovely one, at last. You have not forgotten that we
are to play piquet tonight?"

Miles thought he saw a momentary consternation in the
young woman's face before she smiled at the aging exquisite
who had approached unnoticed from behind her, and said
composedly, "Some evening, yes, Monsieur le Compte, but as
you see, we are very crowded tonight, and my father, unfortunately, is not here. I shall be needed to—"

"Captain Marple has assured me that you can be spared for
an hour or two to provide amusement for one of your establishment's most faithful patrons, my dear mademoiselle. Shall
we retire to the alcove in the other room, where we shall not
be disturbed?"

The suave voice of the French nobleman contained an un-
dertone of coercion that, coupled with the reluctance Miles
sensed in his countrywoman for the proposed tête-à-tête,
caused him to step forward and intervene. "If this gentleman's

. . . request is unwelcome to you, ma'am," he said in English, "I will be happy to explain the matter to him for you."

He could sense the rising hostility with which Louis was regarding the count's sneering mien, but Pelham's gaze never left the girl. Her eyes had widened at hearing her own language, and alarm flashed across her countenance before she said softly, "Thank you, sir, but that will not be necessary. I did promise the Compte de Bouchardet a rubber of piquet sometime." Here she shrugged her shoulders in the French fashion and produced a tiny smile. "If I can be spared from my duties, it might as well be now."

Miss Herbert placed her fingers on the count's proffered arm without looking at his satisfied expression. She murmured a polite greeting to a discomfited Louis and directed a fleeting glance at Miles before walking off with her head erect and her lovely face devoid of all expression.

The Englishman remained watching the young woman's departing back until, turning to address her escort, she presented him with a glimpse of a serene profile as the pair passed through the archway between the rooms. He turned to the dejected man beside him. "It seems we were both correct in our estimation of Miss Herbert, Louis." At his friend's look of incomprehension, he continued evenly, "She is certainly as attractive as you said, and has apparently closed with a better offer as I predicted. Shall we join the action at one of the tables?"

When Louis would have launched into an impassioned defense of Miss Herbert's moral character, the Englishman silenced him with a smiling challenge. "Did you not promise me an evening's entertainment, *mon vieux*? I am in a mood to test the tables of this delightful establishment."

The men remained at the gaming house for another two hours, sampling the play at various tables. Louis gave the appearance of a man wrestling with a private dilemma, and he paid for his lack of concentration by finding himself poorer by nearly six hundred francs at the end of this time. Miles, on the other hand, never varied his demeanor of imperturbable affability and walked away enriched by more than three hundred francs when they left.

The curtains across the alcove in the first room remained

closed during all this time and, though a woman's light laugh could occasionally be heard from within the enclosure, they did not see Miss Herbert again that evening.

Nothing on earth, no temptation nor torture would induce her to look back at the disdainful Englishman, Claudia vowed as she walked with stiff spine and clenched teeth toward the private cardroom. Her body felt rigid and brittle with rage against the whole male gender. Her father's partner, well aware that she detested the lascivious count, thought nothing of offering her upon a platter in order to retain his patronage; the cynical nobleman, convinced his wealth could purchase anything he desired, including another human being, had no scruples about commanding her company, however reluctant; and the Englishman was the worst of all, presuming to condemn her morals without a trial. Something inside her had crumbled when she'd seen the admiration in the stranger's eyes turn so swiftly to contempt, but she must not permit herself to dwell on that devastating moment. Anger would serve her much better in the ordeal ahead. She would have need of all the feminine wiles and stratagems she'd had to cultivate since entering a gaming house to help her father, simply to preserve her person from the Frenchman's roving hands.

That wasn't enough, she decided, another wave of fury burning through her veins. She owed it to herself to avenge the insult by trouncing him at piquet. If she could maintain her concentration while destroying his, she believed her skill at the game was equal to the task, barring a run of ill luck.

Buckling on her feminine armor, Claudia turned to her escort with a smiling remark as they exited from the larger room through the archway.

When she left the gaming house several hours later, Claudia's jaw ached from forced smiling and her spirit and soul were bruised by the bantering, innuendo and barely disguised propositions she'd had to parry during an extended match with the Compte de Bouchardet, not to mention the added strain of having to speak French throughout. The experience left her feeling besmirched, despite the grim satisfaction of winning several hundred francs from her opponent, whose judgment had become somewhat clouded by the time he'd finished his second bottle of wine. She had steadfastly refused to partake herself, falsely claiming that even one glass of wine produced a blinding headache that would compel her to retire from their contest. She had needed to keep her wits about her to concentrate on the cards while at the same time deflecting de Bouchardet's numerous attempts to initiate a seduction.

Nor did the night's trials end when the slightly unsteady nobleman was tenderly assisted into his carriage by Captain Marple. She had remained in the alcove and was sitting with eyes closed, attempting to relax her taut muscles and summon the composure to face the rest of the evening, when her father's partner returned.

"My congratulations," he said, pulling the alcove curtains completely open. "I'd made up my mind that it would be worth a few hundred francs to keep de Bouchardet coming back to our faro table after he strongly intimated that he'd play elsewhere if denied your company, but you actually fleeced the old goat. I'll take the money," he added, holding out his hand.

Claudia had been expecting no less, but the bald demand increased her resentment at the treatment she'd received at Marple's hands exponentially. She got to her feet and edged out of the alcove, meeting the proprietor's glance squarely. "I think not," she said. "You knew I've been avoiding the count's advances for weeks, yet you forced that repugnant encounter on me without a thought for my feelings or reputation. I earned this money, and I intend to keep it."

He seized her wrist between steely fingers then and reminded her that she'd been playing with house money, but she refused to back down. Realizing that she was prepared to create a scene if pushed, Marple released her arm and stepped back to allow her to pass, but not before issuing a low-voiced promise to take up the matter with her father on the morrow.

A few moments later, when Claudia came out onto the quiet street in the company of the groom porter, whom she'd requested to accompany her the short distance to the lodgings she shared with her father, she was still endeavoring to subdue her racing pulses and maintain a calm demeanor. The soft

night air was like balm to one who had been confined in a
stuffy room with uncongenial company for hours. She lifted
her face, dislodging the hood of her cloak in the process, and
relished the slightly damp breeze on her heated skin, noticing
as she did so that clouds had come in to veil the moon. In other
circumstances she's have enjoyed leaning over the railing of a
bridge and watching the moving water until peace stole over
her spirit, but all she wished at the moment was an end to a
horrible evening with its humiliations and confrontations. She
quickened her step and was soon at her own door, where she
thanked and dismissed her blessedly silent escort.

A single branch of candles provided sufficient light to show
that the reception room was empty when Claudia entered the
apartment she shared with her father and his former batman,
who willingly set his hand to any task needed in the small
household. She cast a jaundiced eye around the room as she
removed her evening cloak and gloves. Her attempts to render
their furnished lodgings more homelike had been largely
thwarted by inadequate resources and the indifference to creature comforts engendered in her father by many years of living
as a bachelor in military quarters since her mother's death.
During most of those same years while she had lived with her
mother's elder sister's family, certainly since she had grown
up, she had prayed for the war to be over and dreamed of making a real home for her remaining parent. While the present
impersonal surroundings provided a welcome antidote to the
somewhat tawdry atmosphere of the gaming house, they fell
far short of a home to her way of thinking.

Claudia straightened her spine and lifted her head as she
gathered up her cloak and gloves before heading for her own
room. She hesitated outside her father's bedchamber, one
closed hand upraised but motionless. The leg wound he'd received at Waterloo had ached so badly today that she'd persuaded him to stay home and rest tonight. With no wish to
disturb him if he slept, she finally tapped once very softly on
his door.

"I'm not asleep, Claudia. Come in, my dear," Major Herbert
replied in a normal voice.

On entering, Claudia saw that her father had not retired for the night, but was sitting in a green brocade *bergère*, attired in a dark blue dressing gown that set off his bright blue eyes and wavy auburn hair that showed no trace of gray. Despite his lame leg, he looked far younger than his forty-eight years, and she had become accustomed to exclamations of disbelief when she was introduced as his daughter.

Major Herbert closed his book on his index finger and looked over at the clock on the bedside table. "You are back early tonight."

"Yes." Instead of addressing the question in his voice, Claudia asked one of her own. "How is your leg now, Papa?"

"Much better. Buckley rubbed it for me earlier, and that helped considerably. You are looking rather tired tonight, or perhaps dispirited would be a more apt description. Is something wrong, love?"

"No, I . . . nothing out of the ordinary, I suppose. It was simply that I . . . no." Claudia shrugged and came to a full stop.

"You must see that you cannot leave it like that, my dear. You are clearly upset, and it is my right and, yes, my duty to know what has happened to overset you."

Her father's concern united with still simmering anger at her recent experiences to overcome her habitual reluctance to complain about any aspect of her present life. Claudia related the events of the evening, except that she omitted any mention of the contempt she had detected in the attitude of the tall Englishman accompanying Monsieur Louis Frenier, for that was of no lasting import, however galling to her self-esteem. She finished with an account of the clash with her father's partner over her winnings.

"Perhaps I should have turned it over to him, or half of it at least, but I was so angry, Papa, that I desired only to extract a revenge on him—well, not *only* revenge, of course. There are a number of bills owing."

Major Herbert's brow had grown thunderous as her narration progressed, and now he snapped, "No, you keep that money. I shall have something to say to Marple tomorrow, you may be very sure. I will not have my daughter treated as a Cy-

prian whose favors are available to the likes of de Bouchardet
for a price. I am frankly astounded at Marple's effrontery."

"It wasn't like that in the beginning." Claudia hesitated after
her hasty assurance before asking timidly, "Is the venture failing, Papa? I know there have been several people who have
won quite large sums of late, and it does seem to me that attendance has been declining over the past few months, though the
rooms were crowded tonight."

"Gaming houses always go through such periods, my dear.
It is in the very nature of the business, fortune being such an
unpredictable commodity. Do not trouble your head over a
temporary downturn. We shall come about," her father assured
her. "Go to bed now, love, and put this upsetting evening behind you."

The heartwarming smile on her father's handsome face
elicited a rush of emotion that drove away the bitterness as
Claudia responded to his outstretched hand with a little dash
across the space separating them.

After she had kissed his cheek, Major Herbert took her hand
in his and swung her around in front of him, studying her appearance with pleasure. "You look very lovely this evening in
your new gown, very like your mother when she was your age.
It is not to be wondered at that you dazzled the eyes of the
Compte de Bouchardet, as well as every other man in the
place, I'll go bail."

Claudia dimpled and accepted this gallantry as the very partial opinion of a loving parent. "Thank you, Papa. It is a lovely
dress," she agreed, running a smoothing hand down the soft
silk skirt, "but I am persuaded I should not have listened when
you told me we could afford to purchase a gown from Mme.
Charpentier. Her clothes are shockingly expensive."

"Never mind the cost. It was worth every centime. Now off
to bed with you."

Claudia squeezed his hand and headed for the door, her
world restored once again to the happy state that the long-
delayed reunion with her parent had created.

Her hand was on the door when her father's voice stopped
her progress. "By the way, Claudia, was Lord Selkirk there
tonight?"

"Yes, Papa, and Lady Selkirk, too, in all her diamond splendor."

"Did he win any considerable sum, do you happen to know?"

"I fear I did not linger long enough to inquire about such things, Papa. I was too intent on escaping, and, in any case, it was still early when I left. Has Lord Selkirk been a frequent winner?"

"Yes, too frequent. Never mind," Major Herbert reiterated. "It is of little consequence. Off to bed with you."

Seeing that her father had opened his book again, Claudia swallowed the questions she would have liked to ask and left the room with a murmured good night.

Chapter Two

Claudia went to bed that night nearly restored to equanimity, thanks to her father's ardent support. It had been the worst night of her stay in Paris, one she hoped never to repeat, but apart from a small bruise on the inside of her wrist administered by Captain Marple, she had suffered no damage except to her pride. Even in that department she had actually avenged herself on two of her recent antagonists, at least financially. Oddly enough, the last thing of which she was conscious before drifting off to sleep was a mental image of the unknown Englishman, the third man who had struck at her *amour propre*. His tall, resplendent person had suddenly appeared in her line of vision that evening as the embodiment of a young girl's dream of masculine perfection. She'd been overtaken by surprised delight and had turned eagerly toward him, a spontaneous reaction that now filled her with shamed fury in the light of what had followed. For the space of a heartbeat she'd glimpsed a duplication of her own wonder in his eyes before the Compte de Bouchardet's voice had shattered the magic. It was the stranger's face as she had last seen it, however, frozen in an attitude of cold disdain, that filled her dreams and appeared in her memory upon awakening.

Over the next sennight the Englishman's disturbing image gradually receded from Claudia's consciousness as life settled into a pleasant enough pattern once more. Since joining her father six months before, she had made some friends with whom she exchanged visits, mostly former military families who made up part of a growing English colony in Paris. Her small circle even included a few native Parisians who had been kind and tolerant of her early struggles to become comfortable in their language. It was a source of pride that her fluency had improved to the point where she could now enjoy an evening at the Theatre Française. One of the most delightful experiences in Paris in Claudia's view was the opportunity to dine at an elegant restaurant like Beauvillier in the rue de Richelieu or the Rocher de Concalle, which boasted one of Napoleon's former cooks.

More often than not, though, she spent her evenings in the gaming house. Although she tried to conceal her trepidation from her father, she had dreaded returning there in the wake of the humiliating night when she'd been maneuvered into the piquet match in the private alcove. To see the tall Englishman's contempt replicated in the faces of other patrons would have taken more courage to withstand with composure than she believed she possessed. As it happened, Claudia's fears proved groundless on this score, and she was not called upon to demonstrate the requisite bravery. No one looked at her askance, and no speculative twitterings circulated behind raised fans when she moved through the rooms, performing small courtesies to ensure that the patrons were neither neglected nor bored if delayed from participating in the game of their choice because of temporary crowding at the tables.

Nor did her erstwhile opponents repeat their offenses. The Compte de Bouchardet came to the house only twice in the next fortnight. Though he sought out her company in the intervals he was not engaged at play and plied her with elaborate compliments as before, he did not propose another private game. Her father's close attendance guaranteed that the nobleman's poetic flights of fancy did not receive a private audience. From her father she learned that the count experienced a run of luck at the faro table that more than recouped his losses to her.

Captain Marple ignored her existence whenever possible, a circumstance that would have been eminently satisfactory, had she not occasionally intercepted an expression of patent dislike in his eyes when he thought himself unobserved. This actually came as no surprise to her. On first meeting her father's partner soon after her arrival in Paris, she had experienced an inexplicable and unsettling antipathy to the brusque, cold-eyed man, a revulsion she had striven to conceal from her parent. It had soon become clear that the disaffection was entirely mutual as she and the former officer settled into an enforced intimacy characterized by a wary civility on her part and an ironic formality on his. Improved acquaintance had convinced her that Captain Marple had little liking or respect for females in general, a disquieting conclusion at best, but one that absolved her from any pangs of guilt at her inability to detect any virtue in the man's nature. To her consummate relief, he did not again refer to their clash over the money she'd won from the French count.

Though Monsieur Louis Frenier was occasionally to be seen in the rooms, he did not again have his censorious English friend in tow, a circumstance, Claudia assured herself, that commanded a similar degree of relief.

Claudia slipped smoothly back into the routine she had established over the months of her stay in Paris. Once the balm of passing time had soothed the sores of concern for self, she relaxed and began to observe her surroundings and the persons who populated them with renewed interest, taking in nuances and details that had escaped her notice previously. Unhappily, the result of her observations was a growing conviction that all was not going well with the business at present. She was persuaded her father's smiling bonhomie as he moved about the rooms was assumed to cover mounting concern, but he dismissed her fears and brushed aside her questions.

Captain Marple's behavior was altered, too, but in his case it took the form of an almost tigerish alertness in his manner. He seemed to be everywhere at once, checking on the status of play at the various tables. She noted that he frequently stationed himself where he could overhear the conversations being carried on by various patrons. She suspected his covert attentions were directed most particularly at Lord Selkirk, who was now a confirmed habitue of the card rooms, appearing at least three times each week, alone or with a party of friends. This realization triggered a memory of her father questioning the viscount's presence on the night of her ordeal, and his subsequent response to her inquiry that Lord Selkirk "won too often."

At the time the abruptness in his voice had added weight to the reply, but she had been very full of her own humiliation just then, and it had fled her mind almost immediately. Once Claudia pieced together her recollections and observations, however, Lord Selkirk's recent flirtation with Dame Fortune marched to the forefront of her concerns.

Claudia had to confess that she found neither Lord nor Lady Selkirk to be persons of particular amiability, despite being predisposed toward fellow countrymen. The viscount's forced jocularity was as grating as his lady's conscious condescension. Of course it was not necessary, or even desirable, to form personal attachments to the patrons of a gaming house, but there were any number whose company and conversation made them more agreeable than the English couple.

Observing the viscount more narrowly as opportunity presented, Claudia felt herself becoming infected by the malaise that gripped the partners. She was in the habit of leaving the establishment well before it closed its doors each night, since she had no wish to lie abed all day, missing the delights Paris offered. Her father had lately grown very closemouthed about the business, however, fobbing off her attempts to ascertain their financial standing with cheerful platitudes meant to reassure her but falling increasingly short of their aim.

On the night Lord Selkirk won six thousand francs from Captain Marple at piquet, Claudia had remained into the small hours. Taking a turn at presiding over the faro table, she was pleased after her stint to be able to report that no streaks of luck had deprived the bank of its percentage of the money wagered that evening. By the time she finished, however, the rooms were abuzz with the news of Lord Selkirk's marked success during a marathon session of piquet. After her first start of dismay, she'd encountered her father's warning glance and reined in her emotions, mimicking his professional graciousness as they bade good night to the last of the gamesters within the half hour. She did her best to avoid looking at Captain Marple, whose icy control was belied by a feral glitter in light blue eyes that were every bit as menacing as the darkest Latin orbs were reputed to be.

When Major Herbert would have detailed the last of the waiters to see his daughter home, Claudia protested, "Please, no, Papa. Let me wait for you. I have a right to know how damaging Lord Selkirk's unprecedented run of luck is to the business."

"Run of luck! Is that what you call it, Miss Herbert?"

As he whirled on her with a bark of angry laughter, Captain Marple's teeth snapped together, and his mouth contracted to a sneering line.

Emboldened by her father's proximity, Claudia subdued a craven impulse to retreat before a bubbling volcano. "Are you saying it is something else, Captain Marple?" she asked, keeping her eyes on his, despite the trembling in her knees.

"The man's a Greek—a cheat! He's been rigging—"

"You know we have no evidence that Selkirk is cheating, Harry," Major Herbert broke in before turning to wave the goggle-eyed waiter away. "We'll see you tomorrow then, Dufresne. Good night." When the retreating man's footsteps were heard on the staircase, he resumed in reasonable tones. "Only sealed packs of cards are used at the tables, and the dice are changed regularly as well. I would swear that no substitutions have been possible under our scrutiny."

"I'm not implying that he's been able to fuzz the cards," Captain Marple said through gritted teeth. "In any case, his luck at faro, you will have observed, is inconsistent, and he's never spent much time at hazard or other dice games. Without exception his big wins have been at piquet, and then only when that so-called secretary of his, Cavanaugh, has been at his elbow. The man never drinks anything stronger than water and has eyes like a ferret."

"But even if Cavanaugh has occasionally managed a glimpse of our hands, there has been no communication between them during play. Indeed, I cannot recall having heard the man utter two words running. He is a veritable shadow."

"I'm convinced he's a walking memory, and I'll stake my life that there is communication between them, although obviously not verbal. Selkirk plays his cards well enough, but you will have observed that where he has the edge is in guessing what his opponent holds and keeps. He does *not* exhibit this skill at those times when Cavanaugh is not with him, however, and as soon as his losses mount, he drifts over to one of the other tables on those nights. No, by God, Cavanaugh is signaling to him in some manner. I may not be able to prove it, but he is not going to get away with it any longer."

Glancing away from the furious resolution in Captain Marple's tight-lipped face, Claudia said, "Why can we not simply deny admission to Lord Selkirk, Papa?"

"Without convincing proof of cheating, such an action is unthinkable, my dear. It would ruin us faster than absorbing any losses, once the word got out. Do not concern yourself needlessly over this affair, Claudia. We shall ride out the storm."

"Ride it out, be damned," declared Captain Marple, his agitation confirmed by this deplorable lapse of conduct in the presence of a lady. "I intend to put a stop to the business once and for all."

"How? What do you have in mind?" demanded Major Herbert.

He was to remain unsatisfied on this vital point that evening. Captain Marple, apparently recalling Miss Herbert's presence, gave her a darkling look that caused a shiver to run up her spine, and turned on his heel. "It will keep," he said with less heat than he'd so far exhibited. "I'll see you tomorrow, John." He made an ironic bow in Claudia's direction and stalked out of the room.

Claudia stared in appeal at her father, but Major Herbert shook his head wearily. "Leave it for now, my dear; it is time we went home."

Claudia nodded and slipped off to retrieve her shawl and the stick her father used when walking on the uneven pavement stones. When she returned, he was standing where she had left him, staring into space, so deep in thought that she had to speak twice before her voice penetrated his absorption.

"Papa?"

"Eh? Oh, there you are, my child." Major Herbert accepted the heavy walnut stick with its wide top carved in the shape of a duck's head, laying a caressing hand on her cheek for a second as he did so. "You go on ahead, and I'll blow out the last candles and lock the doors."

Major Herbert rejoined his daughter in the lower hallway, and they set out together in nearly total silence except for his query about her comfort in the paisley shawl that was all she wore over her gown. Claudia longed to give voice to the fears and questions rioting around inside her head, but her father's air of brooding worry gave her pause. The realization after a few moments that he was leaning more heavily on his stick than was his habit sealed her lips. She could not add her qualms to his burdens tonight. She slipped her gloved hand inside his elbow and was comforted when he pressed it to his side. Tomorrow was soon enough to confront the problem of Lord Selkirk's alleged cheating.

An air of grave resolution settled over Claudia as the carriage rumbled across the bridge onto the Île. Tonight she would—she *must*—convince her father to share with her any decisions he and his partner had taken regarding Lord Selkirk's cheating. Several days had elapsed since the viscount's crippling win, days filled with vague apprehensions and nights haunted by a recurring picture of Captain Marple's menacing expression when he had proclaimed his intention of stopping the Englishman's success. She had not been privy to any of the partners' subsequent conversations, nor had she succeeded in several attempts to induce her father to address the burning issue. He had evaded her in the nicest possible manner, but with a gentle finality that the habit of filial deference had not been able to challenge.

Though heartfelt, her sigh barely disturbed the air in the carriage. Claudia shivered a little and drew her evening cloak closer to her throat. The promise of summer had not lasted, and there was a chill dampness to the night air tonight. Similarly, her initial euphoria at being reunited with her father had withered a bit in the austere reality of the lives they led in Paris. There was no lack of affection; she felt secure in her father's love and reveled in his inordinate pride in her in the face of her own knowledge of her ordinariness. A difficult honesty compelled her to accept that they had not grown closer over the past months, despite her best efforts to bridge the years of separation. Perhaps her father had been too long without a family to be able to share his life except on the most superficial level. Theirs was the intimacy of loving strangers, a seeming contradiction, but she could find no other way to describe their shared existence. He would probably deny in good conscience that he considered her still a child, but it had not occurred to him to try to discover how her mind worked. Though generous and concerned for her well-being, he seemed content to have his daughter's inner life remain unexplored territory. Sadly, he appeared not to recognize her tentative efforts to widen or deepen the communication between them.

Tonight was a case in point. It being Sunday, the gaming rooms were closed. The Herberts had been invited to a small dinner party given by the major's old comrade, Colonel Lord Malmsey. Claudia would have preferred to spend the evening exclusively with her parent, but she had acquiesced with a show of pleasure, only to find that her father begged off at the last minute with a flimsy excuse of some neglected duties. He wouldn't hear of her reneging, so she had made the best of it, hiding her disappointment. The Malmseys had been most kind to her throughout her stay in Paris, and she generally delighted in being a temporary member of a large, lively family such as she had never known. That had been true today, too, while she visited with the three youngest members of the family and their governess before sitting down to dine with the adults and several other guests. As the evening wore on, however, her thoughts tended to return to her father during any momentary lull in the conversation, and she found it necessary to dissimulate her gratitude when the first guests began to take their leave at a reasonable hour.

Lord Malmsey always insisted on sending her home in his luxurious carriage, and Claudia usually enjoyed watching the passing scene, but tonight she was so taken up with her own problems that it came as a surprise to her when the carriage stopped with a jingle of harness that was the only sound in the quiet street. Glancing at her mother's gold watch pinned to her bodice, she was pleased to see the hour was still early. As she accepted the coachman's hand in descending the steps with a smile and a murmured thanks, she promised herself that her father would not fob her off tonight.

Claudia's smile faded as she saw a man leave by the door she was approaching and hurry down the street to the left without so much as a glance in the direction of the carriage. Oh dear, it had not occurred to her that her father might have company, but the owners of the building were away at present, and the only other tenant was a widow who lived with her three children across the hall from their apartment. Poor Mme. Renaud seemed to have no social life at all, which doubtless meant the man she had just seen must have been visiting her father.

All this flashed through Claudia's mind as she entered the building and began to ascend the stairs. Suddenly, a noise drew her eyes upward, and she found herself moving quickly to her right to get out of the path of a man running down the stairs, his eyes on his feet. She knew he sent her a glance as they neared each other, but her eyes were glued to his right hand briefly clutching the railing. The man's hand was disfigured by a puckered red scar across the back of it, in addition to dark smears of some sort on the thumb. By the time she raised her eyes in curiosity, the man had gone past her. An instant later, the lower door opened and closed.

Claudia hurried up the stairs, driven by vague alarums that coalesced into a heart-stopping premonition of disaster as she espied the open door to their apartment. After an instant of frozen terror, she dashed inside, her heart now racing with her feet.

The scene that greeted her was appalling enough to bring Claudia to a halt once more. One hand went to her throat, as if to keep her heart from pounding its way out of her shaking body as she gazed wide-eyed about the salon. Disorder was everywhere; overturned tables and chairs were strewn in her path, the desk in the far corner spilled its contents and drawers onto the rug, even the curtains had been pulled from the windows, puddling on the floor beneath.

Claudia assimilated these details in one sweeping look and promptly forgot them as her eyes came to rest on one shoulder and bent elbow of a figure lying on the floor beyond the settee. "No, oh please, no," she moaned, plunging across the room, dodging large obstacles and kicking aside smaller objects along the way. "Papa!" she cried the next instant, falling to her knees before her father's supine form, her eyes staring in horror at the spreading red stain on his shirtfront.

Major Herbert's eyes, which had been closed, opened at his daughter's agonized cry and the touch of her hand on his cheek. His pale lips stretched into the semblance of a smile. "I'm glad you came, my love," he whispered.

"Do not try to talk, Papa," Claudia implored, placing her fingers on his lips. "I must get help. I'll ask Mme. Renaud to send one of her sons for a doctor. I'll be right—"

"No, Claudia, it's no use." As her eyes filled with tears and she started to rise, Major Herbert moved his hand to cover hers. "Please, dearest, there is so little time and I must tell you . . . beg you—"

"What happened, Papa? Who did this to you?" Although quaking like an aspen, Claudia managed to slide her arm under her father's shoulder and push a pillow under his head to ease his breathing.

"Thank you, that's better. After you left this afternoon, I went to Harry's lodgings to have it out with him about this Selkirk affair. He'd refused to tell me what he had in mind to do. Today he was exultant, said he'd gotten our money back. He laughed when I asked how he'd accomplished this and said I was better off to remain in ignorance, but I pressed him, and finally he said he'd sent someone to break into Selkirk's house. He took a thick wad of banknotes from his desk while I stood there, stunned. His servant came in then with a message, and he left the room. The desk drawer where he'd had the notes was still open a bit, and I saw . . . I found the—"

"Don't talk anymore, Papa, rest," Claudia urged as a cough racked his body and his breathing became more labored.

"Must tell you . . . Marple had the Selkirk diamonds. I insisted he return them, we quarrelled, and finally I planted him a facer, took the jewels, and left." Drained from his efforts to tell his story, Major Herbert's eyes closed again.

"Papa, are you saying *your partner* stabbed you to get the necklace back?" Claudia gasped, forgetting in her horror her earlier plea that he should not tax his strength.

"I don't believe murder was his intention. He sent hired ruffians to get the jewels back, not that you will be able to bring it home to him. He will have an alibi for this evening, and his henchmen will disappear back into the underworld. But they didn't . . . get it . . ." Claudia heard the triumph in his weak voice, but she could only stare in despair from his ashen face to the wadded-up handkerchief he'd put across his chest, now soaked crimson.

"Papa, I must get help for you," she pleaded.

"You can help by returning the necklace. It's in . . . the handle of my cane."

"Yes, of course." She possessed herself of his pointing hand and spotted the bottom of the cane sticking out from under the settee. "But now—"

"I . . . I have neglected you all your life, and now I've brought you danger and scandal." As she protested vehemently, his eyes closed, but his lips still moved. Claudia leaned closer to hear. "Forgive me, my love . . . go to M . . . Malmsey . . . he'll take . . ."

A smothered oath from the doorway brought Claudia's head around over her shoulder. "Buckley! Thank heavens you're back. Go fetch a doctor immediately. My father has been hurt, stabbed—" Her voice broke off as she returned her eyes to her parent's still face.

A moment—or an eternity—later, Buckley removed her father's limp hand from Claudia's desperate clasp. "A doctor won't do no good, Miss Herbert," he said in a shaken voice. "The major's gone."

Even before she had finished packing a small bag to take with her to the Malmseys, Claudia had determined on a course of action. Based no doubt on the condition of the salon, Buckley had assumed that thieves had followed her father home and set on him, killing him in the struggle that ensued. With her father's tormented prediction of danger and scandal ringing in her ears, she had not disabused the batman of his theory. Obviously, she was in danger while Captain Marple believed the Selkirk diamonds to be in her possession. Accusing him of the theft would boil down to his word against that of a girl anxious to clear her dead father's name. That the necklace was in her possession would be seen by many as proof that her father had indeed been the thief. Lord Malmsey would believe her story, but there was no guarantee that the Selkirks would. At the very least, any accusations by her would inevitably result in the scandal her father had dreaded for her sake. For *his* sake she would see to it that this did not happen, she vowed, silent tears dribbling down her face as she removed the necklace from the head of the walking stick in her bedchamber. The flow of tears increased in volume as she wrapped the loathsome jewelry in her stockings and tucked the bundle into the valise with her clothing. Obviously, the necklace must be returned anonymously to prevent any breath of scandal from touching the gambling club, even though this would mean that the sole adverse consequence of his heinous crimes would be the loss of the diamonds' value to Captain Marple. Primitive anger burned through her body at the thought that such evil should go unpunished, but she could think of no other course that would bring about his punishment, and certainly none that would avoid the scandal her father had deplored with his dying breath.

Claudia's fingers caressed the cleverly carved duck's head of her father's walking stick before laying it gently on her bed and closing her valise. It occurred to her that in order to end her own personal danger, she would have to apprise Captain Marple of her action after she returned the necklace. Her teeth ground fiercely together as she contemplated the satisfaction this would afford her. Not enough, not nearly enough; nothing short of that malevolent brute's horrible death would appease her consuming rage or lighten her loss. If she were a man, she would kill him with her own hands, she assured herself, bemoaning the misfortune of her weak, feminine nature.

Buckley's tap on her door to inform her that he had hired a vehicle brought Claudia's bloodthirsty imaginings to an abrupt cessation. As she followed him out of the apartment past her father's body, now covered with a blanket, her vague dreams of vengeance gave way to acute misery once more, and she stumbled over something as tears blinded her. She blinked them away and walked with rigidly set face out of the only parental home she'd had since her mother's death when she was nine years old.

Claudia performed her unhappy duties in a purely mechanical fashion over the next few days. After the first wild paroxysms of grief over her father's lifeless body, she did not again make a display of her feelings in front of others. By the time Buckley had conveyed her to the Malmseys' house that night, she had imposed a rigid control over her features and her tongue, though it was as well for her pride that she could not see the suffering that was clearly reflected in her eyes.

The Malmsey family earned Claudia's undying gratitude during this unhappy period, performing all those acts of necessity and many others of consideration that confirmed the high degree of friendship and respect in which they held her father. Lord Malmsey consulted her wishes in making the burial arrangements and supported her during a difficult interview with the French authorities. It would have been a relief to confide the whole truth to him, but Claudia resisted the temptation to unburden herself, when doing so would serve only to add to her host's burdens. She mentioned the two men she had seen leaving her building, both of whom had also been glimpsed in passing by his lordship's coachman, but neither she nor the driver could supply a detailed description. She was less forthcoming when asked what the thieves might have been after.

"Why, money, I assume," she had replied with a practiced air of bewilderment that she had maintained upon being informed that a sum of money had been found in her father's undisturbed bedchamber. Lord Malmsey had come to her rescue, strongly stating his opinion that the sounds of the carriage stopping outside had frightened off the bungling thieves, who had just become murderers.

Discerning her exhaustion after this ordeal, Lord Malmsey had proposed that he convey her regrets to her father's partner when he called that afternoon to condole. Claudia seized with trembling relief upon his offer to act for her in any necessary business transactions with Captain Marple. She had been terri-fied that she would not be able to sufficiently disguise her anger and loathing in a meeting with Marple, which would have alerted him to her knowledge of his perfidy. Lord Malm-sey believed his old comrade had been dead when his daughter returned, and this vital lie was the only reply Marple's ques-tions would elicit from her host.

Nothing untoward had upset her plans so far, but Claudia knew she would not be free to mourn until the diamonds were back in Lord Selkirk's possession. The achievement of this crucial objective was proving anything but simple, however. A casual question to Lord Malmsey had discovered the Selkirks' direction, and she had found a small box and some paper to wrap the necklace in, but a method of conveying it to its owner had so far eluded her. It was inconceivable that she could slip away on a secret errand and return to this house unobserved, and that would in any case compromise the vital anonymity, unless she were heavily disguised. She also shrank from trying to bribe one of the servants to act for her, considering this an offense against the Malmsey's hospitality.

Claudia was beginning to fear that she would have to enlist Lord Malmsey's aid in the end, a particularly distressing op-tion when the poor man was already heavily embroiled in her problems at a time when he was trying to get his own affairs in order before embarking on a trip with his family to Italy for the summer. Unexpectedly, it was Lady Malmsey who came to her rescue with the practical suggestion that she should send a maid to her guest's lodgings to pack up the rest of her clothes and any possessions of her father's she desired to keep.

"I quite understand that returning to the place where your father was killed would be an insupportable agony at present, my dear, but this unhappy chore must be accomplished soon. If you are able to give Marie a list of what you wish to re-move, that would be best; otherwise, she and your manservant will pack up everything and bring it all here until you feel up to the task."

Here was the solution Claudia had vainly sought these past days, her brain so intent on restoring the diamonds and keep-ing scandal at bay that she'd spared no thought for mundane matters. Buckley would be at the apartment, and he was the one person she could trust to deliver the package to Lord Selkirk. Claudia gathered her wits together and succeeded at length in convincing her hostess that she was equal to the ordeal of disposing of her father's belongings.

Had her mind not been so taken up with her sacred mission, she would have found this final service heartwrenching beyond all bearing, Claudia acknowledged, fighting back the threatening tears as she went through her father's dresser drawers a few hours later. Marie was packing Claudia's clothes in her bedchamber, and Buckley was on his way to Lord Selkirk's house with the package containing the necklace. There was actually very little for her to do. Apart from his wardrobe that she was giving to the servant, her father had accumulated pitifully few possessions during his military career. For many years he had sent money to his sister-in-law for his daughter's keep, but he owned no property and had sold his horses to increase his stake in the gaming house. There were a few books, his prized gold-and-enameled snuffbox that Lord Malmsey might like to have as a keepsake, a few items of personal jewelry, including the gold watch her mother had given him on their marriage, and the miniature painting of her mother that had accompanied him all over the Iberian peninsula and recently into Belgium and France. These she would keep, along with the walking stick that had been his constant companion during their too brief reunion. She walked over to the bedside table and retrieved the miniature in its ormulu frame. The lovely smiling face in the portrait blurred suddenly as Claudia lost the battle to restrain her tears. She pressed the painting to her breast and gave way to a short spate of silent weeping.

She was just beginning to regain control when footsteps sounded in the hall between the bedchambers.

"Are you there, Miss Herbert?"

"Yes, Buckley, come in."

Claudia was attempting to mop her face with her handkerchief as the servant entered, and it was a moment before she noticed the small package he was holding out to her.

"I'm sorry, Miss Herbert, but I was unable to deliver this to

Lord Selkirk. There was only a caretaker at the place who told me the family what was living there had left two days ago."

"Left?" Claudia echoed blankly.

"Yes, ma'am. According to this French cove, they went back to England."

Chapter Three

The crowning achievement of Claudia's short—she trusted—career of deception was convincing the hospitable Malmsey family that she really preferred returning to her relatives in England rather than joining them in their upcoming Italian sojourn. For their part, the Malmseys endeavored to persuade their guest that she would be the one conferring the favor by providing companionship for their eighteen-year-old daughter during the summer. Fortunately for Claudia's dogged purpose, her understandably low spirits had been further depressed by the initial failure of her mission, to the point that her worried hosts at last came to agree among themselves that she required those close to her by ties of blood to support her during this unhappy period. For the remainder of her stay in Paris, Claudia clung to the quiet heroism it took to maintain this necessary fiction. She promised herself the indulgence of a full accounting of the affair by letter once she had delivered the necklace to the Selkirks in England. Meanwhile, she tried to convey her feelings of gratitude and affection to her hosts as she prepared to leave France in the company of her father's loyal batman, whom Lord Malmsey had charged with her safety during the return journey.

The evening before her scheduled departure, Lord Malmsey talked to Claudia about her finances, apologizing for his inability to promptly convert her father's investment into accessible funds for her use. "Captain Marple assures me he is endeavoring to find another partner to take over your father's share of the business, Claudia. You understand that it is impossible at present to recover your father's investment, which has not been recouped as yet. To divide the assets now would mean the end of the business and a significant loss to both parties."

"It was my impression from my father's comments that the rooms were not proving profitable of late," Claudia replied, choosing her words with care.

"Captain Marple was frank in disclosing recent losses due to several unprecedented runs on the bank, but he assured me they had weathered the temporary crisis and had begun to reverse the situation. You have given me the power to act in your interest, and I intend to leave someone in my employ here to monitor the rooms while I am away this summer. Also, Captain Marple requested your aunt's direction in England so that he might personally keep you informed of his search for a new partner."

Claudia looked away quickly to hide the shock that rippled through her at the news that her ultimate sanctuary had been stripped away. All her desperate evasion of her father's partner had been for naught, a child's denial of a threat by closing her eyes and refusing to acknowledge the presence of the danger. Captain Marple had simply bided his time and made his plans for the moment when she would not be so closely guarded. It took her a few seconds before she could trust her voice to remain neutral as she said, "I comprehend that Captain Marple knows that I am returning to England tomorrow . . . through Calais?"

"Yes, and he desired me to convey his regrets that your continued indisposition has prevented his expressing his sincere condolences to you in person. He went on to extend his earnest wishes for your safe return to England." Lord Malmsey's eyes reflected nothing save kindly concern as he unknowingly delivered the well-disguised threat that made Claudia's blood run cold.

She produced a conventional response and managed to escape to her room before the trembling that had started to overtake her soul and body at this latest catastrophe became apparent to everyone else.

Claudia stared wild-eyed about the pretty bedchamber that had been her refuge—a false refuge, as it turned out—while she fought down successive waves of fear that produced a

metallic taste in her mouth, and attempted, unsuccessfully at
first, to control the twitching in her limbs. It was nearly a half
hour before she gained enough mastery over her bodily reactions for her brain to begin to function coherently once more.
In the interval she had several times come close to rescinding
her reasoned decision not to divulge the true situation to Lord
Malmsey, once even going so far as to open her door, intend-
ing to seek another interview with him. She had stood in the
doorway for minutes on end, a prey to doubts and indecision,
before closing the door again with soft finality. At last she was
able to bend her mind to considering ways to avoid the fate
Marple was planning for her. She would *not* walk tamely into
whatever trap he was devising. There must be some way to
elude him or his henchmen.

Claudia's eyes narrowed, and she gnawed on her lip as she
concentrated on the essentials of the situation. Captain Marple
knew she was leaving tomorrow—there was no changing this
without involving her hosts more deeply in the affair. He was
expecting her to proceed to Calais, where she would cross to
Dover, so *that* must not happen. Somehow she must contrive
to change direction en route and sail from Dieppe or Le Havre
instead. Marple was acquainted with her father's batman,
therefore she must dispense with Buckley's services as escort
and protector. It would be necessary to give Buckley the slip
and prudent to alter her appearance as much as possible to
make it more difficult to trace her movements, though her
name would of course be on her passport. If she could get
enough of a start on Marple, she would be able to travel under
a false identity once she arrived in England.

Claudia walked over to the satinwood dressing table and
stared into its scrolled ormolu mirror, sighing for the bygone
era of wigs as she regarded her bright hair that was frequently
a source of comment among the French. She must cover it, but
not with clouds of black veiling. Marple would expect her to
be swathed in mourning.

Hope stirred in her suddenly as she envisioned the Malmseys' governess, Miss Elvira Weedy, a tall formidable figure
in an outsize cap and spectacles. Those features were really all
one noticed about Miss Weedy when first meeting her. Even

now Claudia could not with confidence describe that lady's hair or eye color. She pulled open a drawer in the dresser, revealing her father's reading spectacles lying next to his watch. She fingered them briefly before closing the drawer again and heading abruptly for Miss Weedy's room, driven by a sense of purpose. She *would* get away from the loathsome Captain Marple. The element of surprise would be on her side. Surprise and speed, God willing, would be her allies.

She had come to France in the company of a family of her aunt's acquaintance, Claudia recalled as she got ready for bed later that evening. Youth, excitement, and a happy anticipation had insulated her from the rigors of traveling; in fact, she had thoroughly enjoyed the novel experience. She still had youth on her side, she acknowledged with a bitter twist to her lips, as the ever-ready tears crowded behind her eyelids. She could not afford to dwell on the difficulties and dangers that might beset a woman traveling alone. Resolutely, she beat back all qualms that arose to torment her on her last night in Paris, but sleep was well nigh impossible in her current state, and she arose in the morning less refreshed than when she had first laid her weary head on her pillow.

Odd snippets of conversation drifted away from the indistinguishable hum of noise in the Winchester inn's busy public room and sounded clearly in Claudia's ears, to be followed by other fragments, unrelated but equally distinct, a moment later. The aroma of coffee tantalized her nostrils as she raised her cup to her lips and took a satisfying sip of the hot fragrant brew. Warmth spread through her body along with an unfamiliar sensation she identified tentatively as pleasure. She tried to keep the feeling with her a little longer, sitting nearly motionless, except for her roving eyes, at a small table tucked into a corner formed by the huge jutting fireplace that dominated the back wall of the room. With gratitude she probed the absence of the fear that had tormented her every waking moment since her father had died in her arms in Paris.

From the instant she had entered the carriage Lord Malmsey had hired to bring her to Calais, fear had been her invisible companion every mile of the journey out of France, despite the

presence of her father's armed batman during the initial stage
to Amiens. She had slipped out of that city at night, boarding
the *diligence* bound for Rouen while Buckley slept, leaving
him some money and a lying note that proclaimed her sudden
decision to spend time with friends outside Amiens before returning to England.

There had been ample opportunity during the uncomfortable
ride on the lumbering stagecoach to writhe under the sting of
shame at the way she had repaid the people who had her best
interest at heart. Worse still had been those moments of heart-
tripping fear at each change of horses or whenever a new passenger entered the coach. Although she had made significant
changes in her appearance before sneaking out of the inn at
Amiens, a gentlewoman traveling alone must always stand
out. At least the drivers and guard on the *diligence*, if questioned by pursuers, could honestly deny carrying a young
woman dressed in mourning among their passengers. The vo-
luminous mobcap and unbecoming felt hat she had purchased
from the Malmseys' governess entirely covered her hair. Combined with darkened and thickened eyebrows and her father's
spectacles, Claudia felt confident that no casual eye would detect her Parisian persona in her present guise. Her father's cane
had posed a problem, being too long to fit in her bags. Apart
from a sentimental attachment to the stick, Claudia could think
of no safer hiding place for the Selkirk diamonds. In desperation she had begged some bandage cotton from a housemaid at
the Malmseys' before her departure and had used it to wrap
her ankle to give visual legitimacy to the walking stick when
she left Buckley at Amiens.

While her eyes continued to survey the lively scene in the
dining room, Claudia felt surreptitiously for the cane leaning
against the wall. Reassured as to its presence, she took another
sustaining sip of coffee, savoring the deep flavor. Nothing had
tasted this good in recent memory, certainly not since that
dreadful Channel crossing, the mere recollection of which
caused her to shudder. After the easy crossing from Dover to
Calais last year, she had been woefully unprepared for interminable hours of constant pitching and rolling as the packet
plowed along the longer route from Dieppe. Upon reaching

Newhaven at last, she'd been too sick and shaken to embark immediately on the overland trip to Maplehurst, the Selkirk seat near Litchfield in Hampshire, despite the most urgent desire to complete her mission. Almost as horrible as her sufferings at sea had been the day she'd spent recuperating in a dismal inn at Newhaven, fearing that each new sound from outside or below stairs signaled discovery by Captain Marple or his hired ruffians. With no way of knowing exactly where Marple had planned to overtake her on the way to Calais, she could not assume that she had more than a day's start on her pursuers at best.

Fearing that her funds would not be sufficient to see her safely to her aunt's home ultimately, she had elected to travel by stagecoach, though chaffing at the slowness and discomfort. The trip had been blessedly uneventful so far, and with something less than twenty miles to go, she was aware of a growing sense of excitement. Soon, this very day, she would be free of this horrible obligation. She could not allow her mind to venture into the void that was her future until she had performed the duty her father had laid upon her with his dying breath, which was just as well, she admitted drearily before mentally turning her back on that line of thought. The London-bound stage would leave Winchester within the hour. Already her baggage was in the courtyard with that of several other passengers, but she would leave them before Basingstoke. She planned to hire a local vehicle to take her the last few miles to the Selkirk estate.

As Claudia pulled her father's watch out of her reticule to check the time, a man entered the coffee room, pausing in the doorway to sweep the room thoroughly with a pointed gaze before he headed toward the empty chair at the table under a window overlooking the inn yard. She lowered her eyes to her cup as he neared her table, but not before his dark unshaven visage had registered in her mind. He wore leather breeches and mud-stained boots like a number of the men present, but there was something . . . alien about his appearance nonetheless. Behind her cup Claudia eyed him uneasily, aware of a slight film of perspiration above her lip suddenly. When the newcomer ordered a tankard of ale in accented English, a little worm of apprehension gnawed at her insides. She tried to dismiss the inappropriate reaction—the man was paying no mind to her or anyone else. After that first searching glance that had penetrated every corner of the room, he had kept his eyes on the window, presumably watching the activity in the inn yard.

She wrenched her eyes from the unprepossessing man and took another sip of her coffee, but a few seconds later when the barmaid brought his ale, Claudia found herself covertly watching him again as he raised the tankard to his mouth, his sleeve falling back.

For what seemed an eternity Claudia sat frozen in witless terror before she raised trembling fingers to her face and lowered the spectacles that blurred her vision the fraction of an inch necessary to confirm that the individual seated less than six feet away from her was the same man she had seen fleeing from her building after her father's murder. She utterly rejected any coincidence that could have placed another man with an identical puckered scar on his right hand in her path. Fear and a strong instinct for self-preservation kept her motionless while she mustered her scattered wits. Obviously, Captain Marple had assumed that her disappearance on the way to Calais meant that she still had the necklace in her possession and intended to deliver it to Lord Selkirk in England. His source of information being as good as her own, he had dispatched his henchman—perhaps more than one—to Hampshire, where the viscount had his county seat, to keep her from accomplishing her mission, she realized, fighting down a rising panic. She would not, she vowed, swallowing with difficulty, give way to the terror that was making her feel nauseated. The man had not recognized her; she still had a chance to elude him, but there was no time to lose.

Even with echoes of dire urgency resounding inside her head, Claudia found it nearly impossible to make her petrified limbs obey her commands. Her movements were slow and heavy as she resettled the spectacles on her nose and eased herself out of her chair, shifting the walking stick to the hand farthest from the killer's table. She could feel his eyes on her back as she walked out of the room with a more pronounced limp than she had used on entering. At least it kept her from running pell-mell, which some craven part of her brain was insisting on doing.

Safely in the vestibule, Claudia paused just inside a door leading out into the inn yard and summoned one of the ostlers with a raised arm. After ascertaining that there was a livery stable on the next street where she might find a carriage for hire, she gave him some money to remove her baggage from the pile awaiting the London coach and to see it delivered immediately to the stables. Grateful for the ostler's incurious acceptance of the commission, Claudia left the coaching inn by the door that opened onto the street and proceeded on foot to the stables, forgetting in her haste to maintain her limping gait until her eyes lighted on the stick clutched in her hand, whereupon she slowed her pace considerably.

Twenty minutes later, when the carriage she'd hired entered the toll road, Claudia drew her first easy breath since spotting her father's killer in the coaching inn. She was ahead of the stagecoach and would be leaving the turnpike after a few miles in any case. The owner of the stables had assumed, on noting her two valises, that she was going to stay at Maplehurst, a misapprehension she allowed to stand. Somehow she would have to get herself back to her aunt's home near Aylesford, but at this stage of the adventure that was a mere bagatelle, she concluded wryly, turning her attention to considering what would be her best course once she arrived at the Selkirk estate.

Now that she was so near her destination, the disguise that had bolstered her courage in France might prove a handicap. Regarding her bandaged ankle with a thoughtful frown, Claudia decided that this at least could be discarded, and she proceeded to unwrap the bandage, delighting in the sense of freedom that ensued as she flexed her foot in its sensible leather half boot.

There had been oceans of time during this interminable journey to reexamine her decision to return the diamonds anonymously. The Malmseys had removed from Paris by now, the Selkirks were back in England, she would soon return to the obscurity of a Kentish village, and nothing could hurt her father any longer. The decision to tell the truth had been sneaking up on her over the past week, she realized all at once

as she glanced inattentively at the verdant Hampshire countryside through which the road ran. How to deal with the question
of the partners' suspicions that Lord Selkirk had cheated at
cards was, however, an extremely delicate point and one that
challenged Claudia's ingenuity, while the hired carriage left
the turnpike with, thank heavens, no sign of pursuit.

They had not gone more than a couple of miles along the
country road when Claudia noticed a figure tramping ahead as
they rounded a curve. Her teeth and sinews tightened, then relaxed as she saw that the person, though undoubtedly male,
was just a lad. He was carrying a valise and limping quite noticeably. Claudia's instinctive response to the boy's predicament was to rap on the roof of the carriage with the handle of
her cane.

The youth had pressed himself up against the hedgerow as
the coach drew near, alarming two feathered inhabitants who
flew out uttering complaining squawks. His expression became hopeful as the driver pulled the pair to a halt a short way
ahead, and he hobbled up to the door when Claudia beckoned.

"I can see that an accident of some sort has befallen you,"
she said, noting the grimace of pain he couldn't suppress as he
shifted his weight. "May I be of assistance by bringing you
nearer to your destination? I am going a bit past the road to
Litchfield if that will help."

"Then you will go right past the entrance to my uncle's estate just beyond Overton, ma'am," the youth said eagerly,
though he made no move to touch the carriage door until Claudia bade him enter.

"There is room inside for your bag also," she added, moving
her cane to accommodate this item as the boy climbed awk-
wardly in, holding one leg stiffly and sinking onto the seat
across from her with an audible sigh of relief.

Claudia had had time to study him closely without appearing rude during this uncomfortable exercise. The result of her
stocktaking was positive; though not at his best with rivulets
of sweat running down his face and his mouth set hard against
pain, her passenger was clearly a handsome young man. Beneath an unruly mop of curly dark hair his light gray eyes were
startling against unusually tanned skin. They were very fine

eyes, large, well opened, and full of awareness undimmed by his present physical discomfort. He was of medium height with the slenderness of adolescence, but the width of his shoulders gave promise of superior strength at maturity. She judged him to be not much more than sixteen, though possessed of a poise and easy bearing rather unexpected in one of his tender years.

"Thank you, ma'am, for taking me up with you," he said now, his lips widening in a friendly smile as he wiped a handkerchief over his face. "It is a relief to take the weight off this wretched leg for a bit."

"What happened to it?" Claudia asked, returning his smile with interest.

"A sporting carriage came bowling along around a curve a mile back, and the horses spooked at the sight of me. The driver had trouble controlling them, and I had to scramble out of the way in a hurry. I wrenched my knee somehow, and it has stiffened up on me. It will be fine after a little rest," he predicted cheerfully. "By the way, my name is Julian Brewster."

"And I am Claudia Herbert," Claudia replied, recalling too late the assumed identity under which she had been traveling. "If you think it might help to wrap your knee, I have a bandage here that you are welcome to take," she added quickly, pulling the bandage out of her reticule.

The boy blinked, then chuckled. "Now, that is what I call being really prepared for emergencies, ma'am. You are doubly my good angel. If I wrap my knee, there will be no problem at all in walking to the house from the entrance. Thank you again."

"As for that, Mr. Brewster—Julian," she amended, in response to his quick demur, "I shall certainly convey you to your front door. You must stay off that leg as much as possible for the next day or two." She firmly squelched his embarrassed protest that he could not impose so needlessly on her kindness and changed the subject.

"Did I understand you to say this is your uncle's house? Are you paying him a visit?"

"No, that is, not precisely. We—my sisters and brother and I—are living with my uncle until our parents return from

India." He looked up from his task of wrapping the injured knee to add, "I have been at school in Winchester. Oh, thank you." He accepted the pin she held out to him and attempted unavailingly to secure his handiwork tightly.

"Here, let me do that for you." Claudia took the pin back, saying casually, "I would have thought it a little early for the Easter term to be over," as she bent forward to affix the pin. "There." Looking up, she saw a trace of embarrassment in his eyes.

"The term doesn't finish for another week, but I received a letter from my sister Susannah—my twin, actually—that had me thinking I'd better get back quickly to keep her from doing something stupid, so I . . . just left."

It was Claudia's turn to blink. "Without getting permission from the school authorities?"

"They wouldn't have given it," he said gloomily, "but my uncle is away at present, and our great aunt has no idea how to control Susannah's starts. There'll be all sorts of rumpus at school when they discover I'm gone, of course, but it cannot be helped. I'd spent all my allowance, so I couldn't buy a ticket on the stage, but I got a ride part of the way with a farmer taking his pig to market. Everything would have gone swimmingly except for that cow-handed curricle driver." He lapsed into silence, evidently oppressed by his cumulative woes.

Claudia regarded her passenger with sympathy, while curiosity warred briefly with good manners and emerged victorious. "I do not wish to appear vulgarly inquisitive," she said gently, "but I cannot help wondering what your sister might do—what you *fear* she might do—that would warrant such an impulsive and potentially costly reaction on your part."

"I am persuaded she is contemplating eloping with some court card she's been meeting on the sly."

Julian's bald pronouncement routed Claudia's inner amusement. "Good heavens, she cannot surely be more than six . . . seventeen," she amended, not wishing to insult the youth by underestimating his age.

"She's sixteen, and her head's stuffed full of romantical nonsense," Susannah's exasperated brother declared.

"I believe most girls' heads are full of romantic notions at this age, Julian, but that does not mean they could be persuaded into an elopement."

"Most girls haven't had men making idiots of themselves over them since they were fourteen."

"I apprehend that your sister is very pretty?"

"Too pretty for her own good and without even the wit of a widgeon, which at least knows better than to flirt with everything in pants, especially when my uncle is away."

Claudia's appreciation for the boy's genuine concern for his lovely sister's safety enabled her to conceal her amusement at this linguistic flight of fancy. "Well, she will soon have her brother's protection. Tell me about the rest of your family. How many of you are there?" she asked in the hope of lightening his despondency.

"Five. Susannah and I are the eldest, our brother George, who is at school also, is fourteen, Roberta is twelve, and Esther is nine."

"And you are all newly come from India to stay with your uncle and aunt?"

"Great aunt," he corrected. "Our uncle is unmarried."

"It must be a very great change for all of you."

"Yes. Susannah and I are the only ones who remember England at all. Roberta and Esther were born in India. Esther misses our parents dreadfully, being the youngest, but the rest of us are enjoying being in England now that we have become more accustomed to the cooler climate and all the rain."

"Are you enjoying school?"

Julian shrugged. "It's all right," he said, meeting her interested gaze squarely. "Though all the chaps seem to have known each other forever. George likes it better; he has made some good friends already. Most of the masters are a bit . . . stodgy, but the cricket is great. I don't quite like leaving the girls on their own at Beechwood however."

"Do your sisters have a governess?" she asked when his voice trailed off and the worried look crept back into his eyes.

"Not at present. The one we had in India traveled with us to England, but she and Susannah were forever at odds because there were several youngish men sailing, not to mention some

of the ship's officers, who were falling all over themselves to
engage Susannah's attention whenever we were on deck. And
Susannah *would* flirt with all of them, mostly to annoy Miss
Chester. I must in fairness to my sister explain that Miss
Chester was generally abrupt and unconciliatory in her manner
toward Susannah, although she was kind enough to the
younger girls. Not that that excuses Susannah's behavior, of
course."

Claudia produced some understanding murmurings, although her unspoken sympathy was solidly behind the poor
creature who, for a mere pittance, had found herself in the unenviable position of bearing full responsibility for the moral
and physical well-being of a provocative honeypot such as Julian had described, in addition to shepherding four other children halfway around the world.

"When we docked, Miss Chester turned us over to my uncle
and resigned on the spot, declaring she would sooner starve in
a ditch than travel another step in Susannah's company."

"Your uncle must have been rather taken aback at such a
turn of events."

"Not a bit of it," Julian responded, more cheerfully than before. "Uncle Miles is a great gun. He never turned a hair, just
looked in a very piercing way from Miss Chester to Susannah,
and accepted the resignation on the spot, stopping Miss
Chester in midflight when she launched herself into a denunci-
ation of Susannah's character and conduct. My uncle simply
smiled at her and made her a formal speech of appreciation for
her loyalty and devotion to us that mollified her enough that
we were frightened for a moment because we could see that
she already regretted her outburst and would have reconsid-
ered if he had asked her to stay. Uncle Miles immediately
summoned a porter to take her bags and told us to make our
adieus and thanks while he sent his groom to arrange for collecting our baggage. I saw him give some money to Miss
Chester when the children were looking at something happening on deck. The second Miss Chester turned to leave us, Susannah threw herself into my uncle's arms and kissed him."

"So your uncle succumbed to your sister's charms also?"
Claudia said with a lift of one eyebrow.

Julian laughed, looking all at once like the carefree youth he should be. "Uncle Miles pinched her chin and warned her not to try her tricks on him. He also promised to find another governess who would keep her sewing samplers and practicing on the harp twice as often as Miss Chester had."

"But he has not, I gather, been able to secure such a dragon as yet?"

"Actually, there have been two so far, according to Susannah's letters, but neither could deal happily with our aunt." Julian leaned forward suddenly, his eye on the passing scene. "I *thought* I recognized that wall. The entrance to the estate is just around the next bend, Miss Herbert, but I assure you there is no need to drive in. I shall do splendidly with my knee wrapped."

Claudia ignored this bravado, having noticed the wince he'd tried to prevent when he moved his leg. She rapped on the ceiling again and gave the driver instructions where to turn when he slowed to a walk shortly thereafter. Closing the window again, she caught Julian's eye on the stick in her hand. "I have recently recovered from a sprained ankle myself," she remarked offhandedly, adding, "the stick may make it easier for you to climb down presently."

"Thank you, ma'am; it's very handsome." The boy's slender fingers ran over the duck's head carving.

"It belonged to my father."

He must have detected the pain beneath the words because he said softly, "Is he recently deceased, ma'am?" At her little nod, he added, "I am very sorry."

"Thank you," Claudia said with a wobbly little smile, realizing that this well-bred youth with his frank manner and rare sense of responsibility was the first person she'd encountered since she'd left the Malmseys who had evoked a feeling of shared humanity in her. She would be sorry when Julian Brewster went out of her life in a few moments. She stared unseeingly at the well-tended grounds through which the entrance road passed until the horses slowed once more.

When the carriage stopped in front of a sizable dwelling, Claudia motioned Julian to remain seated and set down the steps herself, descending with an agility that belied the story of a tender ankle. She stood ready to lend a hand, but Julian managed to get himself out with the aid of the cane, though perspiration stood out on his upper lip again. He gave her a game smile and extended his hand.

Julian had scarcely begun his fervent thanks when the entrance door opened and a soberly clad man of three score or more years hurried down the steps, exclaiming, "Is it you, Master Julian? We were expecting the doctor."

"The doctor? Is someone sick, Jimson?"

The butler, if such he was, held out a gnarled hand that shook to take the valise Julian was wrestling down the carriage steps. "It's Miss Esther, not to say ill, but I fear her leg is broken—at least the coachman says it is, and Calloway is quite familiar with broken bones—on the animals, you understand."

"Where is she and where is my aunt?" the boy demanded, whirling about to follow the servant's movements to the detriment of his own precarious balance. Claudia put out a hand to steady him as he grunted in pain.

"Lady Powerby is prostrate on her bed, having succumbed to spasms when word was brought to her of Miss Esther's accident. The groom and one of the footmen carried Miss Esther to her room, but the poor child has been weeping since it happened."

"Where is my sister?"

The butler's watery blue eyes shifted momentarily, passing over Claudia, who had stood silent throughout the meeting. "Miss Susannah doesn't seem to be on the grounds, Master Julian, or within earshot at least. Two of the maids are out looking for her. Miss Roberta is with Miss Esther. Calloway sent a groom for the doctor nearly an hour ago."

To his credit, Julian did not lose his presence of mind under this succession of blows, but his face was now pasty under the tan, and he was visibly trying to gather his wits as he assimilated all the information. "I'll go up to Esther now, Jimson."

As he turned to Claudia with the evident intention of bidding her farewell, he put too much weight on the wrenched knee. In the face of his obvious discomfort and with a picture of an injured and frightened nine-year-old with no one to succor her save her twelve-year-old sister in her head, Claudia said impulsively, "Would it help if I were to stay for a little while—just until the doctor has attended your little sister and the household has come to grips with the situation?"

Hope leapt into his face. "Would you, Miss Herbert? I should be eternally grateful. If you send your carriage back now, you may take one of ours to your destination when you leave."

"Give me a moment with my driver, and then we'll go straight up to Esther," Claudia said, burning her bridges behind her. She put her hand on the lad's shoulder. "Everything is going to be all right shortly, Julian."

Chapter Four

"Claudia, my leg is hurting, and I'm very hot."

The weary and incipiently teary little voice behind her penetrated Claudia's abstraction. She turned away from the window that looked across a terraced lawn and a small lake and walked over to the bed, pausing to pull the bell cord before taking the chair snugged up against the bed.

"I hoped you were still napping, my pet," she said, smiling at the woebegone face on the pillows as she smoothed damp strands of auburn hair away from the child's equally damp brow.

"I tried, but I couldn't sleep; I am too uncomfortable. I wish my mother were here." Tears spilled out of round blue eyes, wetting the lower half of the child's face.

Claudia silently echoed Esther's fervent wish as she mopped up the tears without appreciably stemming the flow. "I have been thinking of ways to make you more comfortable, love. Would you like to hear my plans?"

At that, a glimmer of hopeful interest appeared in Esther's swimming eyes as she nodded and took the handkerchief from Claudia, absently taking over the mopping operation as the latter explained, "I rang for Josie, who is going to bring some lovely cool lavender water upstairs in a few minutes so that I may bathe your face and neck to cool you down. Also, I am persuaded you will feel much cooler in bed if we braid your hair and fix it on top of your head. Then we'll change that heavy bedgown for a lighter one and carry you over to the chair near the window. Julian has brought up that large ottoman from your uncle's library for your poor leg to rest on." Affecting not to have noticed the fear that had leapt into Esther's eyes at mention of moving her, Claudia continued gaily, "There is a slight breeze from the window now, which you will enjoy while you drink a special concoction that I promise you will ease the discomfort in your leg. And while you are doing this, Josie and I shall change your bed linen and move the bed nearer to the window to catch the breeze during this unseasonable hot spell."

Claudia had her back turned to the bed as she chatted brightly, gathering up hair brushes and bedgown, when the anticipated complaint came that her young patient did not wish to drink any nasty medicines, even if they were called concoctions. She returned to the bed and said gently, "I know it is never quite pleasant to drink odd . . . mixtures, love, but I prepared this medicine myself from the roots of the butterbur plants Roberta gathered for me from the stream banks yesterday. We all—your brother and sisters, the entire household—want to help you to feel better as quickly as possible. Can you not trust us to do what is best for you, and cooperate like a brave girl?"

"Will this truly take away the ache in my leg, Claudia?"

"Yes, my pet, for a few hours, so you may rest and get stronger," Claudia replied, her glance steady in the face of the demanding stare of childhood. "Every day the ache will diminish as the bone knits together again. Soon you will scarcely notice it at all, I promise you."

"Then I will drink your concoction even if it tastes horrid," Esther promised solemnly, dropping the enormous weight of a child's faith on Claudia's slim shoulders.

"I have added honey to help it go down more easily, and cook has made some strawberry ice for a special treat for you afterward," she said, accepting the burden and bestowing an affectionate smile on the little girl.

An hour later, Claudia sat limply in the chair next to the recently repositioned bed, grateful for the faint stirring of air in this part of the room as she gazed upon the sleeping child of whose existence she had been unaware four days ago, but who had moved into her heart in that short span of time.

Sweeping her eyes around the quiet room, every item in which was now completely familiar to her, Claudia still found

it all but incomprehensible that she had come to Beechwood
so recently and by the merest quirk of fate. Prior to this experience she could never have conceived of thrusting herself into
the middle of an unknown family and instantly becoming an
integral part of its existence. But thrust was the wrong word; it
would be more accurate to say she had been sucked into a
whirlpool, so compelling had been the circumstances of a ter-
rified, pain-racked child whose immediate well-being depended on the doubtful ministrations of inexperienced siblings
and servants who looked for authority to an hysterical woman
too engrossed with her own hypothetical ailments to extend
herself in the service of another sufferer. Without conscious
decision on her part, Claudia had found herself cradling and
comforting a sobbing child, then assisting the physician in the
painful process of setting a bone, and eventually becoming the
repository of the doctor's instructions when he had finished
with his small patient.

By the time Esther had sunk into a laudanum-induced sleep
and a subdued Susannah had returned with a tale of a trip to
the village to buy embroidery silk, the dinner hour was upon
them. In the void occasioned by Lady Powerby's abrogation of
her hostess functions, Susannah, under discreet prompting by
her brother, extended a cordial invitation to Claudia to stay at
Beechwood overnight. With nowhere to go and no transport of
her own, she had accepted gratefully. The wisdom of her decision had become manifest when Esther, awakening in the middle of the night, had succumbed to pain and homesickness,
rejecting all her siblings' attempts to comfort her, her sobs escalating rapidly into hysterics. Claudia, aroused by the resul-
tant commotion, had administered hot milk, accompanied by a
combination of motherly solicitude and authority that had at
length succeeded in returning the little girl to a somewhat restless slumber for the remaining hours of darkness.

Before this episode Claudia had spent a pleasant evening
with the other three Brewster children. Perhaps their familial
habit of conviviality among the English in India had made
them more outgoing than the majority of their contemporaries;
whatever the reason, there had been no such constraints as
might have been expected between chance-met strangers

forced into a quasi-intimate association. The children had entertained her with stories of their lives in a completely alien environment and had quizzed Claudia eagerly about Paris in their turn.

It had struck Claudia then that an unexpurgated account of her Parisian adventures might not be considered appropriate fare for children by their guardians. When general descriptions of the city scene had only whetted their appetites for specifics, she had in desperation donned the invisible mantle of Miss Elvira Weedy once again and appropriated that worthy woman's life in Paris as her own.

This fictional history had rebounded on her the next morning when Lady Powerby, having evidently quizzed her eldest niece earlier, had summoned Claudia to her quarters and questioned her closely about her supposed employment in the Malmsey household. Claudia had hung onto her temper with some difficulty under the pointed barrage, only to be overset presently by her ladyship's prompt offer of a position at Beechwood, subject to her nephew's approval. It had required all Claudia's powers of invention, plus dogged determination, to convince Lady Powerby that she could not accept the flattering offer.

Recalling that interview now, Claudia smiled somewhat wistfully, surprised to discover just how appealing the idea of being governess to the Brewster children had become in the few days she had spent with four of them. They were all different personalities, each one interesting, and there was no reason to suppose the absent George would be less appealing than his brother and sisters. It was impossible to remain at Beechwood, of course, apart from her probable lack of academic qualifications for the position. If Lady Powerby had an inkling of the truth about Claudia Herbert's existence in Paris, she would withdraw the impulsive offer on the spot. Besides, Claudia must not lose sight of her pressing mission just because a detour had proved heartwarming. Her life lay elsewhere, and she must shortly set a time for her departure from Beechwood. Esther would begin to improve rapidly now, and it was inadvisable to let the homesick child form an attachment to someone who was simply passing through her life.

Claudia's mouth drooped at the corners as a picture of her future began to emerge unbidden and unwelcome. She could not give way to this line of thought. Delivering the diamonds to the Selkirks was still her first priority. How odd that she had almost forgotten her obsession these past few days. A sennight ago she would not have believed it possible that anything could have pushed this obligation to a position of secondary importance even temporarily.

A soft tap on the door brought Claudia out of her chair in a flash. She sprinted across the room, replacing the spectacles she had caught up with one hand over her eyes before pulling open the door and putting a cautionary finger to her lips as Susannah opened hers.

"Is she asleep?"

"Just. Come in, Susannah."

The girl entered silently, glancing in some surprise at the odd placement of her sister's bed. In the same breathy voice she said, "My aunt would like to see you in her rooms, Claudia, as soon as possible. I'll stay here with Esther." She watched as Claudia brushed a streak of dust from the skirt of her dark cotton dress and moved over to the mirror above the washstand to straighten her cap and tuck a few stray wisps of hair back under its enveloping gathers. "You are looking worn to a thread, Claudia," she said on a rush of sympathy, "and no wonder. You have scarcely been out of this room for the last three days and nights. I'll sit up with Esther tonight if you'll show me what to do for her if she should wake. You really must get a good night's sleep or we'll have your collapse on our consciences."

Looking in the glass at Susannah's reflection, Claudia was touched by this evidence of thoughtfulness and amazed as always by the girl's glowing beauty. Like her twin brother, Susannah Brewster had nearly black hair, worn piled on top of her head in an artless profusion of ringlets, and eyes that had scarcely more color than rainwater, made more startling by virtue of a narrow dark outline around the iris. Her creamy complexion bore no evidence of a long stay in a hot climate, unlike Julian's. Everything about her was exquisite from the delicate modeling of her features to the lovely proportions of her body and the liquid grace inherent in all her movements. Claudia now comprehended why Julian was overwhelmed with the responsibility for his lovely sister's safety.

Claudia turned and smiled at the earnest girl. "Thank you, Susannah. If you'd like to stay here while I go to see Lady Powerby, that would be a help. As for tonight, I am fairly confident that Esther's sleep will be more restful than the last few nights, and since I am in the next room now, it is a simple matter to leave my door open so that I can reach her quickly should she waken. Now I had best not keep Lady Powerby waiting any longer. There is a book of poems on the table if you get bored," she added with a nod of her head before whisking out of the room.

There was no spring in Claudia's step a few minutes later as she approached the wing containing the principal guest chambers of the house, where Lord Pelham's aunt was installed in comfort, surrounded by choice furnishings and lovely objects. It was not that she had taken Lady Powerby in dislike; indeed, she could only pity someone whose energies were entirely concentrated on discovering evidences of failing health with every breath she took and who tried to draw all with whom she associated into endless discussions of possible treatment plans and the ultimate ramifications of each. Having considered this, however, there was no denying that Lady Powerby's acquaintance was rather a trial to be borne than a boon.

To Claudia's knowledge the woman had not ventured out of her own suite since Esther's accident. Obviously, she had not found it necessary to reassure herself personally as to the quality of the care the child was receiving under the direction of a total stranger. Claudia pitied the unknown Lord Pelham profoundly if he had counted on receiving any practical assistance from his aged relative in lightening the burden he had assumed when he'd agreed to take on the care of his sister's children for a prolonged period. She could not help but wonder why his choice had devolved on such an unsuitable candidate—mayhap he was one of those hearty sports-minded men who had gleaned little understanding of the female of the species. From things the children had said, it was patent that to a man they adored their uncle, which was reassuring at least. In another day or two she would have the household running smoothly again. Mrs. Trowbridge, the housekeeper, was a very good sort of woman who managed her staff efficiently.

Claudia's comfortable optimism about a quick return to normal at Beechwood received a decided setback when she entered Lady Powerby's suite and discovered that the woman's habitual languor had been replaced by a state of agitation. True, she was lying back against pillows on a rose-colored chaise longue, a wet cloth to her forehead, but she was clutching a filmy handkerchief between fingers that were constantly twisting and untwisting this item, and her thin features were drawn into a mask of horrified protest.

"Oh, Miss Herbert, you are here at last! The most dreadful thing has happened. How could he do such a thing without first consulting me—and on such short notice too! Oh, I shall go perfectly distracted—I can already sense one of my spasms coming on—and just when I was hopeful that the relief provided by that herbal tea you sent up to me—I have forgotten what it was?"

"Cowslip," Claudia murmured, seeing that her ladyship actually expected an answer in the middle of her tirade.

"Yes, well, as I was saying, I was beginning to entertain the hope of a steady improvement in my digestion when the letter arrived, and it has completely overset my nerves as you can see. My head is pounding—"

"What letter, ma'am? From whom?" Claudia ruthlessly interrupted what promised to be a catalogue of symptoms.

"From Miles, my nephew." Lady Powerby untwisted the fingers of one hand from the tortured handkerchief and searched among the folds of her mauve silk peignoir, emerging after a few seconds with a crumpled sheet of paper that she held out to the younger woman. "Take it, read it—I cannot bear to gaze further upon such a monstrous missive. How could he have so little consideration for his own flesh and blood?" Lady Powerby raised the handkerchief to her face, her breathing increasingly rapid and shallow.

The letter was quite short; Claudia would have mastered its contents in one swift perusal had it been less wrinkled and had one worried eye not kept returning to the afflicted woman on the chaise. After a second reading she turned an uncomprehending gaze on Lady Powerby. "It seems that Lord Pelham has written to advise you that he will be returning to Beechwood tomorrow with two guests and has desired you to direct Mrs. Trowbridge to prepare certain rooms for their reception," she parroted, ending on a questioning note.

"To bring anyone here when the household is at sixes and sevens is inconsiderate enough—"

"But surely Lord Pelham cannot know about Esther's accident—unless you wrote to him, ma'am?"

"How could I write to him when he didn't even deign to inform me of his destination when he rode off nearly a fortnight ago—and he scarcely back from France at the time. Very odd he was, too, on his return, restless and absentminded, quite unlike himself, and so I told him more than once. Then to turn around almost immediately and leave me here again with full responsibility for these children when anyone with the least degree of sensitivity would know that I could not be expected to cope in my delicate state of health. But this, this latest affront is beyond imagining! I knew he was dangling after the Hingham girl in London this spring before the children came—Mrs. Miccleston could not wait to inform me, though her letter was only two days in advance of one from my niece Letitia to the same effect—but I was persuaded the advent of the children had turned his thoughts away from that madness. He never stirred from Beechwood for over a month when they first arrived. And I must say in justice to Miles that he is very good with them and does not permit that spoiled young madam, Susannah, to wind him around her little finger, but *this*," she declared, coming back to her grievance, indicating the letter in Claudia's hand with a pointing finger and a fulminating eye, "is beyond anything! To invite that woman under this roof and expect me to act as her hostess—oh, it is too bad of him!" Lady Powerby's meager bosom heaved with resentment.

"I apprehend that you . . . you do not care for Miss Hingham, ma'am?"

Thinking she had at last uncovered the nugget of gold in the confusing torrent of complaint, Claudia was put right when

Lady Powerby snapped, "I have never met the Hingham girl, but if she is anything like her harridan of a mother, then I pity Miles from the bottom of my heart, even while I marvel at his gullibility to be so taken in by their shabby gentility."

The situation now being clear in her mind, Claudia devoted her best efforts to reconciling Lady Powerby to her distasteful duty as her nephew's hostess. These efforts included additional cups of cowslip tea to combat her ladyship's gastric distress and a soothing draught for her headache. These ministrations were accompanied by encouraging words of support, reiterating as often as necessary Claudia's confidence in Lady Powerby's generous nature, and her ability to set aside her personal prejudices in order to perform a role for which she was uniquely qualified by virtue of the innate graciousness and dignity that Claudia had remarked on first meeting her hostess. Her subsequent offer to deputize for Lady Powerby in apprising Mrs. Trowbridge of Lord Pelham's instructions succeeded in turning the tide after more than a half hour of judicious flattery and persuasion. Wanly but bravely, Lady Powerby declared herself prepared to undergo the great personal sacrifice required to fulfill her beloved nephew's wishes in the face of her undying conviction that he was acting in the grip of a dangerous delusion if he thought any daughter of Sophia Hingham would be a suitable wife to a man in his position.

Claudia rose from her chair in the charming boudoir with its rose damask draperies and smiled widely at the courageous figure on the chaise. "If you need to conserve your strength tomorrow, ma'am, I shall be happy to do the flowers for you. I am persuaded there will be ample time before I leave Beechwood."

"Thank you, Miss Herbert, that is most accommoda—*leave*? What do you mean? How can you think of deserting me—and the children—Esther!—at such a time?" Lady Powerby sat up straight, her whole being eloquent of wounded disbelief.

"But . . . but naturally I must be leaving, ma'am. My being here at all is the merest happenstance. I am very glad to have been able to be of service in an emergency, but Esther is much better now, and Lord Pelham will be here tomorrow. You must see that it would be most . . . most disconcerting for him to find a strange female established in his house when he is bringing his betrothed—at least someone he is considering as his future wife," she corrected in the face of the older woman's ardent protest, "to be presented to his family."

The baron's venerable relative could not be brought to acknowledge the reasonableness of Claudia's scruples, however; indeed she began to show alarming signs of relapsing into the highly strung nervous condition in which Claudia had found her. Against her better judgment the younger woman agreed to remain at Beechwood in the unofficial role of nurse and temporary governess until Lord Pelham returned home, although she resolved privately that she would be packed and ready to depart the instant she had given his lordship an account of her brief stewardship.

As Miles Pelham leaned down to brush a fly off his horse's neck, his line of vision changed to include the young woman he had asked to become his wife, her serene profile framed in the carriage window. It was a good profile, perhaps a bit too long in the chin for real beauty, but clearly defined, as was everything about Miss Hingham—Martha, he amended, his eyes taking in the modest straw bonnet adorning the lady's fair curls. His proposal, though unproductive as yet of a favorable reply, had at least gained him the privilege of Miss Hingham's Christian name, after due consultation with her mama.

Though not rating himself a real prize in the Marriage Mart, Miles had been forced to acknowledge a certain chagrin these past few days at Miss Hingham's—Martha's—hesitation in accepting his offer, based on what he had obviously misread as ladylike encouragement in her cordial reception of his attentions this spring. He had not committed the error of believing her to have formed a romantic attachment to him; he'd accepted that her feelings were as tepid as his own, but he'd assumed that the suitability of the match would appeal to the rational judgment of a young woman still unwed in her fourth Season and not possessing any extraordinary degree of beauty or a large portion that might command a more advantageous offer.

He had no earthly right to resent Miss Hingham's exercising

the prudence and rationality that had commended her to him in
the first place, Miles admonished himself, and he would be
very uncomfortable indeed to be the recipient of ardent affec-
tions when his own attachment was of a significantly cooler
nature. Innate honesty, however, compelled recognition of, if
not pique, uneasiness at least in the face of Miss Hingham's—
Martha's—evident intention to weigh the desirability of his estate against the familial encumbrances of which he had
dutifully informed her before casting her lot with his. Not that
any such indelicate explanation had been given for her post-
ponement of a decision until she had visited Beechwood. Indeed, her maternal parent had nearly drowned him in an ocean
of circumlocution designed to sugarcoat the commercial nature
of the projected transaction, stressing, as she did at great
length, the necessity of subjecting their impetuous emotions to
the test of the practical realities of the projected union. Revolted by the woman's arch hypocrisy, he'd taken a small
measure of comfort in his prospective bride's refusal to echo
or endorse the views set forth by her mother. Her refusal to
cloak the decision process in sham sentiment had gained his
admiration for the integrity of her mind.

Miles's interest in Martha Hingham had developed very
gradually over a period of several years' acquaintance. He had
come to appreciate the self-command that enabled her to conduct herself appropriately as the situation demanded. It was
not simply a matter of behaving with propriety. He'd never
seen her display moodiness or give way to sulks or hysterics as
other young ladies were wont to do when events did not fall
out according to their wishes. She listened and spoke with
equal intelligence, to his mind a rare combination in a woman.
Her temper was equable and her nature cool and reasonable, in
marked contrast to that of a number of females he'd observed
over the years who had made life a merry hell for some of his
closest friends who were floundering in the grip of blind infat-
uation with sparkling eyes and smiling, teasing lips. He had no
intention of putting himself at the mercy of the sort of selfish,
false-hearted females who seemed to throng society these
days. It was his experience that these unappealing tendencies
increased in direct proportion to the degree of beauty pos-

sessed by a young woman. Though he'd certainly enjoyed his share of amorous adventures with flirtatious charmers in his salad days, he'd decided quite some time ago that they'd have no part in the task of selecting a wife. Naturally, a man must marry, but such a far-reaching decision should be made by the intellect, not left to the senses, which were notoriously unreliable.

Miles had long held this unshakable conviction, but had been in no great rush to implement it, something his more outspoken female relatives had commented on with increasing frequency over the past few years. Even early in the spring of this year he would have denied, if challenged, that his discreet attentions to Martha Hingham were in the nature of a courtship. It was not until his recent brief trip to Paris had demonstrated that, at the advanced age of thirty, he was still susceptible to a pair of beautiful hazel eyes and bewitching dimples—Louis's *fossettes*—that he had decided it was more than time to put such temptations behind him and set about acquiring a wife in earnest. If in the hidden recesses of his heart a faint hope of finding a suitable bride who could also set his pulses clamoring had persisted down through the years, Miss Herbert's willingness to sell herself to an aging French libertine had given this pathetic puerility the coup de grâce it deserved.

Suddenly, the dilatory attitude he'd taken toward arranging his domestic future vanished, replaced by an urgency to get the deed done with all due dispatch. Once he'd set his mind to the task of evaluating suitable candidates, however, he'd made the rude discovery that the list of potential brides, seemingly so long in his youth, had shrunk drastically of late. Natural attrition accounted for a fair proportion as the eligible girls he'd once known had married in turn. There were still plenty of marriageable young ladies to be seen during the London Season each spring, but whenever he dredged up a name from his memory, it proved to belong to a girl he recalled as being nearly as young and silly as his niece Susannah. By the time he'd been back at Beechwood for a few days, it had become dismayingly clear from the process of elimination that the only female who came anywhere close to meeting his requirements in a life partner was Martha Hingham.

Casting his mind back to the day he'd arrived at the momentous decision to pay court to Miss Hingham, Miles could clearly recall that his primary emotion at the time had been relief to have the matter in a way to being settled. He'd plunged into a veritable furor of planning and making arrangements to ensure that the estate would run smoothly during his absence. Within another few days he had hightailed it to London where the Season was still at its height and had initiated his courtship in earnest. His plan had received a temporary setback when Miss Hingham mentioned that the family expected to return to the country within a sennight, but Miles had had no difficulty in wangling an invitation to their home from Mrs. Hingham, who had tacitly let it be seen that she favored his suit.

As he rode beside his traveling carriage on an unseasonably warm day in early June, Miles admitted to himself that his initial sense of relief at taking action had entirely evaporated, starting with Martha's unexpected refusal to give him a definite answer to his proposal. Obviously, something quite apart from his personal qualities would be the crucial factor in her decision, a sobering reflection at best. Proud though he was of the gracious house built by his grandfather in the middle of the last century, he could not whip up his usual happy anticipation today as they drew closer to Beechwood. With each rotation of the carriage wheels a chill hollowness seemed to be spreading inside him, and a question was repeating itself endlessly in his brain like a persistently unmelodic refrain. *What had he done?*

Chapter Five

As always, his first glimpse of the rosy brick gateposts at the entrance to Beechwood quickened Lord Pelham's senses despite the hazy misgivings recently articulated concerning this particular homecoming. A delicious coolness embraced him once they entered the avenue of copper beeches planted by his grandfather nearly sixty years ago, and he felt the furrows in his forehead smooth out as the leafy canopy filtered the sun's fiercest rays. They left the shady avenue after a few minutes to join the carriage drive that circled the entrance front of the house and soon came to a stop opposite the main door.

By the time Jimson and two footmen reached the arriving party, Miles had let down the carriage steps and was assisting Mrs. Hingham to alight. He performed the same office for Miss Hingham and their abigail before turning to greet the members of his household with a smile.

"Ah, there you are, Jimson. Morris and William can manage the baggage, I believe, and if you will summon Mrs. Trowbridge to see that the ladies' abigail is settled in her quarters, I'll escort Mrs. and Miss Hingham to the saloon, if that is where my aunt is waiting. I am persuaded they will like a cup of tea after a rather hot and dusty drive."

"Very good, sir," Jimson replied, bowing to the ladies. "Miss Susannah thought your guests might find the garden room appealing on a warm day. She is waiting there now, and her ladyship will be down directly. If you will follow me, miss, the housekeeper will be in the hall by now," he said to the small thin abigail, whose eyes were darting all around her surroundings from the open door behind the but-

ler to the smooth lawn stretching away beyond the graveled
drive.

The baron turned his horse over to one of the footmen and
offered an arm to each of his guests. "I am persuaded you will
find the garden room inviting. It was my mother's favorite
room, especially in the summer."

By now both ladies had had time for a leisurely look about
while their host was organizing his servants' activities. As
they walked up the shallow entrance steps, Mrs. Hingham said
approvingly, "These modest dwellings built in the mid-
eighteenth century have much to recommend them, I find.
Beechwood is particularly well-proportioned, and that triangu-
lar central pediment breaking into the roofline gives the facade
a definite elegance that some of the more austere examples
don't possess."

When had he grown so sensitive that he discerned a hint of
condescension in Mrs. Hingham's generous praise for his
house? Miles wondered with some dismay. It was true, as
some of the more acid-tongued women of his acquaintance
held, that Mrs. Hingham was sure to have an opinion about
every subject under the sun and that she was animated by a
corresponding willingness to communicate them to anyone
who could be brought to listen, but Miles had always attrib-
uted such remarks to a peculiar tendency in many females to
be lacking in charity for members of their own sex. He was not
pleased to think he might share this tendency toward one who
most likely would become his mother-in-law in the near future. He reminded himself that she was a sensible, well-
informed woman as he banished all trace of stiffness from his
response, saying cheerfully, "My grandfather appreciated the
fine proportions and symmetry in the original design, but
thirty years later my father indulged his desire for comfort and
light in the back of the house as you will see shortly."

"I assume the avenue of copper beeches was your grandfather's inspiration, it is so well grown," Miss Hingham said as
they went into the entrance hall together. "It's quite lovely,
majestic really. We have nothing to equal it back home."

"Yes, those trees were my grandfather's delight," Miles
said, smiling at the attractive young woman at his side. "I

often wish he could see them as they are today." He ushered his guests past the graceful main staircase to the back of the original house and thence into a wide passageway that branched into a wing that had not been visible from the center of the carriage drive. They passed several doors on the left, and on the right a number of large windows looking out into a garden. Paintings lined the walls on either side, but Miles did not encourage the ladies to linger over interior or exterior views in the light-flooded area, promising them an early opportunity for a better look. He led them through the wide archway at the end of the passageway and halted just inside a room that ran the entire width of the wing.

"What a delightful room," Miss Hingham said with uncharacteristic enthusiasm, her eyes making a rapid survey of the sunny room with multiple sets of French doors on three sides giving onto lawns and gardens that in June were a riot of color. There seemed to be almost as many flowers inside as out, what with floral-patterned chintz upholstery on some of the sofas and chairs scattered about the large area and several massive arrangements of flowers placed on side tables. "It is aptly named the garden room," she added with a smile that showed small white teeth.

"Yes, delightful indeed." Mrs. Hingham echoed her daughter's sentiments. "Was your mother especially fond of flowers, Lord Pelham?"

"She was an avid gardener in her youth, ma'am, but, unhappily, she suffered from a severe arthritic complaint dating from my early childhood that eventually made all movement difficult and painful. My father planned this room so that she could enjoy the gardens daily and even go outside in her wheeled chair when the weather was clement." He nodded toward a small dining table in one corner of the room. "We even got into the habit of dining here in her later years if there were no guests expected."

Just then a breathless voice from the passageway brought all three heads around. "Oh, Uncle Miles, I meant to be here waiting when you arrived, truly I did, but I tore a section of my flounce, and I had to run upstairs so that my maid could sew it. I'm so glad you are home. We missed you so much."

Two similar pairs of light blue eyes rounded as the Hingham ladies watched a dark-haired vision in pink hurl herself into their host's arms while she delivered this gay explanation-cum-apology. Their surprise increased when Lord Pelham returned the girl's embrace, kissing her on both cheeks before he removed her arms from around his neck and turned her to face his guests. "Mrs. Hingham, Miss Hingham, may I present my eldest niece, Susannah Brewster?"

The ladies arranged their features into expressions of cordiality as Susannah, beaming a friendly smile at them, dipped a curtsy to Mrs. Hingham and then extended her hand to Miss Hingham. Both murmured appropriately.

The introductions completed, Susannah apologized again for not being present to greet the guests. "Do come inside," she urged, stepping back to allow their progress into the center of the room. "My aunt . . . is on her way down. I believe you will find this chair comfortable, Mrs. Hingham. If you will ring the bell, Uncle, Mrs. Trowbridge will know it is time to serve tea," she added, glancing over her shoulder at the baron, who was handing Miss Hingham to a chair.

"I believe Jimson has already alerted her to our arrival," he replied, concealing his amusement as he seated himself once his niece had settled onto a sofa. Susannah consciously playing hostess like a little girl presiding over a doll's tea party was really very sweet. Possibly the visitors had missed her sidelong sweep of the room and brief hesitation when mentioning her great-aunt, who should have been present. He listened with grave attention as Susannah made courteous inquiries into the travelers' comfort on the short journey, speculating idly on what she would next consider offering up as a topic of general consideration.

In the event, Mrs. Hingham rescued her young hostess by seizing control of the conversation. "My daughter and I were expressing our pleasure in this delightful room when you arrived, Miss Brewster. I am struck by admiration for the lavish floral arrangements, particularly the one on the bombe chest under the large mirror, containing a profusion of daisies and delphinium set off by red roses and brilliant yellow lilies. Indeed, I wonder can there by anything left in the cutting garden?" She bared her teeth in an arch smile. "Is yours the creative hand responsible for these lovely arrangements?"

"The cutting garden is quite extensive at Beechwood, ma'am, and the mirrored background, you know, doubles the effect of the flowers. I am afraid mine was merely the helping hand in creating these arrangements, which were the inspiration of my friend Claudia. She has the knack of making even a few blooms look marvelous in small containers. She did the flowers in your bedchambers also."

"Your friend has a real flair for floral design," Miss Hingham said pleasantly.

"Claudia?" Lord Pelham repeated, a puzzled line between his brows. "Is she the daughter of one of our neighbors?"

"No, Uncle Miles, she—"

"Oh, dear me, I do beg your pardon for being so tardy." Lady Powerby followed her quavering voice into the room. "My maid is getting old, and she simply cannot be hurried, especially in this terrible heat."

Despite the heat, her ladyship trailed a long silk shawl that kept slipping from her sloping shoulders as she tottered up to the group that had risen at her entrance.

"Well, you are here now, Aunt Sophronia," Miles said soothingly, putting a supporting hand under her elbow. "I believe you are acquainted with Mrs. Hingham?"

"Yes, of course, although it is several years since we have met. How d'you do, ma'am."

Mrs. Hingham met the limp fingers extended to her with two of her own. "I believe it is exactly four years since I last had the pleasure of meeting you in London, Lady Powerby. At that time you were troubled by some physical complaint as I recall. It is nice to see you looking recovered."

Nothing could have been more calculated to offend Lady Powerby than having improved health imputed to her. She drew back, sighing. "Regretfully, that is not the case. I fear my general health is much debilitated in recent years." Her voice grew stronger as she added, "You appear to have put on a little flesh since last we met, ma'am."

"My weight hasn't varied by even one pound in fifteen years," Mrs. Hingham rebutted in her turn, keeping a smile fixed on her lips.

"Really? I beg your pardon; appearances are often deceiving, are they not?" Lady Powerby said sweetly.

The honors now being more or less even, Lord Pelham judged it time to take a hand. "May I present Miss Hingham to you, Aunt?"

"How d'you do, Miss Hingham. You have a great look of your mother about you."

As Martha Hingham returned a polite reply, the sound of tinkling china outside the room put an end to the opening formalities. Lady Powerby seated herself beside her niece on the sofa behind the tea table, and the others returned to their chairs.

Miles sensed that Jimson's entrance with the tea tray was a welcome diversion to everyone, with the possible exception of his doddering aunt, whose habitual lassitude had unaccountably given way to what he could only term a thinly veiled antagonism toward his guests, an attitude that, if permitted to continue, could doom this visit from the start. He participated in the tea-drinking ritual, his bland civility covering puzzled speculation as he observed his female relatives. Susannah was all sweet graciousness as she pressed refreshments upon the Hingham ladies, while his aunt exhibited a punctilious formality that was equally unexpected as she presided over the teapot with more energy than he had yet seen her display during this stay at Beechwood. Was it his own faint unease about the visit of the Hingham mother and daughter that was making him more alert to nuances of behavior, or was there something odd in the atmosphere of his home today?

At that moment a brief exchange between Susannah and Martha Hingham about one of the flower arrangements recalled another small oddity to Lord Pelham. "That reminds me, Susannah. Just before Aunt Sophronia came down, you were about to tell me of this friend of yours, Claudia, is it? I gather she is staying somewhere close to Beechwood at present?"

Susannah's pretty laugh rang out. "Very close indeed, Uncle; she is staying here."

"Here? At Beechwood?" Dumbfounded, Miles glanced from his aunt to his niece, but it was Lady Powerby who rushed into speech.

"Yes, Miles, and you must persuade her to remain. Miss Herbert has been a godsend. I vow I would not have survived these past terrible days had it not been for the herbal medications she prepared for my stomach and my nerves. And she knew just how to cope with Esther, which I never could have done in my weakened state. I have begged her to remain as the children's governess, subject to your approval, of course, but she insists she cannot, though she has admitted that she is not en route to another post but only her own home. You must persuade her to stay. She has the household running smoothly in spite of . . . of complications," she finished lamely, avoiding the eyes of her nephew's guests.

The name Herbert had struck Miles's ears as though they had been plucked harp strings and the vibrations skidded along his nerve ends. Herbert was not an uncommon name, he reminded himself sharply; the likelihood of any connection between this woman and the gaming-house beauty in Paris was extremely remote. He struggled to extract the essential facts from his aunt's disjointed speech and found the most crucial fact missing.

"How came this woman to be at Beechwood? You say she is a friend of yours, Susannah?"

"Yes, but not *previously*, if that is what you mean, Uncle Miles. Julian brought Claudia to Beechwood—or rather she brought him in her carriage, for he had hurt his knee and could scarcely walk—"

"*Julian!* Is he home?" asked Miles, fastening onto another anomaly.

"Yes," Susannah replied, but he noted a certain evasiveness in her eyes before she continued brightly, "it was the most fortuitous thing. Julian and Claudia arrived just after Esther's accident, and with everything at sixes and sevens here, Claudia offered to stay until after the doctor had come, but it—"

"Accident?" Miles interrupted again. "What happened to Esther?"

"Did . . . did Jimson not tell you that Esther fell out of a tree and broke her leg?" Susannah faltered.

"No one told me until now." Miles forced his voice to evenness as he glanced from his niece to his aunt, both of whom looked somewhat discomposed under his scrutiny.

It was Lady Powerby who rushed into the breach, her manner redolent of injured dignity. "Had you left word where you could be reached, Nephew, I should naturally have written immediately to inform you of Esther's misfortune." Her ladyship allowed her eyes to drift over to the Hingham ladies, who were following the conversation with rapt attention.

"When did all this take place, and how is Esther now?"

"The accident was five days ago, and Esther is on the mend now, thanks to Claudia's constant care and ministrations." This from Susannah.

"Yes, Miles, Esther would permit no one else to care for her," Lady Powerby interposed, "but Miss Herbert is planning to leave today. You must beg her to stay."

"I see." The baron rose to his feet and smiled at his guests. "My apologies, ladies, for clouding your welcome with a tale of family misadventure." He acknowledged their polite disclaimers with a bow. "I know you will forgive me if I leave you to enjoy your tea while I run up to check on my youngest niece. Susannah, may I count on you to show Mrs. and Miss Hingham to their rooms presently and see Mrs. Trowbridge about any requirements they may have in that respect?"

"Of course, Uncle."

Miles started for the door, pausing after a few strides and half turning back toward the now all-feminine group. "By the way, Susannah, do you happen to know where Julian is at the moment?"

"I believe he went riding with Duncan Marshall after lunch."

"I see. Thank you."

Lord Pelham had entered the main block of the house when he was hailed from behind. He turned and waited for his smiling nephew, who had entered from the courtyard door, to come up to him.

"You're limping," he said by way of greeting as they shook hands.

"Oh, it is nothing at this point," Julian said, "although I did wrench my knee quite severely. Claudia had me apply compresses of comfrey or some such plant, which really helped heal it quickly."

"Claudia being Miss Herbert, I take it?"

"Yes. Have you met her?"

"I have not yet had that pleasure."

"She's a real trump," Julian declared with simple enthusiasm. "I don't know what we would have done these past few days without her."

"I gather it was you who introduced this paragon into the family. Tell me about it."

Julian obeyed this request, recounting his meeting with Miss Herbert and describing the chaotic situation that greeted them at Beechwood and his relief when his new friend offered to remain until the initial crisis had been weathered. "By the time the doctor left and Esther had calmed down somewhat, it was really too late for her to resume her own journey, and in any case I had told her to dismiss her hired carriage, promising that we should send her on in ours, which is what I thought you would wish me to do," he ended on a questioning note. His uncle nodded, and the boy continued his tale. "It all worked out for the best because poor Esther woke up in the middle of the night and none of us could comfort her, except Claudia. And after that she just stayed on to take care of Esther. She is planning to leave today now that you are home," he added with a worried air, "but I don't know how Esther will take this news. She was crying for our mother a lot at first, and it is my belief that she now regards Claudia almost as if she were Mama. I am very glad you are back."

"So am I." His uncle put a reassuring hand on the lad's shoulder. "And now perhaps we should discuss the matter of your early and . . . unauthorized? return," he added, watching a guarded look come into the honest gray eyes.

"Yes," Julian replied. "I have had plenty of time to ponder what to tell you, and I do not wish to tell any lies."

"That's fortunate because I don't care to hear any."

Taking heart from this nonjudgmental stance, Julian swallowed and began slowly, "I was afraid that Susannah needed me, needed my help, and . . . and knowing you were away, I felt I must get back here. I knew the Head would never let me go without permission from home, so I just left."

"And did Susannah need you . . . your help?" came the gentle question.

"I . . . I am not absolutely certain, but I believe my being here was important. Will you accept that I really cannot say more?"

The boy's trusting eyes met his uncle's searching blue gaze unflinchingly during a silence that stretched long enough to make him sweat a little.

"Yes," Lord Pelham said, convinced of Julian's integrity and alerted to a need for closer supervision of his beautiful but rattlebrained niece. "I imagine the school authorities have tried to get in touch with me since you left?"

"There is a letter from the school on your desk," Julian said with a little grimace.

"Did George know you were leaving?"

"I told him before I left. There is a letter from him on your desk, too."

"I'll attend to both shortly, but now I think it is time I met your Miss Herbert."

"She's always in Esther's room, except for dinner. Susannah and I have insisted that Esther allow Claudia to take her meals with us."

What role had his aunt played in these makeshift household arrangements occasioned by Esther's accident? the baron wondered as he climbed the main staircase in company with his nephew, who was enthusiastically describing his friend Duncan's new hunter. Julian had the liberated appearance of someone who has just had the world's burdens lifted from his shoulders, which served to deepen the sense of guilt that had begun to prick his guardian as the events of his absence were revealed. It was being borne in on him that he'd blithely accepted the sole charge of his nieces and nephews with only the haziest conception of the responsibility involved. The picture had just become a lot clearer, he acknowledged, his mouth taking on a grim set. He would not again leave Beechwood until a competent governess had been installed, one who could deal happily with the children and his aunt. It was only a stroke of divine intervention that had placed this Miss Herbert on the spot to discharge his responsibilities so capably—perhaps more capably than he could have done, he thought, shuddering at the mere idea of coping with an inconsolably homesick child with a broken leg. If he'd understood his aunt correctly, the woman had been a governess in the past, but was not actually seeking a post at the moment. Perhaps she already had a position lined up after this visit to her home. If her character references were acceptable, he would offer her more money to take charge of the Brewster children, he had nearly decided by the time Julian gave a soft knock on the door to Esther's bedchamber. At least three of the children evidently held her in some affection after only a few days' acquaintance.

Make that four of the children, he amended a moment later when he spotted young Roberta curled up at the foot of her little sister's bed, happily listening to the story being read aloud by a woman wearing a hideous mobcap that riveted his gaze. As Roberta dashed across the room to throw her arms around his waist in greeting, Lord Pelham saw the woman grope for a pair of spectacles on a table beside her chair, which she donned before rising and turning toward the door.

Judging by her lithe movements, she was younger than he would have expected, he guessed before giving Roberta a kiss and heading for the little girl on the bed, who was clamoring for his attention with the unnecessary announcement that she had a broken leg.

"Have you, my poor pet? But you are looking very blooming for all that," he declared, bending down to kiss the piquant little face beaming up at him, aware at the same time of a sharply indrawn breath from the woman who had moved aside to ease his passage.

It was not until Miles turned from the bed and glanced at the white-faced female standing as though petrified, her hands gripping each other tightly in front of her waist, that suspicion stabbed him. Her hair was completely hidden by the monstrous cap, and the spectacles she apparently did not require for reading disguised her eyes, but she could not cover the telltale dent in her chin. She was not smiling at the moment, but he would wager his best hack that a smile would reveal a matching dent—Louis Frenier's *fossettes*—in her right cheek. Shock was transforming itself into cold rage as he considered the sheer effrontery required to turn up on his doorstep. Her eyes clung to his as though mesmerized; she did not move a muscle as Julian proceeded with the superfluous introduction.

"Miss Herbert and I were nearly introduced once before," the baron said softly, but his tone brought the woman's chin up and firmed her soft lips. Even that slight movement was enough to cause the dimple to appear in a shallow version in her cheek, not that he had needed this confirmation of her identity.

"You *know* each other?" Julian's initial amazement was replaced by a look of puzzlement as he addressed Miss Herbert. "Why did you not tell us you were acquainted with our uncle, Claudia?"

Miss Herbert emerged from her stupor and looked at the boy, some semblance of life coming back into her face, although her voice held a shaky note at first. "Because we are not acquainted, Julian. Your Uncle and I once attended the same . . . affair in Paris, but I never learned his name."

And that's a damned lie, Miles thought furiously, curling his lip, but he merely repeated in careless tones, "I said we were *nearly* introduced, Julian. Something . . . intervened to prevent it."

Miss Herbert was glaring daggers at him for the oblique reference to her tête-à-tête with the middle-aged French roué, when a clear little voice from the bed bubbled over with delight. "Isn't it wonderful, Roberta, that Uncle Miles knows Claudia? Now she can stay here forever."

Chapter Six

Dismay speared through Claudia, just one more in a series of unpleasant sensations prompted by the appearance of Lord Pelham, but she drew a sustaining breath and dropped to her knees beside the bed, taking one restless little hand in hers.

"I am afraid that is not possible, sweetheart. I told you I would have to leave when your uncle returned home, remember?"

"But . . . but not *now*, not when Uncle Miles *knows* you. He will wish you to stay with us, won't you, Uncle?"

"We'll talk in a little while, Esther. Right now I must speak with Miss Herbert alone. Will you remain with the girls until I come back, Julian?" Lord Pelham asked as he put a hand under Claudia's elbow and urged her none-too-gently from the room without responding to Esther's continued protests.

Claudia jerked her arm out of his hold the second they stepped into the corridor. "You need not grip me like a jailer," she hissed in case they could still be heard inside the bedchamber. "I assure you I am nearly packed and ready to leave."

He ignored her assurance. "How dare you follow me to my home and try to pass yourself off as a governess?"

"How dare *you* make such an infamous suggestion—one that you know very well to be impossible?" she flared back, spitting mad.

"How is it impossible?" he asked with icy gentleness.

"How? I did not even know your name until a moment ago!"

"Why should I believe that among your other lies? You could have learned my identity merely by asking Louis Frenier."

"To what end, pray enlighten me? Why should I wish to meet someone who had clearly demonstrated that he held me in contempt," she ground out between clenched teeth, keeping a firm grip on herself to control the urge that was churning inside her to do him a violence.

"I don't know that yet, but I shall have an answer before we are both much older."

"You shall have nothing further from me, sir. I am nearly packed. I can be out of this house in fifteen minutes."

"Do not be ridiculous. You'll leave when I say you may leave."

"I can make that ten minutes, Lord Pelham," she replied coldly, turning her shoulder on him and walking with conscious dignity down the hall.

He caught up with her as she turned the handle of the door to the next room. "Where do you think you are going?"

She looked pointedly at the restraining hand on her arm, but did not deign to struggle with him. "Into my room to close my bags and put on my hat and gloves," she replied in the patient tones people use to those incapable of grasping simple ideas.

"There will be time for that later. After we get to the bottom of this matter, I shall put my carriage at your disposal to take you wherever you wish to go."

"Thank you, but I'd prefer to walk to the nearest town with a livery stable, rather than accept a favor from you."

"Don't be childish," he snapped.

"And I suppose you are the voice of sweet reason with your melodramatic vows to 'have the answers' and 'get to the bottom' of things?" Her voice dripped poisoned honey, but she was put out of countenance when her antagonist laughed in real amusement.

Lord Pelham seized the momentary advantage. Releasing her arm, he admitted ruefully, "Guilty as charged, I fear. Do you suppose we might both get to the bottom of the matter with a little plain speaking, Miss Herbert?"

Claudia glanced up at him in reluctant amusement. "I do not know what to call what we have been doing if not plain speaking, sir, but I promise you there is no 'matter' to get to the bottom of. My coming to Beechwood was entirely accidental, whatever you choose to believe; I shall leave very shortly, and that will be an end to what little 'matter' there was." She refused to be cowed by the inquisitorial stare he leveled at her, merely raising her eyebrows after a moment. "Would you excuse me now, sir? I am persuaded Esther will welcome your presence. The poor baby has had a difficult time of it. Please be gentle with her; she is terribly homesick in addition to her injury."

"Wait," he said as she opened her door. "Will you answer one question?"

She sighed heavily. "Yes?"

"If you were not trying to worm your way into my house, why did you tell the children you were a governess?"

Claudia was disposed to bristle at his words, but the underlying tone was not accusatory in this instance. She shrugged. "It was all I could think of that first day when the children were questioning me about Paris. I did not think their guardians would welcome tales from a gaming house, so I borrowed a friend's identity."

"Why did you leave Paris?"

"That is two questions, Lord Pelham," she said wearily. "I see no point in telling you the story of my life when our paths are about to diverge forever. I believe I hear Esther becoming a trifle agitated. She needs you, sir. Will you excuse me, please?"

Not waiting for his dismissal, Claudia went into the bedchamber that had been hers for the past few days, thankfully closing the door behind her when he made no attempt to prevent her escape. She slumped against the door, weak and trembling in reaction to a confrontation like nothing she had ever experienced before. She could feel her heart pounding under her hand, although there had been no unusual physical exertion involved. Anger had been the emotion uppermost during those horrible moments, but it had arisen, she realized now, from a painful humiliation at being misjudged for the second time by a man whose name she had not even known, but who obviously considered that he understood her well enough to judge her as lacking in moral fiber. A large portion of her rage was directed inward for allowing herself to be wounded by the unflattering opinions of a stranger. Futile, wasted emotions—it was time to end this brief detour and move on in every sense of the word.

When Claudia's heart had resumed its normal beat, she straightened up and walked dispiritedly over to the satinwood dressing table, where her hair brushes still reposed on its polished surface. She glanced in the wall mirror and was revolted by the white-faced, sad-eyed image looking back at her. If you continue to look like a figure of tragedy, my girl, you will be letting that horrid man think he is correct in his estimation of you, she flayed herself mentally. And don't dare to lower your eyes in his presence or slink out of this house with your tail between your legs either. You know you have performed an act of simple human kindness at Beechwood without any ulterior motive. Lord Pelham's mistrust and dislike cannot alter that. Moreover, the children and Lady Powerby are grateful and cherish only the warmest feelings for you.

With this defiant affirmation to bolster her spirits, Claudia made a face at the girl in the mirror and turned away to bring her brushes over to the open valise on the bed. She began a methodical check, pulling out drawers to make sure she had left none of her possessions behind.

Claudia was engaged in this activity when the escalating level of sound coming from Esther's bedroom, which communicated with her own, invaded her preoccupation with the evils of her personal situation. At first she tried to ignore the sounds. Whatever was going on next door was no longer any affair of hers. Her self-assumed responsibility for the Brewster children had ended with the arrival of their guardian. Even when she could no longer ignore Esther's crying and pleading, Claudia set her lips firmly and continued about the business of completing her preparations for departure, but her ears were actively listening now and her nerves were at the stretch as she apprehended that the little girl was rapidly becoming hysterical. She was crying for her mother again, something she had not done for the past two days. Claudia bit her lip nervously, recalling the great difficulty she'd had calming Esther then and the aftermath of lethargy that had been nearly as frightening.

She strode over to the door, then hesitated with her hand

outstretched, torn but reluctant to intervene after she had declared herself finished with Beechwood business.

Claudia was saved the decision-making dilemma when a loud knock sounded on the door. She pulled it open and stared into Julian's anxious eyes on a level with her own. "Please, Claudia, can you help? I am afraid Esther will make herself sick if we cannot stop her weeping."

Claudia's gaze flew over his shoulder to the bed where Lord Pelham was trying to gather a sobbing, struggling Esther into his arms. His eyes met hers over the child's head, and he rose, indicating that she should take his place.

"Oh, Esther darling," pleaded Claudia, sitting on the bed, her arms sweeping around the thrashing, out-of-control child, "you know all this wild crying is bad for your poor leg and it does no good." She rocked the little girl as much as their respective awkward positions permitted, and Esther's struggles subsided somewhat, though her tears did not cease. She continued to gasp out disjointed pleas and complaints while clutching Claudia convulsively.

Lord Pelham stood off to the side, watching the tableau taking place, glancing from Roberta huddled at the bottom of the bed, her frightened eyes never leaving her sister, to Julian, another silent, anxious spectator. His gaze returned to the central pair.

"Roberta will find Josie and have her bring some camomile tea up to you, sweetheart," Claudia said, nodding over Esther's shoulder to the child at the foot of the bed, who slipped off at once and left the room. "Then you will have a nap, and you will feel much better when you wake up, I promise you."

"No, I won't feel b . . . better; everything will be worse, Claudia, because Uncle Miles says you won't be here when I wake up. And I will have to stay up here in bed all by myself while everyone else entertains the guests who have come. I c . . . can't have my mother, and now I can't have y . . . you either." Esther's words ended in a wail, and she buried her head in Claudia's shoulder, her thin body heaving with the ferocity of her sobs.

"It won't be like that, sweetheart. Soon you will be much better if you do not make yourself ill with all this crying. You

will be able to go downstairs and visit with everyone, too."
Claudia, continuing to murmur comforting phrases and
promises, did not see Lord Pelham come up beside her, and
she jumped when he put a hand on her shoulder. She turned to
find herself staring into a pair of blue eyes much like Esther's.

"Miss Herbert, if I were to go down on my knees, would
you reconsider your decision to leave today? Would you stay
for another day or two until Esther is a bit stronger and has
grown accustomed to the idea of losing you?"

Why, she realized, reading the worry and concern in his
face, he is putting aside all personal considerations, his contempt for me and his eagerness to have me out of his house,
especially now when his betrothed is here. He is allowing none
of this to interfere with what he hopes is best for Esther.

"Please, Miss Herbert," he said softly, misinterpreting her
silence as refusal. There was a note of desperation in the word.

Her arms enfolding the trembling, weeping child, Claudia
nodded her acquiescence over Esther's head and continued to
rock her and croon soothing words. Her eyes did not turn aside
under the searching regard Lord Pelham bent on her, even
when he straightened up again.

"I am greatly in your debt, Miss Herbert, and I always discharge my debts. You will not lose by delaying your departure, I promise you."

Claudia turned her head away so he could not see that his
punctilious offer of recompense had hurt her, but she could not
keep the stiffness out of her voice and manner as she retorted,
"You need not consider yourself in my debt at all, sir. I am remaining solely for Esther's sake."

Now his manner, which had thawed toward her when making his plea, reverted to cold formality as he bowed. "I understand." Glancing again at his young niece, whose sobs had
diminished somewhat as she lay limply against Claudia's
bosom, Lord Pelham said, "At a more convenient moment I
should like to talk with you about the doctor's actions on the
day of the accident and his recommendations."

"Of course."

"Perhaps this evening after dinner?"

"But that would take you away from your guests, sir. You

might stop by this room before you go down to dinner. Esther will spare me for a few minutes, won't you, pet?"

"She will spare you for dinner with the family, which I apprehend has been the routine during your stay."

Ignoring the steel underlying his quiet words, Claudia said quickly, "Oh, but it was different when it was just the children and I here. I assure you it is quite normal for the governess to remain above stairs when guests are present."

"You are not a governess."

"Claudia," hastily interjected Julian, who had been a silent witness to their conversation thus far, "I am all dusty from riding. If there is nothing I can do for you or Esther right now, I'll get cleaned up."

"Nothing, thank you, Julian," Claudia replied with her sweetest smile. She waited until the boy had made his escape before turning back to the man regarding her fixedly but with no discernible expression on his face. "Everyone at Beechwood is in the habit of regarding me as a governess, which will work to your advantage, sir," she pointed out. "It should not be too difficult to avoid your guests for the short time remaining of my stay. That will diminish any slight awkwardness at my being here."

To her surprise, Lord Pelham seemed totally undisposed to avail himself of this expedient course of action.

"You are not a governess," he repeated. "You are a guest and you will naturally dine with the family."

"But do you not see that that would be an even more awkward situation?" she protested, exasperated by his obtuseness.

"I cannot fathom why you should anticipate any awkwardness," he stated coolly.

Claudia maintained a disbelieving silence, letting her skeptical expression speak for her.

When he saw that she had no intention of entering into a discussion of social niceties, Lord Pelham produced a small smile that Claudia considered a self-satisfied smirk at getting his way, and he turned toward the door.

"I'll see you before dinner in the saloon then, Miss Herbert."

Claudia remained silent, merely nodding when his brows climbed toward his hairline and he paused, ready to resume hostilities. She was still watching his exit a moment later when he glanced back around the open door. "One thing more, Miss Herbert. You may now dispense with the disguise." Ignoring her affronted gasp, he added, "I expect to see you *sans* cap and spectacles when we assemble in the saloon before dinner."

An hour and a half later, Claudia stood before the dressing table in her bedchamber, eyeing her reflection with trepidation. She wished now that she hadn't been so quick to climb onto her high horse when Lord Pelham had overridden her advice on the desirability of excluding her from the household activities of his guests and keeping up the fiction that she was a governess. His superior attitude had roused a little demon of opposition in her breast, and she had decided he would be well served if his prospective—or actual—fiancée and her mother were put out of countenance at the appearance of another young female guest at what was designed to be an intimate party. Claudia would have to be stupid or a hypocrite not to know that men found her attractive, although she could name several of her contemporaries who in her opinion quite eclipsed her in beauty. With this in mind, she had done her hair in the simplest fashion tonight, merely sweeping it to the back of her head and confining it in a tight knot at the nape. She wore no jewelry or hair ornaments. Her gown was of black silk and modestly cut, but it had a definite look of Paris about it, she conceded with a sigh. Her choices of apparel were limited to what she had packed into two valises, her trunk having been expressed to her aunt's home in Kent. With that thought, Claudia made a mental note to write to inform her relative of her whereabouts before she retired for the night.

A knock on the door when she was searching for a fresh handkerchief—Esther's trials were rapidly depleting her stock—announced Susannah, looking enchanting in a muslin gown the rich color of buttercups.

"Uncle Miles thought it might be less awkward for you if we went downstairs together, Claudia," she said, advancing into the room. her eyes widened as Claudia straightened away from the dressing table drawer. "I *knew* you did not really need those spectacles," she declared triumphantly, "and it was nothing short of criminal to hide such beautiful hair under that awful mobcap."

Claudia blinked at this display of frankness. "Well, a governess . . ." she began, and then gave up the unequal task of finding a coherent explanation after having been unmasked by Lord Pelham this afternoon.

"But you are not really a governess, my uncle said." Susannah spoke absently, her attention still focused on her friend's changed appearance. "Your hair is a marvelous color," she went on. "At first glance I thought that coiffure too severe, but I can see now that it emphasizes your high cheekbones and the dimples."

Claudia grimaced, deepening the aforesaid features. "There's no doing anything about them, I fear."

"Why should you wish to do something about them? They're delightful."

"They're childish."

"Nonsense. They make you look approachable and friendly."

"And childish," Claudia said laughingly, "but I shall take that in the complimentary spirit in which it was uttered." She added briskly, "Now we had best go down lest we bring disgrace on the household for poor hospitality to your uncle's guests. By the way, what are the Hingham ladies like?"

"Miss Hingham seems very pleasant. Her manner is agreeable and cordial, and she was quite taken with your flower arrangements. I'm not quite certain about Mrs. Hingham though. She smiles a lot and says complimentary things, but there seems to be a little sting somewhere if you examine her remarks closely. I could be wrong about that, but one thing I saw right off. Great-aunt Sophronia dislikes her very much."

"Oh?"

Susannah launched into a lively account of the meeting between the matrons in the garden room, relishing the retelling as they headed for the main staircase.

Claudia listened with one ear while her mind drifted back to the surprising person of her host. Lord Pelham was an odd man, so obviously disapproving of her on the one hand, but

mindful of his duty to her as a guest, albeit an uninvited one.
She appreciated the thoughtfulness that had prompted the gesture of sending Susannah to escort her to the saloon. It would
be idle to deny that she was uncomfortable with her anom-
alous position in the Pelham household, but several months in
a gaming house had taught her to disguise her feelings. It was
time to apply the lessons she had learned in that arena. Claudia
straightened her spine a trifle and assumed a pleasant expression as she and Susannah walked through the archway into the
saloon with its lovely Aubusson carpet and pale elegant bro-
cades covering the chairs. Against her will her eyes sought out
her host, glancing away almost instantly from the brooding intensity in his eyes that signified neither admiration nor disap-
proval.

Claudia arranged her features into an attitude of polite attention as she swung her gaze to the two women who had flanked
Lord Pelham on the gold sofa before he had risen and come
forward to greet her. No, not a beauty was her first impression
of the younger, but very attractive, her appearance and groom-
ing meticulous, her expression composed and affable.

Lord Pelham's voice interrupted her train of thought before
she could form an impression of the elder Hingham lady.
"Good evening, Susannah, Miss Herbert." He offered his arm
to Claudia, who placed her fingers on it mechanically, allowing herself to be led over to the sofa to the accompaniment
provided by his deep voice making the introductions. "Mrs.
Hingham, Miss Hingham, may I present Miss Herbert, with
whom I share a number of mutual acquaintances in Paris."

"Although you appeared not to recognize Miss Herbert's
name when Miss Brewster spoke of her this afternoon. For
shame, sir, forgetting such a charming young person," Mrs.
Hingham said, scolding him playfully as Claudia dropped her
a curtsy.

"I had not previously heard Miss Herbert's given name
when she was pointed out to me," Lord Pelham replied as the
two younger women acknowledged the introductions with
identical civilities. "I assure you I recognized her immediately
when we met earlier today in Esther's room."

"And do I apprehend that you are not after all a governess,

Miss Herbert?" Mrs. Hingham persisted. "How odd that such a mistake should occur."

"I fear the fault there is entirely mine, ma'am," Claudia said before her host could chime in with his version. "The situation when I arrived at Beechwood was rather chaotic. Susannah's little sister, who is but nine years old, was in great pain with a broken leg and quite overcome with hysterics. She was crying pitifully for her mother and refusing to let anyone attend to her. It occurred to me that, lacking a parent or a nurse, a governess might be able to command the necessary obedience to help her to help herself, instead of hindering the efforts of others to assist her."

"Ah, a happy inspiration indeed."

"And not altogether false," Claudia said quietly, having detected, as had Susannah, the sting in the tail despite an impressive display of large teeth produced by Mrs. Hingham's accompanying smile. "After my father's death in Paris, I stayed for some time with his comrade Colonel Lord Malmsey's family and occasionally assisted their governess, a marvelous woman who maintained a firm but loving control over a lively group of children."

Claudia felt rather than saw Lord Pelham's swift glance at her. She kept her eyes on Mrs. Hingham, acknowledging with a murmur and a nod that lady's instant expression of sympathy for her bereavement.

The entrance of Julian escorting his great-aunt at that moment forestalled any further probing into her stay in Paris, much to Claudia's relief, though she foresaw a resumption of interest on the matron's part at a more convenient moment. She was not naive enough to hope that Mrs. Hingham's curiosity about her would be so easily satisfied. Lord Pelham had been shocked at the announcement of her father's death, too, and would certainly refer to it at the first opportunity. Only not here, she prayed, not tonight in front of an audience, not until I've decided how much to tell him.

Fortunately for Claudia's apprehensive state, Lord Pelham, ably assisted by Mrs. Hingham, saw to it that conversation flowed freely and impersonally both in the saloon and later at table. She who had desired and expected to remain mute in

this family party found herself willy-nilly contributing a number of observations of Paris under her host's skillful prompting. Even Lady Powerby was induced to speak of something
other than her poor health when her nephew extracted from
her several recollections of London's social scene as it was a
quarter of a century ago, which sparked a spirited exchange
with Mrs. Hingham. The elder ladies aired and defended their
opinions of the leading actors and musicians of that period.
Clever Lord Pelham, Claudia thought, to manipulate the long-
standing antagonism between the matrons to produce a
rounded picture of a bygone era for the entertainment of all.
Julian and Susannah were sitting entranced at the stories being
recounted, and she could feel herself relaxing her guard and
enjoying the evening she had approached with a reluctance
bordering on dread. Perhaps it was not too much to hope that
she could end her stay at Beechwood on a positive note and
leave in a day or two with the pleasant memories of this most
unlikely experience relatively untarnished by Lord Pelham's
low opinion of her.

The optimistic mood engendered in Claudia by a splendid
dinner and interesting conversation suffered a partial eclipse
when the ladies adjourned to the saloon. Mrs. Hingham displayed every disposition to continue her probe into Claudia's
antecedents, her life in Paris, and the circumstances surrounding her decision to return to England. She was quickly
thwarted in her quest, however, by Lady Powerby who, having
been drawn unwillingly from her cocoon of pampered inva-
lidism to preside over her nephew's table, was now determined to have her resurrected love of music gratified by the
young people gracing her drawing room.

Lord Pelham and Julian rejoined the ladies while Lady
Powerby was quizzing Claudia and Miss Hingham about their
ability and willingness to entertain her, Susannah having already promised that she and Julian would sing some duets.
Miss Hingham, admirably composed under her ladyship's ex-
pectant stare, replied that her singing was nothing out of the
common style, but she would be happy to play for the others,
whereupon Lady Powerby praised her for her becoming modesty and promised that no one at Beechwood would dream of

applying concert standards to what was merely family entertainment. Still in possession of her composure after this cavalier sweep of her defenses, Miss Hingham meekly signified her willingness to participate, thereby earning additional encomiums from her hostess.

When her turn came, Claudia assumed her firmest tone and looked Lady Powerby straight in the eye. "I do not wish to appear disobliging, ma'am, but my performance on the pianoforte is much less than indifferent, and as far back as I can remember, people who pride themselves on having a good ear have been unanimous in urging me *not* to sing in company. Even Esther, who desires the comfort of hearing the songs her mother used to sing to her at bedtime, has requested that I read to her instead."

"Poor Claudia," came Julian's sympathetic voice from the doorway as he and his uncle entered, "I hope you were not hurt by her rejection. That husky quality that makes your speaking voice so appealing seems not to transfer quite . . . successfully to singing . . ." His explanation trailed off as the lad became aware of all eyes and ears tuned to him. A wave of color rose from his throat into his cheeks.

"Perhaps," said Claudia, coming to his rescue, "it has something to do with my inability to carry a tune or stay in key." Her earnestness matched Julian's and drew a chuckle from Lord Pelham.

"After that disclaimer, I believe we shall honor your wish to be excused from performing, Miss Herbert. I am persuaded you have many nonmusical accomplishments. I would venture to speculate, for example, that you play an excellent game of whist and would be pleased to accommodate Mrs. Hingham in this activity at another time."

Claudia could feel her features freeze at this secret shaft, but she kept her head high and murmured an indistinguishable assent in response to Mrs. Hingham's eager question before Lord Pelham returned to the subject of a program of music for the evening.

It was a pleasant evening all told, much the opposite of what Claudia had feared when Lord Pelham had compelled her presence during this afternoon's altercation. Julian and

Susannah sang delightfully with a total absence of self-consciousness, their vocal performance enhanced by the incomparable picture they presented of vibrant youth and beauty doubled by their twinship. Miss Hingham, too, sang and played better than almost any of her contemporaries who had not been extraordinarily gifted in this area. It would have been a treat to lose herself in the pleasures of the moment, content to allow the melodious sounds issuing forth to soothe away a portion of the worries and fears that had beset her since her father's murder.

To some extent this did happen, and Claudia was grateful for even a temporary sensation of peace and beauty. The practical urgencies of her days at Beechwood had pushed her personal concerns into a back room of her mind, a room she had been able to keep locked so far. The homecoming of Lord Pelham could not have been less than awkward, once she had given in to Lady Powerby's pleas to remain, but her grisliest nightmares could not have produced a more lamentable coincidence than to have the master of Beechwood turn out to be the man whose disdain for her had been festering in her mind since the night they had nearly been introduced in Paris. Why could he not have had his portrait prominently displayed in the public rooms at Beechwood like most men in his exalted position so that she could have disappeared before his arrival? A baleful look directed at his handsome profile attentively turned toward Miss Hingham at the pianoforte accompanied this extraneous thought among those roiling about in Claudia's head.

It was no less than sheer malevolence on the part of an unkind fate that he should know so much about her recent life. She had survived their acrimonious encounter this afternoon with her secrets intact, but it was an exercise in futility to hope he would not resume his efforts to discover everything that had occurred since their first meeting that had contributed to bringing her to his doorstep more or less in disguise. She would not put it past him to fire off a letter to M. Louis Frenier requesting an account of her behavior as far as the Frenchman knew it. She would get away from Beechwood before an answer could be forthcoming, of course, but it was vital to conceal her aunt's identity and location. Once she left

Beechwood, she was determined to put herself beyond his reach forever. Just why this seemed so important was a question Claudia did not pursue. It was enough to acknowledge the necessity. She sat unmoving in a Chippendale armchair upholstered in peach brocade, keeping her face relaxed and her hands still in her lap by a stern effort of will, while her brain scrambled to come up with a way to conclude her business with Lord Selkirk without Miles Pelham's becoming any the wiser about the affair.

Claudia was no closer to a solution to her pressing problem when the tea tray arrived, but at least this event provided her with an excuse to make an early retreat.

She rose unhurriedly, addressing her words to Lady Powerby. "If you will excuse me now, ma'am, I will say good night. It is time I checked in on Esther and sent Roberta, who has been keeping her company this evening, off to her bed."

"Surely one of the servants can do that and report back here to you so that you need not miss your tea and cut the evening short, Miss Herbert," Lord Pelham said, glancing at her for the first time since the company had settled into a musical mode.

"I'm afraid I am the only one who can get Esther to swallow her medicine, sir," she replied in the same even tone he had used, "and to confess the truth, I am rather tired myself. The day began rather early." Claudia did not give him a chance to find another argument, but proceeded to issue a general good night to all those assembled. She maintained a steady gait as she left the room a moment later in defiance of a wild desire to flee the effect of a pair of bright blue eyes boring into her back like twin drills.

Chapter Seven

Lord Pelham observed Claudia Herbert's graceful exit with an air of detachment that belied his seething thoughts. By dint of constant reminders, starting from the instant she had stepped foot over the threshold of the saloon tonight looking stunning in the simplicity of black silk, he had managed to keep his eyes from lingering on her, but this was a Pyrrhic victory at best. The stern authority he had exercised over his glance had not extended to his thoughts that, in defiance of all attempts at censorship, had returned again and again to the girl he had believed gone from his life forever. In extenuation of this inexplicable weakness, it could be argued that he was suffering from a series of shocks that had upset the balance of his previously well-ordered existence and destroyed his customary certainty that he was sailing on the proper course.

The first upset, though not precisely a shock, of course, was the eruption of five half-grown children into his quiet life. He had rather prided himself on the rapidity with which he, a bachelor with no previous experience of children, had adjusted to the role of surrogate parent and guardian to his nephews and nieces. There were potential problem areas, of course—he was not so simple as to expect perfection in the children or his makeshift arrangements—but they had all rubbed along fairly well together right from the start.

No, the first event that had set him back on his heels was the unexpected refusal of Martha Hingham to accept his offer of marriage outright. That had been a blow to his conceit of himself as a desirable match, he admitted again, glancing over his cup at the young woman in question, serene and composed as usual as she listened with an air of polite attention to something Julian was explaining with expansive hand gestures. Heaven knew he had deliberated long and hard before proposing marriage; he had no earthly right to resent the same degree of caution on her part before making such a vital decision. The fact remained that her hesitation had left him with second and third thoughts about the wisdom of his own action. Most unsettling of all, he no longer knew what response to hope for from Martha.

He had arrived home in this ambiguous mental state to be greeted by the news that his youngest niece had suffered a serious accident during his absence, and the even more startling news that an unknown woman had apparently taken over the helm of his household with the delighted acquiescence of all hands. There was no denying that these events paled in shock value, however, in the light of his discovery that the acclaimed savior of his happy home was the girl from a Parisian gaming house, whose lovely face had, to his everlasting shame, haunted his dreams for more than a month. Except for an instinctive rush of suspicion at such an unlikely coincidence, which he had voiced in less than civil terms, he could not fault his reactions to her presence. He'd have seen her off the premises in short order with formal thanks for what had been in all truth a crucial service rendered to his family and an offer of pecuniary recompense if she would accept it. He'd gone a fair way toward carrying out this intention before Esther had sabotaged his plan.

He'd been mildly concerned over the little girl's homesickness long before the accident. She was the youngest, timid and small for her age, and very much the petted darling of the family. She missed her mother dreadfully and had lost a familiar governess on arrival in England. Since then there had been two more governesses whose brief tenures and quick departures had most likely delayed her assimilation into her new life. With this in mind, how could he have acted differently today when she had been in a truly pitiable state that aroused fears for her health?

Miles shifted his long legs and placed his empty cup on the piecrust table beside his chair. "That is an astute observation, ma'am," he said in response to something half heard from

Mrs. Hingham, generally a safe enough reply, given the lady's penchant for didactic pronouncements. She seemed to find nothing amiss in his response, and he gathered his wits together to make yet another attempt at concentrating on what was going on around him.

This had been his main difficulty from the moment Claudia Herbert had acceded to his plea to remain a bit longer at Beechwood. He could defend his actions; once the decision to keep her here had been taken, it was imperative to stay as close to the truth as possible. Not for a minute had he considered abiding by Miss Herbert's expressed desire to be treated as a servant and kept away from his guests. His was not some vast ducal estate where poor relatives, old family retainers, and diverse other characters with some claim on one or more members of the family could be maintained away from the public eye for years on end. Nor would he permit his private knowledge of her dubious virtue to affect the way she was treated at Beechwood, whatever the circumstances that had brought her here. She was entitled to every consideration enjoyed by his other guests.

No, it was not his actions in promoting Miss Herbert to the status of invited guest that were indefensible; it was his inability to oust her from his thoughts, the obsessive nature of which would, if not checked, eventually rebound to his discredit in his treatment of his prospective wife and mother-in-law. He looked up to see Martha glancing his way, inviting him to share her amusement at something Susannah had just said. He smiled warmly at her and exerted himself to take a greater part in the conversation for the next few minutes until his aunt indicated that she was ready to retire. This was the signal for all the ladies to declare themselves likewise inclined, and the exodus from the saloon began.

"You look as if you could do with an early night, too," Miles said to his nephew after the women had departed. "Is your knee bothering you? You seem to be favoring it more than you did earlier."

"It aches a little," Julian admitted, rubbing the sore member. "Today was the first time I have ridden since I wrenched it. Claudia suggested I put another compress on it before going to bed. She said she would leave the stuff in my room." He yawned again. "I think I will turn in early."

"Miss Herbert's word seems to have become the law around Beechwood these days," the baron remarked, keeping his tone light.

"It's not that she is bossy—not very bossy, that is," Julian amended with a quick grin, "but she generally seems to know what it the best thing to do when there is a problem."

"She is very lovely to look at, too." Miles watched the boy's face from under lazy lids.

"Yes, I was surprised how good-looking she is without her spectacles and that odd cap."

Well, it isn't a virulent case of calf love at all events, the baron decided, based on Julian's unguarded countenance as he uttered this artless remark.

"Did you read the letter from George yet and the one from the school?" the boy asked a trifle anxiously.

"Yes, don't worry, I'll handle the school authorities. George wants to go home with one of his classmates for a fortnight when the term ends in a couple of days, a boy he referred to solely by the revolting soubriquet of Piggy."

"That is Charles Nettles," Julian informed his uncle with a grin. "He's all right, Piggy, though he has no brains to speak of. He greatly admires George's prowess on the athletic fields."

"I used to know his uncle Charles, who had no brains either. Believe it or not *he* answered to the even more repellent Fish Face at one period of his life if memory serves. George will come to no harm with the Nettleses, though it won't hurt to check that Piggy's parents are aware that they are to have the honor and gargantuan task of feeding George for two weeks."

Julian laughed and bade his uncle good night.

Lord Pelham did not follow the boy upstairs, but headed instead for the library, where he dealt with the two pieces of correspondence that required swift attention before casting a jaundiced eye on the stack that had accumulated in his absence. There was no point in putting off a disagreeable chore, especially when his time would be largely taken up with his

guests and social duties in the immediate future. Sighing, he
pulled the pile toward him and opened the missive on top.

An hour later, when he found himself reading the same so-
licitor's letter for at least the fourth time with only a dim conception of its contents, Miles conceded that it was time to give
up. He swept the messy pile into the center drawer of the desk
and pushed it shut, shoving back his chair at the same time. As
he stretched the kinks out of his shoulders, he acknowledged
the error of permitting thoughts of his duties to his guests to
encroach on his work. The floodgates had opened and destroyed his ability to concentrate. From jotting down ideas for
entertaining his guests, it was a short hop to wondering if
Claudia Herbert would insist on remaining with Esther all day.
And there he was, fighting to keep her out of his thoughts
again.

It was the aura of mystery hanging over her that plagued
him, he told himself. She claimed her presence at Beechwood
was entirely accidental, and Julian's version of their meeting
supported this, but what was she doing in rural Hampshire
when her home, according to what she had told the children,
was in Kent? And why had she left Paris? She had refused to
answer that question this afternoon. Were the black gown and
the story of her father's death true? It would explain the hint of
melancholy in her face when she was not directly engaged in
conversation, but it would still not account for a respectable
young woman traipsing around Europe completely unaccom-
panied. And that, of course, was the crux of the matter—the
question of her respectability.

About to extinguish the lamp on his desk, Miles paused,
then sat down again in sudden decision. He would have to
begin with Paris. He found a sheet of paper and took up his
pen once more.

It was nearly midnight when he finished his letter to his old
friend Louis Frenier, and the long day of traveling was taking
its toll. Miles rubbed his eyes and headed upstairs with a candle. His aunt and his guests were established in the new wing,
but he slept in the main house to be near the children. He did
not go to his own rooms immediately, having formed the habit
early in their stay of checking on the two youngest children

before he retired. They had shared a room before Esther's accident, but Roberta had confided today that she was sleeping
in the small dressing room next to their room until her sister's
leg was better.

He entered the dressing room from the corridor, treading
lightly, and approached the cot that had been set up for his
niece, his lips widening into a smile as he gazed down at her
sprawled form. It must have been warm when Roberta had
gone to bed because she had kicked all the covers off the cot.
She lay facedown, arms upraised, her long auburn hair in a
tangle around her shoulders. Her white cotton bedgown was
hiked up around her knees, the soles of her feet faintly pink,
the toes curving inward. Miles placed his candle on a chest of
drawers and arranged the discarded sheet over the sleeping
child, being careful to settle it lightly over her shoulders.

He retrieved the candle and opened the door to the connect-
ing room, his movements as stealthy and silent as a burglar's.
It would never do to waken Esther after what he had seen
today of the child's fears of being alone. He had not attempted
to get Claudia Herbert aside tonight to question her more
closely about the doctor's opinion of Esther's condition. He'd
realized how particular such an action would appear to Mrs.
Hingham and Martha despite the legitimate need for the interview. He would make it a point to remedy the omission in the
morning.

Miles slipped noiselessly into Esther's bedchamber to be
brought up short by a stifled gasp as he was closing the door
behind him. He spun around, his eyes winging across the room
to the area by the bed that was illuminated by a candle on the
bedside table. Claudia Herbert, the fingers of one hand pressed
against her lips and her eyes enormous, sat bolt upright in a
chair pulled up to the bed where Esther lay sleeping. A slim
volume lay on the rug at her feet, where she had dropped it in
her surprise at his appearance. As he approached the bed, the
baron appraised her, his eyes racing over the slim form entic-
ingly garbed in a pale filmy robe that fell in a drift to her bare
feet. They returned to linger on the ripple of hair gleaming like
molten honey in the candlelight and spilling over her shoulders
and breasts. He bent to pick up the fallen book, aware of her

recoil at his sudden move. He held it out to her, noting that her
eyes glowed green tonight and her soft lips—no, best not to
dwell on her lips.

"Did you think I was a ghost? You look like an apparition
yourself in that pale robe," he added when she did not respond
immediately. His hoarse whisper sounded harsh in his own
ears, and she slid a quick look at the child, putting a warning
finger to her lips as she did so.

"What are you doing here?"

"I always check on the children before I go to bed. More to
the point, why are you not asleep in your bed at this hour?" He
tried to keep his own voice as nearly soundless as hers had
been.

"I did go to bed, but Esther was a bit restless, and I came in
here when she called out. Often just a soothing voice is
enough to settle her down again, but I was waiting for a little
while to make sure she is deeply asleep."

At the mention of her name, the baron's eyes had gone to
his niece's elfin face sweetly asleep on her pillow, but they returned at once to the woman in the chair. The silence between
them now thrummed with unspoken desire as he peered at her
mouth with the intensity of a scientist with a specimen under
his microscope. He examined the twin peaks of her upper lip
and visually traced the long generous curve of the lower,
aware of a sudden infinitesimal parting between them as her
breathing rate accelerated.

Claudia blinked rapidly and cast her eyes down, saying in a
choked whisper, "It is getting very late, sir. I think I will go to
my room now . . . if you will please excuse me."

Miles ignored the implied request that he step back and give
her room to rise. Instead, he extended a hand to assist her.
After a second of mute protest, she put her hand in his, still
avoiding his eyes. The instant he gripped her hand his duty to
a guest and his honor as a gentleman were forgotten, submerged in the tide of desire that had been swelling inside him
from his first glimpse of her, so alluring in her *déshabillé*. One
quick pull and his arms encircled her before she could regain
her balance. He kissed her then, savoring the sweetness of that
trembling mouth for the short space gained from the shock that

held her motionless initially. All too soon she began to struggle however, twisting in his arms and attempting to turn her face away. Something hard that he dimly identified as the book she held in one hand dug into his chest. He fought a wild urge to coerce a response from her, already ashamed of the panic he'd induced, made more pitiable by her frantic struggles unattended by a single sound that might disturb Esther's sleep. He closed his eyes and released her mouth, battling to bring his own breathing under control while he moved his hands from her back to her upper arms and stepped away, removing his hands entirely once she was steady on her feet.

He half expected her to bolt for the door to her own room, but she did not bolt, nor did she cower. When he brought himself to look at her again after raking an unsteady hand back through his hair, it was to find her staring at him with her head held high and her lips pressed together, both hands clasping the book to her bosom. When she spoke, there was only the tiniest tremor discernible.

"That was a dastardly thing to do."

"Yes, it was, and I make you my sincere apologies."

"Why did you do it?"

Why? "Now that is a poser, Miss Herbert," he said after a pause, rapidly rejecting any and all versions of the truth as likely to prove incendiary.

"You must have had a reason."

How like a woman to want to analyze a purely masculine impulse! "Reason did not enter into it, I fear. You must know you are a very attractive—"

"Don't dare to claim that I tempted you, for you know it to be a lie!"

"You did nothing whatever to provoke my reprehensible action," he agreed. "I promise it will not happen again. Now it really is time for you to go to bed."

She continued to search his face for something she did not find while he hung onto his patience, holding his hands tight against his sides to keep them from stroking her soft cheek. At last she turned toward the door to her room, but halted with her hand on the knob.

"Miss Hingham is also a very attractive young woman, but

given the same circumstances, I believe you would not have insulted her in that fashion, Lord Pelham. I had not expected that it would cost me my reputation to be able to live with my father for the first time in twelve years. And it lasted for such a short time." Her mournful words trailed off, and she vanished into her room.

Miles stood by his niece's bed for several minutes staring at the closed door and cursing himself for an utter cad. Claudia had been close to tears at the end; he had heard them in her choked whisper. His instinct was to try to comfort her, but following his instincts had created this situation in the first place.

With a last look at the sleeping child, he left by the door into the hall, walking like a man who had not yet regained his shore legs after a stormy sea passage. Indeed, he was beginning to realize that his experience in the last ten minutes had been akin to being swept up and nearly drowned in a tidal wave before being washed ashore on an alien strand. Whether he ever reached his intended destination or not, his life would be forever changed. That was the one clear thought amidst the muddle in his head.

When Lord Pelham entered Esther's bedchamber the next morning dressed for riding, he received an ecstatic greeting from his niece and a cool nod from Claudia Herbert. In his own quarters late last night he had spent more time than he cared to admit in coming to grips with his stupid—he could find no kinder word for it—behavior with regard to this unwelcome but insidiously attractive visitor. For several hours during the evening he had waged a successful battle against the pleasure he took in gazing upon Miss Herbert's lovely face, and then in less than two minutes in Esther's room he had succumbed ingloriously to a sudden overwhelming desire to kiss her.

One battle did not make a war, however. Now that he had an inkling—to put it mildly—of his weakness, he would take care to guard against a repetition of the circumstances that had given rise to his injudicious and ungentlemanly conduct. The blame was his alone; no matter what he had seen and imagined concerning Miss Herbert's respectability in Paris, she had done nothing to invite his assault upon her person at Beechwood. If his visceral reactions to her potent appeal could so easily get the better of his common sense, then it would behoove him—nay, it was imperative—to eschew any private meetings with the lady. Her apprehensions of awkwardness if she was to go much among the other guests had proved well-founded, though for reasons other than those she had cited.

This hard lesson assimilated, he had gone to bed, only to spend additional restless hours rejecting the enticing images of Miss Herbert that repeatedly presented themselves to his heated imagination. With the increased incentive provided by a disturbed night, Lord Pelham had entered the sunny breakfast room resolved to spend all his energy on devising suitable entertainments for his prospective fiancée and her mother. A swift survey of those around the table had revealed that only his two elder nieces and the Hingham ladies were in attendance. He'd apologized for his own late arrival, adding, "I see some have already finished."

"No, Uncle Miles," Roberta had piped up. "You know Great-aunt Sophronia always has breakfast in her room, and Claudia is having hers with Esther. Julian went riding early. He charmed Cook out of some ham and the best muffins to take with him."

"Such a delightful child," Mrs. Hingham had cooed with a smiling nod toward Roberta. "We are eager to meet the youngest member of the family, are we not, Martha?"

Martha had agreed placidly before raising her cup to her lips.

He'd confided his intention of consulting the doctor on that very point when the medical man presented himself at Beechwood in response to the summons already on its way to his home. He had then changed the subject to planning the day's activities. Behind the solicitous manner of a good host, however, had been an uneasy awareness of the interview he would have with Miss Herbert before he talked with Dr. Martin. This made rather a mockery of his late-night decision to avoid the alluring lady and contributed to the general sense of oppression under which he was laboring on this fine summer morning.

All of this had chased through the baron's mind on the way to his niece's room. As he kissed a beaming Esther on her charming little nose, he slid a sideways glance at her attendant regarding them with a bland composure that rivaled Martha Hingham's, a tiny smile on the lips he had kissed so thoroughly just a few hours before. He returned his gaze to his chattering niece, not wishing Miss Herbert to divine his sour reflections on the remarkable ability of females to recover from seemingly devastating emotional scenes. Last night she had exuded an air of hopeless pathos that had wrenched his heart and conscience, and here she was a scant eight hours later looking fresh as a daisy in her crisp cotton gown and as serenely unruffled as a summer sky.

The gist of Esther's exhortations penetrated his resentful reverie, and he smiled at the eager child. "When Dr. Martin comes today, I shall ask him if we may safely carry you down to the reception rooms, love. Now, I must talk to Miss Herbert for a moment."

As he made a motion to rise from the side of the bed where he had been sitting, Miss Herbert said with smiling quickness, "We need not leave Esther for our talk, sir. She knows that she has a clean break of the right tibia and that the doctor had no trouble in setting it. He was very pleased with her progress when he saw her two days ago. She has not been feverish since the first day, and her appetite has started to pick up lately."

There was nothing a reasonable man could take exception to in this crisp, concise report; therefore, it was disconcerting to the baron to discover that he was not quite the reasonable man he had supposed himself to be. He had intended to conduct a short businesslike interview with the twofold purpose of quieting any fears she might harbor that he would break his promise to keep his distance, and initiating his revised plan to allow her to remain more in the background during her extended stay. She had stolen a march on him.

"A very efficient report, Miss Herbert. Thank you," he said, sensing as her eyes slid away from his that he had not succeeded in suppressing his unbecoming irritation. He hurried on, trying to infuse more warmth into his manner. "Mrs. and Miss Hingham have decided to content themselves with exploring the grounds and gardens today, but they, or Miss Hingham, at least, will ride with me tomorrow morning. We would welcome your company if you would care to join us."

"Thank you, you are very kind, but I do not have a riding habit with me."

"I am sorry," he said with automatic courtesy. "My aunt is writing to some of our neighbors to invite them to dine here tomorrow. Naturally we will expect you to be with us then."

"Do you think that is wise?"

"Must I repeat that you are a guest in this house, Miss Herbert?" He forced a smile as their eyes met across Esther's bed. "Besides, given the rapidity with which news spreads around this community, everyone within a ten-mile radius has already heard that a young woman dropped out of the sky last week, figuratively speaking, of course, to take over the reins of my deserted household and nurse my cruelly abandoned niece." He grinned at Esther, who was giggling appreciatively, before adding, "You are doubtless the object of much conjecture and curiosity hereabouts, one of them at least, Miss Herbert, and I would be loath to disappoint my neighbors."

This attempt at light humor was not a rousing success in one quarter, judging by Miss Herbert's appalled expression. As the baron got to his feet, he noticed a small board with holes in it and some playing cards on the bed between his niece and her companion. "And what is all this?" he asked the child, glad to have a diversion.

"Claudia is teaching me to play cribbage, Uncle Miles. It is much more fun than arithmetic lessons. Claudia says I learn very quickly, and I've already beaten her once."

"Good for you," he said to his bubbling niece, and then in an aside to Miss Herbert as he left the room, "I draw the line at roulette wheels."

Lightning flared in her changeable eyes before she bit her lip and stared at him wooden-faced and mute. Had the woman no sense of humor at all?

He closed the door behind him with a bit more emphasis than was necessary, though it did little to relieve his feelings.

Chapter Eight

The decided click of the door registered with Claudia as she continued to shuffle the cards, but she kept her gaze on her busy hands, wishing her thoughts were under similar control. She had tossed and turned in her bed for hours following the midnight encounter with Lord Pelham, her mind a churning mass of wayward desire and regret. Eventually, these gave way to a rising tide of self-disgust at her inability to stop reliving those few seconds in the baron's embrace before sanity had reasserted itself.

She had been kissed on three occasions in England during her youth when eager awkward young men had surprised her defenses. None of those fumbling forays had tempted her to the slightest degree of cooperation. In Paris she had been uniformly circumspect in her dealings with the male gender, aware that her position in the gaming house left her open to advances men would not make to the young women they met in a family setting. Moreover, she had been intent on rebuilding the ties of affection with her father that had attenuated over the years of his absence. It had even crossed her mind once or twice that she might be one of those women who were basically immune to masculine charms.

This tentative theory had been disproved at the instant her eyes locked onto Lord Pelham's in a dingy, crowded room in a Parisian gaming house. Her breath had caught in her throat, her pulse rate had accelerated, and all sounds in the room had faded away. The sensation of being on the brink of some earth-spinning experience had lasted just a few seconds before being obliterated by a rude reality in the form of a middle-aged roué who demanded her attention and company. Reality had rapidly grown much crueler in the weeks that followed, stifling any foolish inclination to dwell on what might have been.

And now fate had thrown her into Lord Pelham's orbit once more. Claudia was too honest to deny the attraction that had sparked between them, not after what had happened last night. Nor could she deny the bitter truth that attraction was all it was for the baron, and a mighty inconvenient one at that. The proof was clear in his cool demeanor this morning after his midnight lapse in propriety. She could only hope that she had projected a matching nonchalance just now.

After a disturbed night she had awakened with a firm resolve to conduct herself in precisely this fashion. At all costs to her nerves, she must continue to conceal the horrifying discovery she had made last night that it was not simply attraction on her part. For a few ecstatic moments in Lord Pelham's embrace she had experienced a sensation of homecoming; nothing had ever felt as perfect as his lips on hers, no place as safe as the circle of his arms. Fortunately for her battered self-respect, her reason had not been entirely swamped by amazed delight. She had been able to rally her defenses to deny her pleasure and fight against him, her determination augmented by the knowledge that she meant nothing to him. She had submerged her despair and mustered the temerity to confront him, a futile action that had elicited worthless compliments and assurances she would be foolish to put any faith in. At that point rising despair drove her to escape from his presence before she lost every shred of dignity. At least the hours of unhappy reflection had strengthened her determination to leave Beechwood with her pride intact, whatever the condition of her heart and spirit.

"Claudia, is it necessary to shuffle the cards so many times before you deal them? My fingers are not very clever at it yet."

Claudia blinked and gazed down into Esther's worried face. As the meaning of the child's words sank in, she laughed. "No, sweetheart, not at all. I must have been thinking of something else." As she proceeded to deal out six cards each to Esther and herself, she coached the neophyte. "Remember now, you want to try to make runs of three or more or keep cards that add up to fifteen, but you do not want to give me a pair or a five for my crib. Sometimes you must sacrifice your own point count to avoid giving your opponent points." She watched the little girl's lips move silently as she added up her hand and deliberated over what to throw in the crib.

The game ran its course with Esther squeaking with glee as she edged out her opponent. She was dealing the cards for another game when Roberta strolled into the room, nibbling on a piece of fruitcake that she offered to share with her sister and Claudia. Both declined the treat, and Roberta looked at the cards on the bed.

"What are you playing?"

As Esther rushed into a disjointed explanation, Claudia gazed at the second youngest Brewster child with indulgent affection. Both girls had curly auburn hair and bright blue eyes, but there the resemblance ended. Esther was delicately made and mercurial in nature, while Roberta was sturdy and even-tempered. She had been unfailingly sweet and patient with her little sister during this trying period and had been an enormous help to Claudia in her unfamiliar role of trying to keep the household machinery from breaking down in the master's absence.

"Let me retie your ribbons, Roberta; your hair is sliding out," she said now.

Unlike her elder sister, Roberta took little interest as yet in her appearance, putting on the first items of clothing that came to hand each day, regardless of their condition or suitability. She plunged into activity with the same wholehearted abandon and with predictable results to her person and garments. At the moment there was a fresh scrape across two knuckles of the hand holding the fruitcake and a smear of something, possibly the cake, on the shoulder of her crumpled blue muslin dress. Unconcerned by either blemish or, more likely, Claudia guessed, unaware of either, Roberta was avidly attending to Esther's lecture on cribbage, her brow puckered in concentration. Claudia was too slow to prevent additional damage to the dress as Roberta dropped the last hunk of cake into her lap in order to reach for a peg in the cribbage board. She removed the sticky mass to a bowl on the table and handed Roberta the damp cloth hanging over the edge.

"Here, pet, clean your hands before you touch those cards that Julian appropriated from your uncle's library," she instructed. "Would you like to try playing a game with Esther? I'll coach you for a hand or two until you understand how it is played."

Both girls being amenable, Claudia's plan was instituted. The three spent an enjoyable half hour together before Claudia recalled that she wished to speak to the laundress about an article of clothing that had been misdirected.

"Perhaps you ought to go to the kitchens, too, Claudia," Roberta said without looking up from the discards she was putting in her sister's crib. "Cook was in a dreadful state when I was there just now."

"What is the problem?" Claudia asked, her heart sinking. His lordship's cook was only marginally less difficult to deal with than his aunt. She did not relish a session of peacemaking in the kitchen, something that, if it came to Lord Pelham's attention, would only serve to confirm his suspicion that she was trying to worm her way into his household for some nebulous but undoubtedly nefarious purpose of her own.

"I'm not quite sure, something about salmon . . . and Greataunt Sophronia, I think."

In no way heartened by this vague reply, Claudia sighed and rose to her feet. Her exit from the room was accompanied by Roberta's triumphant call, "Thirty-one for four points."

Several hours later, Susannah arrived to take over in the sickroom for an hour while Claudia went for a walk, a practice the young girl had insisted on almost from the beginning. She had overridden Claudia's conscientious demurs and her little sister's initial hysterics at even the temporary loss of the being she had quickly decided belonged exclusively to her. Esther had recognized Susannah's unbending determination, however, and accepted the inevitable with only token resistance after the first day.

Claudia greeted her smiling substitute with even more gratitude today. Cook had indeed been in a state earlier, chaf-

ing under Lady Powerby's unrealistic orders concerning the
menu for tomorrow's dinner party. The scullery maids, having borne the brunt of her ill temper, were scurrying around,
trying their poor best to follow her directions for luncheon
preparations while keeping out of her reach. It had taken
much tact and patience, seasoned with large pinches of flattery, to restore the cook's equilibrium, in the course of which
Claudia had promised to convey to Lady Powerby that
salmon was not available locally at present. By the time she
had left the kitchen, the artist in charge of this domain was
determinedly bent on creating what she declared would be
the world's finest cream of mushroom soup to impress their
neighbors. She also agreed that the menu would feature the
new peas and strawberries that were now at their peak in the
garden.

Lady Powerby had not yet left her rooms when Claudia
knocked, which made the task easier, but might be considered
as rather slighting to her nephew's guests. Before Claudia
could begin to discharge her own errand, she found herself listening to a string of complaints about Mrs. Hingham's character and conduct in the first twelve hours of her stay at
Beechwood. It would have been injudicious to admit that she
shared some of her ladyship's opinions; her job was to lend a
sympathetic ear while rallying her ineffectual hostess to better
serve her nephew in this role. When Lady Powerby paused to
draw breath, Claudia jumped in and launched her own campaign to this end. She was rather limp by the time she left
Lady Powerby's suite, but she had the satisfaction of seeing its
resident on her reluctant way down to the reception rooms,
swathed in shawls and fortified by her indispensible vinai-
grette.

Claudia had returned to the sickroom to find its small occu-
pant launching a campaign to be taken downstairs herself.
Though rejoicing at this evidence that Esther was no longer
much troubled by discomfort in her injured leg, Claudia had to
counsel patience since the doctor's expected call had not yet
taken place. Esther received this unpalatable advice with the
same lack of enthusiasm children have displayed down
through the ages. Claudia dismissed the faithful Roberta to

luncheon with the adults and exercised the despised virtue of patience herself while the small sufferer sulked through her own meal until she finally nodded off to sleep.

Though she was relieved at the temporary cessation of calls upon her diplomatic skills, Claudia found no peace in the somnolent atmosphere of Esther's room that day. The glimpse of the gardens from its window presented a lovely rich tapestry of color as always, but the turmoil of her thoughts prevented her from deriving much pleasure from the peaceful scene today.

Her stay at Beechwood had jolted her out of the fog of misery in which she had dwelt since her father's horrifying death. Besides providing a respite from the fear for her own safety that had dogged her every step since she had left Paris, the sheer busyness of her days and nights coping with a series of household problems in addition to the stages of Esther's recovery had occupied her mind almost to the exclusion of thoughts of self. The temporary nature of this respite had never been in question, yet ever since the baron's return yesterday she had been mentally moping as if she had lost something precious, which was ludicrous and pathetic. The man despised her, for heaven's sake, and even if he did not, he was betrothed or as good as betrothed. The sooner she left Beechwood the better for her self-respect if nothing else.

The day continued unseasonably warm and yesterday's relieving breeze had vanished. Esther awoke from her nap hot and perspiring. She was quite willing to submit to being bathed and having her hair washed by Claudia while Josie changed her bed linen and regaled her with news of the visitors from the servants' perspective, including the information that the Hingham ladies' abigail had already made herself unpopular in the servants' hall by adopting a superior air that fooled no one. Claudia intervened before the maid could recite a detailed indictment of the newcomer's misdemeanors for the child's ears, directing the conversation to more general matters.

When Susannah entered the room a few minutes later, Esther was established in a chair with her legs on the ottoman and her long hair arranged in a braided coronet. She exuded an air of complaisance and the fresh clean scent of lavender as Susannah, her arms full of flowers, leaned down to kiss her cheek.

"Are the flowers for me?" Esther asked, her eyes huge.

"They are indeed. Mrs. and Miss Hingham asked Uncle Miles if they might pick some to send up to you with their best wishes."

"How very thoughtful of them," Claudia said warmly. "Is this not a lovely surprise, sweetheart?"

"Oh, yes. May I hold them for a minute?"

"With my blessings. Mrs. Hingham sent me back to the house for the shears, and then they kept piling stem after stem into my hands," Susannah said, brushing a couple of torn leaves from her arms after transferring her colorful burden to her sister's lap.

"What shall we put them in?" Claudia gazed around the room without discovering anything that might serve as a container for such bounty.

"I met Josie on my way up here and sent her to fetch a large vase. Miss Hingham offered to arrange the flowers, but I said I thought Esther would enjoy doing it herself."

"Yes, I would. And then may I go downstairs to thank the ladies, Claudia? Cannot Julian or one of the footmen carry me?" Esther pleaded. "My leg doesn't hurt at all today."

Claudia hesitated. "Your uncle said you must wait until after he speaks to Dr. Martin, love. Has he been here today?" she asked Susannah.

"Not yet. Why don't you go for your walk now, Claudia. I'll stay and help Esther arrange her flowers."

"I do not like to take you away from your guests."

"They are not my guests," the girl said promptly, "although they might as well be. I conducted them through the house this morning while Uncle Miles went out to check with his farm manager and my great-aunt remained behind because she said her leg was bothering her too much to walk for long. Uncle didn't return for lunch. Thank heavens the ladies retired to their rooms for a couple of hours this afternoon. When they returned to the saloon after their rest, I showed them around the gardens until Uncle Miles joined us a few moments ago. They won't miss my company now."

"You have more than done your duty," Claudia said with a twinkle in her eyes.

"Well, I think I have. Miss Hingham is perfectly agreeable and conversable, though not very . . . very spontaneous. Her expression never varies whether she is speaking of something wonderful or lamentable. Mrs. Hingham is quite another matter, however. I am tired of being cross-questioned by her on every aspect of our lives."

"Cross-questioned? Isn't that a bit strong, my dear? Naturally Mrs. Hingham is interested in Lord Pelham's family, but I am persuaded she means no impertinence by it."

Susannah tossed her head and her beautiful dark eyes flashed. "Whatever she means by it, it is none of her affair why our parents sent us back to England or what became of our governess or how long we shall live with Uncle Miles, and I was horribly tempted to tell her that."

"I am glad you had the good manners to refrain from doing something that would cover your uncle with shame," Claudia said as she walked over to the mirror to check her appearance. She made a minute adjustment to the watch pinned to her gown and took her leave of the sisters with a smile.

Claudia's feet became lighter and picked up speed as she came down the main staircase and headed to the garden entrance at the back of the house. It would be good to have some time to herself in the fresh air.

Once outside, Claudia lifted her face to the sun, undeterred by its burning heat. It occurred to her that she should have worn a hat—Susannah had sported a charming chip straw bonnet with yellow ribbons—but she was loath to waste any of her precious freedom in going back inside to fetch one. As a concession to prudence and, she acknowledged guiltily, to avoid the Hingham ladies and Lord Pelham if they were still in the gardens, she set off in the direction of the orchard, where there would be ample shade.

She nearly made it. Her hand was on the latch of the door in the brick wall at the end of the cutting garden when Lord Pelham's voice arrested her progress.

"Ah, Miss Herbert, how nice that you have come out to join the ladies in their tour of the gardens."

Sighing in resignation, Claudia turned to see the baron and his guests coming through the opening in the hedge that bordered the rose garden. She retraced her steps slowly, noting without surprise that both Mrs. and Miss Hingham wore wide-brimmed straw hats to protect their complexions from the sun's rays.

They met next to a bed of yellow dahlias a shade darker than Miss Hingham's crisp muslin gown. Claudia smiled at the women, but addressed the baron. "Actually, sir, I was about to take my daily walk while Susannah keeps Esther company." Her smile grew warmer as did her voice when she turned to the women. "Esther is thrilled with her flowers. It was so kind of you to think of her. When I left her room, she and Susannah were busy arranging them in a vase."

"Naturally Martha and I are excessively sorry for the poor little thing and hoped to brighten her spirits with the flowers. How is she today?"

Claudia was giving them a comfortable account of Esther's progress when Roberta came hurrying up to the group. "I've been looking everywhere for you, Uncle Miles. Dr. Martin has arrived. He is waiting in your study."

Lord Pelham smiled at his niece. "Thank you, love." He sketched a bow to his guests. "If you will excuse me, ladies, I have been hoping to have a word with the doctor. I'll leave you in good hands. Roberta already knows every inch of the estate."

While the Hingham ladies responded graciously and followed their host's hasty departure with their eyes, Claudia was taking stock of the child unconcernedly eating an orange as she stopped to tug an audacious weed from the dahlia bed. Her lips parted, but it was too late to issue a warning as the damp soil clinging to the weed's root showered unheeded down onto the hem of the child's dress. It became obvious that this was only the most recent misadventure to befall her attire when Roberta stood up again, revealing a length of torn petticoat ruffle hanging below her blue skirt.

"Are you going for your walk now, Claudia? May I come, too?"

"Of course, but you'd best go back to the house and have Josie pin up that torn petticoat first."

Roberta glanced down in mild surprise at the front of her skirt. "All right, Claudia. I'll be right back."

"Don't run, Roberta, you might trip over that petticoat," Claudia called as the youngster sprinted toward the house.

Roberta obediently slowed her pace.

Claudia, conscious of the silent spectators to the homely scene, sought a trivial remark with which to begin a conversation, but Mrs. Hingham nipped in first.

"I have yet to see that child when she was not eating something," she observed. "It is not a habit that should be encouraged. She is already too plump."

Claudia took care to banish any hint of defensiveness from her voice as she said, "I would guess that Roberta is at that awkward age just before a girl begins her final growth period." It was not her place to display the partiality of a relative in the face of gratuitous criticism. "Did you not find the late Lady Pelham's rose garden a sheer delight?" she added, smiling brightly at both ladies.

"Very nice indeed." Again it was Mrs. Hingham who spoke. "Although some of the bushes show traces of blackspot. As I told Lord Pelham just now, his gardener is being careless in his watering habits."

"Even on a hot afternoon the scents are heavenly in the rose garden," Miss Hingham said, relieving Claudia of the necessity to find a response to the matron's horticultural pronouncement.

"Speaking of the heat," Mrs. Hingham said, "I believe we have had quite enough exposure for one day, Martha. Let us go inside."

"Yes, Mama." Miss Hingham smiled at Claudia. "I hope you will enjoy your walk."

"I trust you will not suffer any serious damage to your complexion going out without a hat or parasol, my dear Miss Herbert," Mrs. Hingham said with a display of motherly concern.

"Thank you for your interest, ma'am," Claudia replied, not to be outdone in civility. "It is very warm this afternoon, isn't it, but I plan to walk in the orchard, where the trees will offer some shade."

As the other women headed toward the house, Claudia moved into the shadow cast by the brick wall to wait for Roberta's return.

Now that she had met all the current residents of Beechwood, Claudia did not find dressing for dinner as worrisome as on the previous evening. Good manners and civil intercourse would be the order of the day, but she could not whip up any enthusiasm for the occasion. It is never a comfortable sensation to know oneself an unwanted outsider, no matter how pleasant one's fellow guests.

The skin on her cheeks felt tight, and a glance in the mirror confirmed that she had not entirely escaped the sun's burning rays even in the orchard. She made a little face at the sight of her pinkened nose and cheeks. A gentle wash in tepid water and the application of a soothing cream did take some of the heat out, but she cherished no illusions that the faint pinkness would escape Mrs. Hingham's eagle eye.

Claudia's thoughts turned to a more agreeable subject, young Roberta Brewster of the awkward manner and loyal heart. Strong ties of affection bound all the Brewster children together, though Julian and Susannah clearly enjoyed an additional bond through their twinship. At the moment Roberta seemed to feel a little lost or left out. Susannah was patient and indulgent with Esther, but she evidently found Roberta a bit trying at this stage. From scraps of conversation over the past few days, Claudia had gathered that Roberta and George, only two years apart, were close companions. Like George, Roberta was athletically inclined, delighting in all physical activity, and she had been in the habit of accompanying her brother on most of his adventures. George was away at school, however, and, Roberta had confided during their walk this afternoon, he was going off to stay with a classmate for a fortnight. The child had made no complaint over what was obviously a personal disappointment, but her wistful air had tugged at Claudia's heartstrings. Before she left Beechwood, she must have a little talk with Susannah and, if the opportunity presented itself, she should bring the situation to Lord Pelham's attention in a tactful manner.

How to accomplish this without appearing presumptuous would take some thought, but Susannah arrived to escort her down to the saloon before she had made any headway on the problem.

Claudia was barely over the threshold when Mrs. Hingham exclaimed in tones of deep solicitude, "Oh, my dear Miss Herbert, it is as I feared; going without a hat this afternoon has resulted in a dreadful sunburn. I have some excellent salve that I shall give you to ease the discomfort."

With all eyes on her face, Claudia was aware that annoyance had most likely deepened the color in her cheeks several shades. She struggled to infuse cordiality into her own voice. "You are very kind, ma'am, but there is no need. I am conscious of no discomfort at all."

"Your stoicism does you credit, but I am persuaded I know better," Mrs. Hingham said with an arch smile. "I shall send my maid to your room with the salve immediately after we dine."

"Thank you, ma'am. I am most grateful," Claudia said, lying through her teeth for the sake of bringing the embarrassing scene to a close.

"I hope it isn't too uncomfortable, Miss Herbert, because the slight color is most becoming," Lord Pelham said, handing her the glass of sherry he had been pouring when she and Susannah entered the room. "It gives you a bright-eyed, healthy look."

"That is just what I was thinking," Julian chimed in.

Rescue came from an unexpected source as Lady Powerby, never one to admit anyone else's sufferings on a par with her own, embarked on a rambling tale of a case of near sunstroke she had suffered in her youth.

Lord Pelham intervened just as his aunt was about to describe her symptoms a second time to an increasingly restive audience. He reported that the doctor was more than pleased with his small patient's progress and, with a gallant bow in

Claudia's direction, the physician had been quick to praise Claudia's skill in keeping Esther quiet during her confinement. Julian and Susannah had seconded this opinion with a spontaneous display of appreciation that caused the fading color to flare up in Claudia's cheeks once more.

The baron went on to say that Dr. Martin had given his permission to have Esther carried downstairs daily so that she might participate in some quiet family activities from a chaise longue. This announcement was greeted by professions of pleasure from all those present, led by Mrs. Hingham who could not have been more enthusiastic had Esther been her own child. Claudia had already heard the good news from her excited patient upon her return from her stroll through the orchard. Her smiling serenity masked an unworthy reluctance to exchange the sanctuary of Esther's bedchamber for the arena of social intercourse. She took herself to task once again for permitting her own inclinations to weigh even a feather against Esther's promised release from a protracted confinement.

The evening was essentially a repeat of the preceding one with music and conversation occupying the hours after dinner. Nothing untoward occurred. Mrs. Hingham and Lady Powerby actually found some common ground in tearing to shreds the character of a mutual and long disliked acquaintance, and the youngsters and Miss Hingham were in good voice. Claudia stayed as much in the background as Lord Pelham's finely developed social sense would permit, which was to say that she was civilly coerced into taking part in the general conversation. Since this never rose above light trivialities, it was no strain on her intellectual faculties to keep pace while indulging in her own thoughts for the most part.

These thoughts included the idle observation toward the end of the evening that Lord Pelham had not so far paid the least distinguishing attention to his purported betrothed in all the time she had seen them together. It crossed her mind that this could be considered carrying his duties as host a bit too far. At least the young woman in question could be pardoned for any slight pique arising from such circumspect behavior on the part of a suitor.

Her covert but pointed observation of Miss Hingham revealed no trace of disappointment in her manner, however, leading Claudia to the conclusion that this was the most anemic courtship, at least in its public stance, that she had ever witnessed.

Chapter Nine

Esther awoke the next morning in a state of eager anticipation more properly reserved for Christmas or birthday morns. Familiar by now with the child's volatile emotions and convinced that nothing awaited her downstairs that could possibly measure up to whatever dimly conceived fantasies whirled in Esther's head, Claudia applied herself to the delicate task of lowering the little girl's expectations without appearing to throw cold water on her enthusiasms. To this end she smilingly seconded all of Esther's pronouncements on the joys of escaping from the prison of her bedchamber, and extended her wholehearted participation in the serious business of selecting a dress for the momentous occasion.

They narrowed the choices to two and engaged in a protracted discussion of the merits of a green-dotted muslin with an abbreviated sleeve versus a soft white Indian cotton boasting an embroidered flounce at the hem. Claudia applauded Esther's eventual selection of the white, based on the news that her mother had embroidered the flounce herself.

"I expect the ladies will be interested to see the lovely work Mama does, do not you, Claudia?"

"I do indeed, and I am persuaded they will admire the pretty pattern of fanciful flowers and leaves as well as the fine workmanship. You must take great care not to crush the soft fabric if you go downstairs this morning because I believe we shall not see Mrs. and Miss Hingham in the saloon until late this afternoon. You would not like to present them with a sadly wrinkled example of your mother's skill."

"Not until then?" Stark disappointment looked out of Esther's blue eyes.

"I am afraid not, sweetheart. Mrs. Hingham was saying last night at dinner that she, too, would like to ride around the estate with your uncle if the heat ameliorated a bit, and I do believe it is cooler. So, in all likelihood there will be only Lady Powerby in the saloon this morning."

Claudia busied herself about the room, putting away the rejected dresses in the clothespress while she gave Esther time to evaluate the altered circumstances. She was not unduly surprised when the child elected to postpone her maiden appearance downstairs until after her postprandial rest. Esther had admitted in the early stages of her recuperation that she was relieved that Lady Powerby did not visit the sickroom because she never knew what to say to her elderly relative. Having discovered early in their acquaintance Lady Powerby's complete lack of sympathy for anyone who did not immediately enter into her own all-consuming obsession with her declining state of health, Claudia was happy to be spared what promised to be an uncomfortable session of monitoring and mediating a conversation between the child and her great aunt. From her own point of view the more people around to smooth Esther's transition into the enlarged family, the better for everyone.

Claudia dismissed all concerns about the inevitable meeting in favor of dispelling the disgruntled mood her charge was now displaying. She had prudently laid by a secret weapon for just such a moment. She opened a drawer in the chest and withdrew it, turning to Esther with the satisfied smile of a successful conjurer, her hands outstretched.

"And now, my love, I have a delightful surprise for you," she announced, putting a sandalwood box into the child's hands. "When Julian went riding with Duncan Marshall the other day, he naturally told his friend about your accident, and Mr. Marshall recalled that his cousin had presented him with a dissected map of Europe once when he was indisposed and confined to his bed. He has sent it to you in the hope that you will find it as diverting and challenging an occupation to put together as he did. Wasn't that thoughtful of him? Shall we try our hand at the puzzle?"

Esther had already emptied the pieces of the map into her lap when Claudia returned with a low table that she drew up to the side of the bed.

The disjointed map had saved the day, Claudia reflected several hours later as she prepared for Esther's descent to the garden room, a venue that Susannah had decided would be the most pleasant for one who had long been confined to an up-stairs room. Child and attendant had worked at putting the map together, enjoying a painless geography lesson in the process, the benefits of which had ultimately extended to Roberta, who had her turn at the puzzle later in the morning. Esther had re-mained tractable through lunch and had even fallen asleep dur-ing a reading of *Waverley*, something Claudia had not dared to hope for, given the child's underlying excitement.

Even with the able assistance of the good-natured Josie it had taken nearly an hour to array the little girl in her finery, following a warm scented bath intended to calm the spirit, but at last she was ready for her entrance.

Looking sideways at her seated patient as she gathered to-gether a number of articles Esther deemed vital to the coming occasion, Claudia thought privately that the youngest Brewster child with her huge, dark-lashed blue eyes and straight little nose, bade fair to rival her eldest sister's beauty in time. The pale porcelain clarity of her skin was enhanced at present by a flush of anticipation as she lovingly fingered the delicate em-broidery on her sash, and her dark auburn hair, freed from the restraint of braids, curled riotously over her shoulders, glinting with red lights in the angled rays of the sun streaming through the window.

Josie had gone to fetch Julian or, failing her brother, one of the footmen to carry Esther downstairs. The little girl's eyes were fixed on the door, and Claudia's ears were primed for sounds in the hall as she added a precautionary shawl to the oddments she was collecting, though she did not really expect that Esther would feel chilled.

When Roberta bounced into the room presently, both its oc-cupants were surprised to see her accompanied by the master of the house.

"Your transport awaits, fair lady," Lord Pelham announced grandiloquently, making his small niece a sweeping bow. "My, aren't you a picture today in that white dress," he added in his normal tones, "and," bending closer, "you smell as delightful as you look."

"Are *you* going to carry me downstairs, Uncle Miles?" Esther asked, eyes wide with surprise.

"It has been intimated that my services in this respect would not be unwelcome," the gentleman replied with a smiling nod in Roberta's direction.

"I told Uncle Miles I thought you would feel safest if he carried you," Roberta explained.

Disarmed by the thoughtfulness of both uncle and niece, Claudia extended her arm around Roberta's shoulders in a quick hug while she beamed a smile at Lord Pelham. Something in his eyes as he returned her smile had her glancing away quickly. "You are a very fortunate young lady," she said to Esther, adding a prosaic warning, "mind you don't wriggle now."

When the baron had scooped up his niece and directed her to put her arms around his neck, Claudia began to pick up the various items she'd assembled.

"What is all that?" asked Lord Pelham.

Claudia grinned. "Like Lady Powerby, Esther likes to be prepared for every eventuality when she leaves her room. Now I know how her ladyship's abigail must feel."

"I'll help you, Claudia," Roberta said, relieving her of the cribbage board and a book.

"Thank you, love. Now I can open the door. We'll let your uncle and Esther go through first, shall we?"

The merry little party descended to the ground floor and proceeded to the garden room in the spirit of a triumphal procession with the baron and his nieces trading laughing banter. Claudia listened with smiling appreciation though she refused to be drawn into the exchange, shaking her head laughingly.

She was bemused at the rapidity with which a bachelor, presumably with little previous experience of children, had gotten upon such close and comfortable terms with his nephews and nieces with their varied personalities and needs. It was wholly admirable, but a little voice inside Claudia's head reminded her that she did not wish to find Lord Pelham admirable. And, another little voice chastised her, *her* attitude was wholly despicable, to accord less than justice to the baron's character simply because it was easier to bear her own unenviable position vis-à-vis Lord Pelham as long as she could pretend to a moral superiority. Yes, it was more than time that she left Beechwood and its intriguing master.

Claudia's somber musings were derailed by an escalating murmur of voices as they approached the garden room. She entered first, casting a swift glance around the large area for the most suitable seating for Esther, noting as she did so that, with the exception of Julian, all members of the household were present.

"Over here, Claudia," Susannah called from a corner near one of the French windows. "Uncle Miles had Grandmother's favorite chaise longue brought in for Esther."

The next few minutes were taken up with making the small girl comfortable after her uncle had deposited her gently on the aforesaid chaise.

"Thank you, Uncle Miles, for carrying me downstairs," Esther said solemnly as she withdrew her arms from around his neck. "Next to Papa, I think you are the best and most handsome man in the world, do you not agree, Claudia?"

"Not having had the honor of meeting your papa, love, it would be improper of me to express an opinion on the subject," Claudia said matter-of-factly, taking care not to glance at Lord Pelham as she took a little extra time tucking a pillow under Esther's injured leg.

His rich chuckle sounded above her ear as she straightened up. "Spare my blushes, sweetheart. I swear I neither beat nor bribed her to garner that endorsement," he added with mock seriousness, addressing the Hingham ladies who had come over to the chaise to meet Esther.

"Of course not," Mrs. Hingham said with an appreciative titter while her daughter merely smiled at his pleasantry. "It is plain as a pikestaff that the child bears a very proper affection for her uncle. Indeed, it gladdens the heart to see the attachment all the children have for you, sir."

"And I for them," Lord Pelham said softly before proceeding to make Esther known to his guests formally.

Mrs. and Miss Hingham proclaimed their pleasure at meeting the child, and Esther repeated her gratitude for the flowers they had sent up to her the previous day. "They are still very lovely, except for a few that wilted, probably because they were picked in the afternoon heat, Claudia said. It was very kind of you to think of me," she added hastily after intercepting the warning look in her friend's eyes.

"Naturally we wished to do something to express our sympathy for your plight, you poor child," Mrs. Hingham said. "It must have been a horridly frightening experience to undergo with neither your parents nor your guardian on hand to support your spirits."

"It was, just at first, but then Claudia came," Esther said simply.

"Yes, I am persuaded everyone is most grateful for the happy accident that brought Miss Herbert to the scene of your distress and for her kindness in looking after you while your uncle was away."

Claudia was spared any extended discomfort by Lady Powerby, who could not long bear to hear of another's suffering eclipsing her own. She launched into a recital of a strikingly similar injury she had undergone in the past when her leg, although not actually broken, according to the medical men, had caused her weeks of agonizing pain. When she contrasted this with the resilience and quick recuperative powers of the very young, her nephew took command of the conversation.

"And thank goodness for that," he said heartily, "if it means that Miss Herbert may finally enjoy an uninterrupted night's rest."

The arrival of refreshments at that moment gave everyone's thoughts a new direction, to Claudia's heartfelt relief.

During the bustle of serving, Miss Hingham, who had taken a seat near the chaise, asked Esther about the piece of wood with the holes that she had by her side.

"This is a cribbage board. If you do not know how to play, I could teach you," Esther offered, producing a pack of cards from under her book.

"Oh, I see, it is a card game. I fear I do not much care for cards."

"It is really a good game. Claudia taught me to play it."

"Perhaps at another time then," Miss Hingham replied with a diplomatic smile as she returned to her former chair.

"I'll play with you, Esther," Roberta volunteered.

This obliging offer produced a collective sigh of relief from the adults in the company, who went on to discuss the evening's dinner party. The topic was initiated by Miss Hingham, who smiled at her host over her teacup and remarked that they could not have wished for a more perfect evening with cooler temperatures than recently, clear skies, and a three-quarter moon expected to aid the homeward drive.

"Yes, we are fortunate," Lord Pelham agreed.

"The dining room looks and smells lovely," Susannah chimed in. "It was an inspiration to cut the last of the late peonies early this morning, Claudia. They have opened beautifully."

Lord Pelham turned to Claudia. "Are the dining room arrangements your work, Miss Herbert?"

"I . . . I helped Susannah with them while Esther napped this afternoon," Claudia replied a bit disingenuously, conscious that once again her actions might be seen as presumptuous. She was grateful when Susannah broke in impetuously.

"That reminds me, Uncle, I counted eighteen places at table when I looked in a few minutes ago," the girl said, a little line of puzzlement between her eyebrows. "There are seven of us; Lord and Lady Rockingham, their son and his friend make eleven; the Marshalls and Duncan make fourteen; and Sir William and Lady Mountjoy and Melissa should bring the total to seventeen." As she finished enumerating the guests, she sent a look of inquiry to her uncle.

"Lady Mountjoy sent a note to say they have someone staying with them, so he makes it eighteen," Lord Pelham replied. "A good sampling of our neighbors for you to meet," he added, smiling at Mrs. Hingham and her daughter. "I hope you will find them a pleasant group."

"Mrs. Marshall is a sensible young woman, but Lady Rockingham would talk the ears off a brass monkey," Lady Powerby said, struggling to her feet. "If I am to preside over such a large group, it is essential that I lie down for an hour to recruit my strength before dressing, so if you will all excuse me now . . ."

While the baron escorted his aged relative to the door, rescuing her shawl as it slipped from her shoulders, the Hingham ladies began to question Susannah about the neighbors who would be dining with them. Claudia edged closer to the children, who were engaging in a rather contentious card game to put a damper on their high spirits, while at the same time distancing herself from the adult group.

Claudia was still mulling over subtle ways to set herself apart from the Beechwood household in the eyes of local society when she entered the main saloon a couple of hours later. Though Lord Pelham's stubborn refusal to relegate her to the anonymity of an upper servant glowed like a candle in the darkness of her heart, she still considered it a mistake. Best for all concerned if she were regarded as a purely transient and accidental presence. She had taken a firm resolution to keep mum in the background tonight, except for the minimum social duty required of any temporary visitor.

Mindful of her determined role, Claudia uttered a quiet greeting to the assembled company, ending in an apology. "An unexpected bit of last-moment mending has made me rather tardy, I fear. I beg your pardon."

"Here you are at last, Miss Herbert, looking charming as ever. Come and sit here and tell me how Esther has weathered her first departure from her room. I do hope the poor child received no setback because of her rashness."

Though surprised by the gushing tones in which it was couched, Claudia complied with Lady Powerby's request and joined her hostess on a sofa. Her cheerful account of the child's improved condition was received with ill-feigned attention, however. A few moments of careful listening to snippets of conversation among the others and Lady Powerby's frigid interjections persuaded her that an earlier altercation must have taken place between the two elder ladies that accounted for the sudden increase in her own popularity. Lord Pelham wore the bland expression of a good host refusing to acknowledge any signs of constraint among his guests. In an effort to assist her host, Claudia asked a question that broke up the tight alliance between the twins, seated together to one side of the fireplace. The more contributors the better.

The butler's announcement a moment later of the first of the invited guests put an end to the awkward situation.

The next fifteen minutes was given over to a flurry of introductions as the rest of the neighbors arrived closely on each other's heels. Though she would never meet any of these people again, Claudia could not in good conscience excuse herself from a fair participation in the social amenities. Consequently, when her turn came, she looked squarely at each guest while articulating the appropriate phrases of greeting. The months she had spent in a Parisian gaming house had taught her the knack of concentrating intently on anyone to whom she was being introduced so she would recall his or her identity at the next meeting. Naturally, it helped her memory if there was something distinctive about a stranger's appearance, especially when she met several at the same time.

Eleven persons represented a real challenge, though mitigated by the prior knowledge that this horde was divided into three families, whose names she had already learned, plus two male guests.

Lord and Lady Rockingham were obviously on the shady side of fifty, despite her ladyship's attempt to cheat the calendar by wearing a youthfully styled gown of pink crape that failed to adequately contain her abundant charms. This unfortunate choice was compounded by the adoption of a girlish manner and a high-pitched laugh, neither of which accorded well with her station or years. Lord Rockingham, thick-necked, red-cheeked, and barrel-chested, making no efforts to disguise his girth or age, greeted everyone with unaffected good humor, patted Susannah's cheek, calling her "pretty puss," then embarked on a discussion of farming with Mr. Marshall.

Claudia judged Sir William and Lady Mountjoy to be several years younger than the Rockinghams. They were apparently quite different in temperament from the elder couple and of a more refined physical type. Sir William, tall and distinguished-looking with iron gray hair, a broad smooth brow, and regular features, was dressed with precision and propriety in a perfectly pressed black coat and sparkling white linen. Tall and slender like her husband, Lady Mountjoy exuded an air of understated elegance in a beautifully cut gown of lustrous gray silk that set off her fair coloring and light brown hair.

Despite the aesthetic appeal of the Mountjoys, Claudia did not find them nearly so attractive as Mr. and Mrs. Marshall who included a welcome element of human warmth among their physical attributes, something the older couple appeared at first glance to lack. Mrs. Marshall, the mother of an eighteen-year-old son, must be coming up on forty, but looked much younger. She had lively gray eyes, a smiling mouth, and a sprinkling of freckles across her nose, these last an honest legacy with the unabashedly red hair that curled wildly about her small head. Her husband's dark hair, faintly touched with gray at the temples, displayed a more restrained tendency to curl. His brown eyes were as alive as his wife's, and his smile as warm when he greeted Claudia. Their son, Duncan, of moderate stature like his father, had inherited a darker version of his mother's fiery curls without the milky skin tones and freckles. His dark eyes and features were strikingly like his father's, and his smile held a trace of shyness when speaking to the ladies that did him no disservice in their estimation.

With so many people meeting for the first time, the formal introductions were of necessity a bit protracted, allowing Claudia time to study each group as they approached. The similarity between parents and offspring struck her forcibly. Mr. Henry Rockingham, a thickset, ruddy-complexioned young man in his early twenties, combined his father's bluff joviality with his mother's vacuous expression and high-pitched laugh.

Melissa Mountjoy, slender and graceful, was a younger edition of her mother, with the same proud carriage and innate sense of style, judging by the simple gown of uncrushed blue muslin that was most becoming to her youthful figure. She appeared to be about nineteen or twenty years old, but had not yet acquired her mother's ability to conceal her feelings behind a mask of stiff poise. Her rather sharp features froze into an expression that Claudia could only describe as alert suspicion as she greeted Susannah, that lightened only marginally when presented to Claudia, although she did manage a thin-lipped smile for the Hingham ladies.

Taking into account that the neighborhood was rife with conjecture concerning Miss Hingham's probable betrothal to Lord Pelham, and acknowledging the truth that, even at sixteen, Susannah Brewster eclipsed all females present *au fait de beauté*, Claudia applied a bit of feminine logic to the occurrence and came to the swift conclusion that Miss Mountjoy must have high hopes of attaching her parents' houseguest, the dark-haired man talking with Mr. Marshall while he awaited his turn to be presented to Lord Pelham's household. Jealousy and lack of confidence were not uncommon emotions to find in a young woman during the uncertain period before the man of her choice made his. Although she did not find Melissa personally appealing, Claudia was aroused to silent sympathy on her behalf, and she made an innocuous observation in an attempt to dissipate the slight awkwardness.

The opportunity to test her theory about Miss Mountjoy's behavior was postponed when the younger Rockingham, who had been enlivening the masculine group with his whinnying laugh, seized his friend's arm and hustled him over to the Beechwood ladies to be presented.

In Mr. Cedric Albertson, Claudia beheld the personification of the English dandy. His neck and jaw were imprisoned behind high, stiffly starched shirt points and swathed in a monstrously wide cravat tied in a more elaborate style than Claudia had yet had the privilege of viewing. The lapels of his coat were wider, the buttons larger, and the fit tighter than that of any other gentleman present. Several fobs dangled below his waist, and the pin in his cravat was the size of a pigeon egg, its colors matching the stripes in his silk waistcoat. He possessed a strong pair of shoulders and good height. There was nothing inherently displeasing about his features, but Claudia considered his carefully arranged and pomaded locks a conceited affectation, and she mistrusted the look in his narrow eyes when he greeted the younger ladies with obvious flattery. When her turn came, she responded with a faint smile and a tiny curtsy and promptly dismissed him from her mind, until she was jolted a moment later to hear Mr. Rockingham say, "And of course you have already met Miss Brewster, Ceddie, that day when we bumped into her in the village."

"Yes, I have enjoyed the incomparable honor of making Miss Brewster's acquaintance and confess to sheer delight at this opportunity to expand it."

Claudia's eyes had flown to Susannah at the beginning of Mr. Albertson's unctuous pronouncement. There was no fault to be found with the girl's smiling acknowledgment of the compliment, but something, perhaps the modest lowering of Susannah's fabulous black lashes, alerted her friend to danger. She knew with the certainty of revelation that this was not just the second meeting between these two. Mr. Albertson was, in fact, the reason for Julian's concern for his flighty sister, the impetus behind his leaving school without permission.

At that instant Claudia became aware that Lord Pelham's gaze was fixed on her. His bright blue eyes were communicating his understanding of the situation to her. She blinked and could feel the muscles of her jaw relax and her lips soften. He knew. Susannah's guardian had not been fooled by the transparent bit of playacting put on by his lovely niece and the town beau currently enjoying the Rockinghams' hospitality. She could leave this matter in his lordship's capable hands.

Claudia glanced away from her host's compelling gaze, and her eyes lighted on the tall, lean man coming toward the group with Sir William. Standing beside Miss Hingham, she had been screened by other persons between them and had seen only the back of his dark head until now. Eyeing him critically, she decided that she approved of Miss Mountjoy's choice. There was nothing particularly arresting about the man approaching, but he had an attractive though serious aspect, and he looked every inch the gentleman.

Beside her, Claudia felt Miss Hingham stir and heard her strangle a gasp in her throat. She turned and saw that the ever-serene Martha was ashen pale, one hand at her throat and her eyes fastened in painful intensity on the man who drew to a stop before them.

"How do you do, Miss Hingham," the gentleman said, bowing. "It is indeed an unexpected pleasure to meet again after so long."

"You *know* Miss Hingham, Edwin?" Miss Mountjoy asked sharply.

"Mr. Carr and my daughter were slightly acquainted several years ago in London," Mrs. Hingham said in firm tones, eyeing Miss Mountjoy briefly before turning a look of command on her silent offspring, whose normal color was now creeping back.

"Then you must not have heard that he is now Lord Frame," Sir William said, addressing Mrs. Hingham.

"No, no, I had not heard," replied that lady stiffly. "My congratulations, sir."

Lord Frame acknowledged this with another small bow. "My father died shortly after I left London, and the two cousins who stood between him and the title were killed last year at Waterloo. My uncle summoned me to Ferndale to learn how to manage the estate I would inherit. I have been there until quite recently."

"And now your uncle is also dead?" Mrs. Hingham persisted.

"Yes. Sadly, I have very little family remaining."

"I am so very sorry for all your losses, sir." Miss Hingham spoke for the first time, softly and with more feeling than Claudia had ever heard from her.

"Thank you." Lord Frame accepted her condolences with another bow and a grateful look.

"We must see to it that you and Miss Hingham find an opportunity to renew your acquaintance after dinner, sir," Lord Pelham said before either Miss Mountjoy or Mrs. Hingham could interject a comment, "but now I would make you known to my aunt, Lady Powerby, my other guest, Miss Herbert, and my niece and nephew."

These final introductions proceeded without further incident, to be followed immediately by Miss Mountjoy drawing Lord Frame away on the pretext of examining the Canaletto over the mantelpiece. Mrs. Hingham did not trouble to invent an excuse for leading her daughter over to a small sofa where she mounted guard until the butler announced dinner. Nor was Claudia permitted an idle moment in which to review the recent scene because Lord Pelham put his hand under her elbow and guided her over to the harp, where the Marshalls stood chatting with Julian. After commanding her in the most civil fashion to describe the joys of a Parisian spring to his friends, he moved off to see that Lady Mountjoy and Lady Rockingham were served sherry.

Chapter Ten

Claudia found the Marshalls every bit as likable as their appearance had suggested. Something of her thoughts at the Turkish treatment accorded her by the baron must have been evident as she stared at his retreating back, for Mrs. Marshall's silvery laugh brought her up short.

"It is my opinion that Miles owes his success as a host to his ruthless insistence that his guests entertain each other," that lady declared, her curls emitting fiery sparks in the candle glow as she shook her head, "but I speak the simple truth when I say that my husband and I are most eager to hear about Paris, Miss Herbert," she added more seriously, eyeing the reluctant smile tugging at Claudia's lips. "Is that not so, John?"

Thus appealed to, Mr. Marshall gave his prompt endorsement to his wife's sentiments. "Yes, indeed. When Julian told us that a lady newly arrived from Paris had come to the family's rescue after little Esther's accident, we were intrigued, having long cherished a desire to see Paris ourselves."

"We were dying to meet you," said Mrs. Marshall, taking over again, "but with Miles away and a crisis situation at Beechwood there was no question of casual callers adding to the problems. Now we need have no scruples about plying you with questions—"

"Within the latitude permitted guests at a dinner party, my dear," Mr. Marshall interjected, favoring his eager spouse with an indulgent smile.

"John is reminding me that I tend to be rather ruthless myself when I am on a quest, Miss Herbert, but I promise to mind my manners and remember my social duty."

"Not ruthless, just a touch single-minded," her husband protested as she wrinkled her charming nose at him. "How long were you in Paris, Miss Herbert?"

"I arrived last November, so I do not know what a Parisian summer is like, but I would advise any visitor to try to see Paris in the spring when the chestnut trees are just coming into bloom and the air smells sweet after the rain."

The small group by the harp was getting along famously when the butler announced dinner. Claudia had been too fully involved with their conversation to take note of the where-abouts of the rest of the company, and she subsequently experienced a little pang of guilt at her dereliction of duty. This lasted only a second before her common sense pointed out that she was not even a secondary hostess at this affair. That role belonged to Susannah, whom a quick glance discovered in the middle of a masculine group consisting of both Rockinghams and the dangerous Mr. Albertson. She dismissed that concern also with a mental shrug. Lord Pelham was eminently capable of protecting his niece's interest and good name. In any case, it was decidedly not *her* concern.

Her eyes drifted to the sofa, where the Hingham ladies had been joined by Lady Rockingham. The conversation at present appeared to consist of a monologue from the last named with the other ladies displaying varying degrees of civil attention. Their host had left Lady Mountjoy to the tender mercies of Lady Powerby, who, if her animated expression was an indication, must be relating a tale of ill health into her patient ears. Lord Pelham and Sir William had joined the young couple near the fireplace and were engaged in a discussion of great painting, judging by their various hand gestures and nods toward the Canaletto.

At dinner Claudia sat between Lady Mountjoy and Mr. Albertson. From her masculine partner she was initially subjected to a persistent barrage of fulsome compliments whose object was to entice her into a flirtation. Had Mr. Albertson's flattery possessed even a spark of originality or a hint of sincerity, she might have gratified him to some slight extent for the purpose of demonstrating to a watchful Susannah that her favorite was an unregenerate philanderer.

Alas, this was not the case. Claudia had had to endure dozens of similar situations during her months in Paris. The overblown tributes to numerous aspects of her anatomy merely insulted her intelligence and inspired her with a powerful desire to box his ears. Naturally, she suppressed such an antisocial impulse and even refrained from delivering the well-deserved setdown trembling on her lips. Instead, she smiled behind tight teeth and sweetly advised him to partake of the cook's famous veal in Madeira sauce before it got cold. Interrupted in full spate as it were, Mr. Albertson blinked and gazed blankly at the dish being offered him by a footman. When he raised his eyes again, he found the back of her head turned to him.

Claudia caught her host's amused glance, and her annoyance increased, unjustly, she was aware, since the seating arrangements had been designed by Lady Powerby. She composed her features into an approximation of polite interest before turning away with slow deliberation. While Lady Mountjoy regaled him with news of local interest, Claudia let her eyes trail around the table, noting with malicious satisfaction that the garrulous Lady Rockingham was seated at her host's right hand. She would not be the only sufferer during this dinner party. Her gaze passed over Mr. Marshall attempting to engage Miss Mountjoy's reluctant attention and focused on the charming picture of Duncan Marshall and Susannah engrossed in a lively conversation. With such an attractive young man almost on her doorstep, why must the girl encourage the odious Mr. Albertson?

This question had no sooner taken shape in her mind than Claudia chided herself for sheer stupidity. What diffident, respectfully adoring youth could hope to compete with a glib-tongued man of the town seven or eight years his senior in the eyes of a sixteen-year-old girl yearning for romance? Susannah was too inexperienced to appreciate the solid worth of the younger man or to detect the hollowness behind the exotic shell of the elder. All would be revealed in the fullness of time, but Claudia feared the Marshall lad was slated to endure the heartburnings of unrequited affection for the present.

Her eyes skimmed past the vivacious Susannah to Mr.

Rockingham stolidly doing justice to the cook's magnificent repast, neglected for the moment by both of his dinner partners. Miss Hingham sat silently beside him, pushing the food around on her plate in a half-hearted pretense of eating, while Sir William on her right was engaged with Lady Powerby. Just then Martha looked up slowly and stared directly across the table through the branching arms of a sliver candelabrum. Under Claudia's bemused gaze the young woman's cheeks reddened, and her lashes veiled her expression as she returned her eyes to her plate.

Her attention captured by this poignant little moment, Claudia cast a quick look around to aid the rapid calculation of the seating chart, in the process of which she received the distinct impression that Melissa Mountjoy's eyes were fixed on the same spot as Martha's had been. It did not take much of a leap of the imagination to conclude that Lord Frame was the recipient of all this feminine interest. Having heard Mrs. Hingham's insistent voice in a lull a moment before, Claudia realized, with a spurt of amusement at the mischievous element of chance, that this lady was seated between the obnoxious Mr. Albertson and Lord Frame in a position to intercept her daughter's languishing—if that was not too strong a word—glance at the latter. Claudia concluded that at this point in the evening there were at least two people, Miss Mountjoy and herself, who did not believe Mrs. Hingham's earlier declaration that her daughter and the former Mr. Carr had been "slightly acquainted" in the past.

Lady Mountjoy's voice on her right recalled Claudia to a sense of her own social obligations just then, and she turned a serenely attentive face to her.

Forgetful of her original intention to remain in the background, Claudia decided to bestir herself when the ladies retreated to the saloon, leaving the gentlemen to their port. Lady Powerby led a glassy-eyed Lady Mountjoy over to a settee and settled beside her for another recital of symptoms, while Lady Rockingham backed Susannah into a corner as she continued with one of her monologues. Meanwhile, Mrs. Hingham, her reluctant daughter in tow, had accosted Melissa Mountjoy and was interrogating her about Lord Frame. Sizing up the poten-

tial for disaster, Claudia sent an unspoken message in the direction of Mrs. Marshall, entering the room last. Making a gesture of her head toward the Hinghams, Claudia interrupted
Lady Powerby with a murmured apology to ask Lady Mountjoy a question about the collection of Sevres statuettes that she
had mentioned at dinner. Mrs. Marshall, quick to sense the
tension in the air, inserted herself into the trio dominated by
Mrs. Hingham with a breezy remark that the two young
women seized on with gratitude. At the same time, Claudia deposited Lady Mountjoy between Susannah and Lady Rockingham with a comment about Mrs. Brewster's talent for
incorporating Indian design motifs into her embroidery. When
Lady Mountjoy obligingly questioned Susannah further, Claudia murmured an excuse and returned to the settee to smooth
over Lady Powerby's pique at being deprived of her audience.

No one would ever mistake the feminine gathering at
Beechwood that evening for one of Mme. de Stael's brilliant
salons, but the ladies managed to sustain several conversations
until the gentlemen rejoined them. Claudia was asked how
long she would be staying in the area, a question she had anticipated and to which she replied with real regret that she expected to leave almost immediately. She appreciated the
kindness behind the polite interest shown in her, but was relieved that the men returned before she had to tell any more
lies about her recent activities abroad.

The next hour passed pleasantly with musical perfor-
mances from several of the young ladies plus a couple of
duets by Susannah and Julian that met with a warm reception. Melissa Mountjoy sang an aria from *Così fan tutte* with
a singular sweetness that belied the tones and expressions
Claudia had seen and heard from her so far this evening.
When not performing, Miss Mountjoy kept Lord Frame by
her side, addressing almost all her remarks to him alone.
There was certainly no opportunity for the tête-à-tête between Miss Hingham and Lord Frame that Lord Pelham had
mentioned before dinner. Claudia was persuaded that Mrs.
Hingham would see to it that no cozy chat would take place
by these two even if suggested. She speculated idly on the
past relationship between them while she sat listening to the

music. Her intuition told her that Lord Frame and Martha Hingham had once regarded each other as more than casual acquaintances.

When she caught herself mentally pursuing this subject, with its possible ramifications for Lord Pelham's betrothal, Claudia slammed the door on the line of thought with self-disgust. *Nothing* that happened at Beechwood could have any relevance to her future life. With a hard-won serenity imposed on her features, Claudia gave her full attention to the musical performance.

During the tea drinking that preceded leave-taking Claudia's composure was blasted to bits. Lord Rockingham's robust voice, intended for his neighbors but pitched to reach all ears, destroyed the sense of security that had crept over her this past sennight in Beechwood's happy atmosphere.

"Have any of you ever heard of a woman called Elvira Weedy, or Tweedy?" he asked his friends as he popped a piece of the Beechwood cook's celebrated fruitcake into his mouth.

Claudia's fingers holding her teacup clenched involuntarily, spilling a few drops of the hot liquid onto her black silk gown. She had the presence of mind to set the cup down gently on the table at her side and take out a black-bordered handkerchief from the reticule hanging from her wrist, which she used to dab at the tiny spots with unhurried motions, keeping her eyes glued to her now steady fingers. She was fairly confident that no one could tell from her quiet presence that her heart was banging against her ribs like a loose window shutter in a high wind, and all her senses were on the stretch, waiting for the answer to his lordship's question.

Murmurs of denial came from several sources, and Claudia was aware that a few conversations continued unabated.

"Why do you ask about this person?" Lord Pelham inquired.

"No reason really, except that I was over at Eldredge's smithy in Mendleship village this afternoon to have the axletree of my work carriage mended, and the lad there was talking about someone—a foreigner, he said—who had evidently been going around asking for this woman at livery stables in the area."

"Why livery stables?" some male voice said as Claudia forced her breathing to a regular rhythm.

"According to the foreigner, it seems the woman hired a carriage in Westminster about a sennight ago to take her to Maplehurst—"

"Maplehurst? Selkirk's estate? Why should that concern some foreigner?" asked another voice, perhaps Mr. Marshall's, though there was now a buzzing sound in Claudia's ears that made it difficult to concentrate.

"She never got there, according to this fellow who's been looking for her. The carriage was returned to the stables in Winchester the same day, but when this foreigner—a real ugly customer, according to the smith's lad—questioned the postilion, he, the driver, didn't recall where she got off, except that it was before Maplehurst."

"What does this ugly brute of a foreigner want with the elusive Weedy-Tweedy female?" Lord Pelham's lazy voice seemed to vibrate all along Claudia's nerve endings, making it a torture to keep her body quiescent. Simply to do something, she retrieved her cup.

"He never said, but the smith's lad vowed he wouldn't want to be in her shoes when the man catches up with her. Especially if she's a runaway wife," Lord Rockingham added with a laugh as he reached for another slice of the cake.

Claudia acquitted him of any intent to be cruel, but as she sent a hooded glance at Lord Rockingham's blunt-featured red face, she experienced a momentary surge of revulsion against the entire male gender, who wielded all the power in the world. Suddenly, she was exhausted, her hand too limp to continue holding a teacup. She set it down again, frowning at the tiny clatter of cup against saucer, and concentrated on maintaining a pleasant expression and a straight back while the evening wound down at what seemed like a crawling pace.

Claudia found the leave-taking an interminable process that evening, though with only three carriages to be brought round to the front entrance no one else felt the inconvenience at all, unlike the situation at town affairs, where the procession of carriages disgorging and retrieving guests was a logistical nightmare for even a modest event. Despite a crying need to be alone, she performed her part in the ritual with what grace she could muster, cheered even in her state of panic by the collective warmth extended to her by all the neighbors as they took their leave of the household on the front steps, it being a perfect summer evening.

As the Marshalls prepared to enter their carriage, Mrs. Marshall paused after expressing their pleasure in the evening to ask Claudia if she thought Esther might benefit from a visit by her ten-year-old daughter at this point in her convalescence. "Lucy is very fond of Roberta and Esther already," she said with a smile, "and has been begging to be taken to see poor Esther this past several days."

"Doubtless both girls would enjoy a visit from your daughter, ma'am, but I . . . I don't think that I . . . I mean, perhaps you should apply to their uncle," Claudia stammered, a trifle rattled at being thought in a position to make decisions at Beechwood.

"That sounds the very thing, Alicia. Send Lucy over tomorrow to play with the girls. Better still, bring her yourself. My aunt may keep to her rooms tomorrow after tonight's exertions, but I am persuaded the other ladies will welcome a visit."

Lord Pelham's enthusiastic tones almost in her ear caused Claudia to start slightly since she'd been unaware of his proximity. He was looking at her now as if for confirmation, and she said faintly, "Of course," softening the bald utterance with a smile for Mrs. Marshall who, with a casual, "That's settled then. Good night until tomorrow, and thank you again for a delightful evening," turned to give her hand to her husband waiting patiently by the open carriage door to assist her to enter.

Surprise had kept Claudia fixed to the spot, and it wasn't until Lord Pelham waved the Marshall carriage off that she realized with dismay that everyone else had already gone back inside with the exception of Mrs. Hingham standing in front of the open door, watching them narrowly. She moved instantly toward the door, though her purposeful gait contradicted an inexplicable shrinking from a brush with the formidable matron.

"Ah, Mrs. Hingham," Lord Pelham said from directly behind her, "I have just made arrangements with Mrs. Marshall to bring her young daughter to play with Esther and Roberta tomorrow afternoon. I hope you ladies will enjoy having a visitor. Alicia Marshall is delightful company, do you not agree?"

Thus represented, civility demanded an agreement from Mrs. Hingham, who gave it with a fair approximation of cordiality, although her thoughtful gaze moved again to the silent Claudia as the trio headed back to the saloon.

Claudia could feel the matron's unfriendly eyes on her during the ensuing two-sided recapitulation of the evening just ended. She was cringing inwardly, but some small corner of her mind could still applaud the skill with which the baron commanded Mrs. Hingham's participation while ignoring her own presence.

When they entered the saloon, only the young people were there talking over the party, Lady Powerby having retired as soon as the neighbors began their departure. Within a very few minutes the others, too, were on their way to their own quarters. Claudia's relief, however, was partially tempered by the impossibility under the circumstances of snatching a private moment with Lord Pelham in which to request an interview in the morning.

Closing the door of her bedchamber behind her that night failed to produce any measurable alleviation in the distressing physical and mental symptoms accompanying Claudia's recent plunge into panic, but at least privacy removed the strain of trying to maintain a pretense of calm. Despite her fatigue, she literally could not remain still, lurching into a mindless interval of pacing that saw her cross and recross the room scores of times while she struggled to bring a rational approach to bear on this new menace.

Rationality seemed to be beyond her reach initially, however, so physically threatened did she feel by the knowledge that her father's murderer was still within a few miles of Beechwood, canvassing the area in a determined search for her. She was shivering in her short-sleeved gown, despite her clammy palms. Barely conscious of the motions, she opened a dresser drawer on one of her aimless circuits and pulled out a wool challis shawl that she wrapped around herself without missing a step.

It was nearly inconceivable that she could have forgotten

her own danger in one short week, but how else could she account for the degree of shock that had exploded inside her at Lord Rockingham's tale tonight? It challenged all belief that the terrible events of Paris and the pursuit across the Channel could have receded so far so quickly that mention of her pursuer should have had this much effect on her. How could she have become so involved with the life at Beechwood that her own predicament could have moved off center stage for even an hour, let alone a sennight? At this point in her self-examination, Claudia was inclined to rate her mental acuity as scarcely above an idiot's.

Gradually, the pacing and raving gave way to the beginnings of a weary calm in Claudia, and she was eventually able to set about the practical task of readying herself for bed while she arrived at the inevitable decision that tonight marked her last day at Beechwood. There was also a shamed acceptance that she must have unwittingly deluded herself into believing that this day need never come. This was the only explanation that could account for weakly allowing Esther's tears and Lord Pelham's arguments to persuade her to remain once he had returned to take over the reins of his household. Fortunately, he had acknowledged the service she had done him and promised to assume the responsibility for her travel arrangements to her home.

She would hold him to his promise. First thing tomorrow morning she would seek him out and tell him she wished to leave immediately.

A recollection of the baron's persuasive powers caused an uneasy pause in her planning momentarily but, she argued, he knew this was no sudden arbitrary whim on her part. She had only remained these past two days at his urgent persuasion. It had been understood that once Esther was able to leave the sickroom, she would be free to leave Beechwood at her convenience. She had only to remain firm in her resolution. Lord Pelham was a man of his word.

At this point in her mental exercises, Claudia's eyes spotted the gleam of silver that was the duck's head top of her father's cane as she bent over the drawer to return the challis scarf. Burning saliva rose in the back of her mouth. She swallowed with difficulty and took the cane from the drawer with every evidence of revulsion. Sinking onto a pink brocaded chair, she rubbed the duck's bill with a fingertip, fighting back a rush of tears. With clenched jaw she unscrewed the top of the cane and removed the chamois bag that held Lady Selkirk's diamond necklace. For the first time since she'd left Paris she looked at the cold stones that had cost her father's life. A mist of tears blinded her after a moment, and she returned the necklace to its hiding place.

A hopeless melancholy overwhelmed Claudia as she climbed into bed a short time later. She had been understandably relieved at Lord Pelham's offer to send her home in one of his carriages, but in her relief she had lost sight of the crucial problem of returning the jewels to Lord Selkirk first. A very few minutes' consideration showed her that there was no way to accomplish this without Lord Pelham's knowledge. With his fine sense of the fitness of things, he was bound to send a maid with her, perhaps even a guard. She did not have enough money to bribe that many people to keep silent, assuming for the sake of argument that his lordship's servants could be bribed to betray their master's trust.

After all she had gone through to preserve her father's good name, Claudia could not bear the thought of disclosing the events leading up to his death and the terrifying aftermath to anyone, least of all Lord Pelham. His low opinion of her hurt more than she cared to admit; something inside her shriveled up with shame when she considered his possible reaction to such disclosures. He might not even believe her; he might think her father had stolen the necklace from Lord Selkirk or that she had and was returning it only out of fear of prosecution.

These specters of future disgrace tormented Claudia for several wakeful hours until she finally reached a compromise that if it did not accomplish her main objective tomorrow, would at least preserve her secret and allow for the fulfillment of her obligation in the future. She would tell Lord Pelham that she had a message to deliver to Lord Selkirk from her father and ask him to allow her the use of his carriage in carrying out this errand on her way to Kent. If he demanded to know more or refused to countenance the detour, then she would take the necklace home and enlist her aunt's aid in delivering it safely to the Selkirks, much as she deplored revealing her father's secret to the sister-in-law who had never considered him a worthy match for her younger sister.

Claudia's last thought before sinking into a welcome oblivion was pitiful regret that Lord Pelham should hold her in scant respect personally even while he considered himself indebted for her practical assistance to his family.

Claudia would have been astounded could she have overheard the conversation taking place in the Marshalls' bedchamber that night at the same time she was mourning the bleakness of her future.

"A pleasant evening, despite being landed between Lady Rockingham and Melissa Mountjoy at dinner," Mr. Marshall said on a yawn, entering his wife's bedchamber from his dressing room, where he had evidently deposited his coat, waistcoat, and cravat. He was unbuttoning his shirt collar as he strolled over to the dressing table, where his wife sat removing a pair of gold filigree earrings.

"Yes, although I cannot say I enjoyed watching my son suffer while Susannah Brewster flirted madly with that objectionable creature staying with the Rockinghams."

"She is just trying out her powers to attract, a harmless enough phase in the very young, my love."

"She is a heartless little minx," declared his love, pulling a brush viciously through her red curls until they fairly sparked.

"Your maternal instincts are rushing to the fore, sweetheart," Mr. Marshall said with a grin. "Do not eat your heart out for Duncan. He'll recover. He is very young, too young to be fixing his interest in any case."

"At least we have the consolation of knowing he had the good sense not to follow that little madam around all evening, languishing like a sick puppy for all the world to witness."

"He behaved just as he ought. We have done a good job with our son—if *I* do say it, who shouldn't."

A soft look came into Alicia Marshall's eyes. "He reminds me forcibly of you when we first met."

"Surely, I had progressed beyond the callow cub stage by the time we met," John Marshall protested and watched the mischievous smile deepen in his wife's eyes. "Minx yourself," he said, moving over to plant a kiss on the nape of her neck. "What did you think of Miles's intended bride?"

"Which one?"

John's startled eyes sought Alicia's in the mirror, and his hands tightened on her shoulders. "I don't understand. You told me when we received the invitation to dinner that Miles had brought a prospective bride to Beechwood."

"That was certainly the word in the neighborhood, but after seeing them all together tonight, I have my doubts."

There was a pause before her husband said slowly, "Then I presume your reference just now was to Miss Herbert, but she and Miles have scarcely known each other for two days. And it was Miss Hingham that he invited to Beechwood."

"I am aware. It is very odd indeed, but several times this evening I saw Miles look at Claudia Herbert in a way he did *not* look at Miss Hingham."

"*What* way?"

"I am tempted to say in an intimate way, but that is not really accurate. He was very circumspect—almost impersonal— with both of them, which is also odd, you will agree, if he is courting Miss Hingham. All I can say with any conviction is that if he does marry Miss Hingham, it will not be a love match."

John Marshall had developed a great deal of respect for his wife's judgment about people over the years, and he ceased arguing, saying merely, "Then I pity them, all three."

"Well, that may not be necessary if my suspicions are correct."

"And what does that cryptic utterance imply?"

Alicia chuckled at the hint of male exasperation in her husband's voice, but replied in a serious vein. "I was seated down at the other end of the table from you tonight, and I noticed Lord Frame looking at Miss Hingham once or twice in a way her purported fiancé did not. Either it was a case of love at first sight, or those two have known each other more than casually in the past."

"Well, they have met before at any event," John said, eyeing his wife with added respect. At her raised eyebrows, he elaborated. "I heard Mrs. Hingham tell Miss Mountjoy before dinner that her daughter and Lord Frame had been slightly acquainted in London, except that she referred to him as Mr. Carr, so the acquaintance must have been before he came into the title."

"So that is why Melissa Mountjoy was in a pet all evening! She could not have shown more plainly that she already regards Frame as her property, though Lady Mountjoy told me he is quite a recent acquaintance of Sir William's. To my mind it would be a very good thing if Miss Hingham were to snatch Frame from under Melissa's nose. She would make him a terrible wife with her airs and selfishness. And I really liked Claudia Herbert, did not you? She is much better suited to Miles than Miss Hingham is. Perhaps we should give a party."

"Alicia, I don't want us to get involved in the neighbors' affairs, especially their *affaires de coeur,*" John protested, alarmed at the turn the conversation had taken.

"Of course not, darling," his wife replied with absentminded sweetness. "It may not be necessary to do anything at all. I'll know better after tomorrow."

"Why do you say that? What is happening tomorrow?" her husband asked, his sense of misgiving activated by her abstraction.

"Nothing at all, except that Lucy and I are invited to Beechwood tomorrow." Before John could comment on this airy reply, Alicia said quickly, "Could you help me unbutton this gown, darling? I cannot imagine what is keeping Molly. I rang for her ages ago."

"I sent her to bed. Tonight I shall be your maid, madam."

"In that case, it is only fair that I return the compliment." With a provocative smile, Alicia rose from the dressing table bench and twisted around to face him in one swift motion. In another second her fingers were busy unbuttoning his shirt as his arms came around her.

Chapter Eleven

Claudia flattered herself that no one could discern the melancholy beneath her tranquil demeanor as she entered the sunny breakfast parlor on the morning after the dinner party. Her smile of greeting was nicely calculated to be friendly without crossing over into a caricature of inane brightness. The smile wobbled when she saw that Lord Pelham was not among those present, but she clung to it as she slid into a chair being held out for her by the butler.

"Thank you, Jimson. Good morning, everyone. It must be later than I thought. I see Lord Pelham has already finished breakfast," she said, directing the last observation to the room at large.

It was Mrs. Hingham who answered, "His lordship was finishing his repast as we entered. He apologized profusely for the sudden emergency on one of his farms and some business that would keep him away from the house until midafternoon."

"Oh."

Claudia must have looked and sounded as nonplussed as she felt at this de facto nullification of her travel plans, for Mrs. Hingham observed with a trace of malicious satisfaction, "You seem quite put out that Lord Pelham will be unavailable to his guests today, Miss Herbert."

The suspicion in the matron's voice and manner helped rally Claudia's wits as she turned to Mrs. Hingham and said quietly, "Yes, you see I had hoped to leave Beechwood today, but—"

"Oh, Claudia, don't go—not so soon!"

Roberta's heartfelt wail drowned out the more restrained protests of the twins at this announcement.

"Sweetheart, please don't cry," pleaded Claudia, flustered

by the violence of Roberta's reaction. The child had pushed away her half-filled plate and was staring across the table with tears raining down her face. "You knew I would be leaving as soon as Esther was well enough to leave her bed."

"But Esther needs you!"

"Only a very little at this point, now that your uncle is home. I promise you she will be getting along famously in a very few days. And you may both write to me in Kent, you know."

"Yes, child," Mrs. Hingham put in sharply. "You must see how selfish it is to keep Miss Herbert from her own home any longer."

"Selfish?" The word brought Roberta's tearstained face around to the older woman briefly before she turned back to Claudia, her voice choked with sobs. "I . . . I did not mean to be selfish, Claudia. P . . . please ex . . . excuse me." She pushed back her chair and darted from the room.

Claudia stared after her in consternation, undecided what she should do until she heard Susannah say with stiff dignity, "I think you do not quite comprehend how very difficult it was for my little sisters to leave our parents and travel halfway around the world, ma'am." She turned to Claudia and added, "I fear Roberta will head straight for Esther's room. I had best go up to them."

"Yes, of course, Susannah. I will come up presently," Claudia murmured, settling back into her chair, though she had lost all appetite. She poured herself a cup of coffee with an unsteady hand, trying not to notice Mrs. Hingham's tight-lipped mien.

"I can see that their removal from India has been very hard on the children," Miss Hingham said into the void, aiming her remark at Julian, who was looking uncomfortable. "Your uncle is to be commended for his care and consideration. I am persuaded he will do his best to make up for the absence of your parents."

"Yes, yes, Uncle Miles is very good to us all," Julian agreed eagerly, sending a grateful smile to the earnest young woman.

Miss Hingham's next comment was on a topic unrelated to the stormy scene just enacted, and again Julian was quick to follow her lead, easing the atmosphere in the room.

Claudia sat, crumbling a piece of toast on her plate, waiting until she could decently excuse herself and follow the girls. After nerving herself up to insist on leaving Beechwood today, she was now thoroughly deflated, her limbs limp as wilted greens, knowing it was all to do over again. She had prepared herself for a difficult session with Lord Pelham because of her desire to detour by Lord Selkirk's estate on her way home, but this still lay in the future. She had known the children would be reluctant to part with her, of course, but had expected to break the news to them after seeing the baron.

Roberta's outburst had been her fault. Claudia censured herself severely for allowing Mrs. Hingham's innuendo to goad her into a public announcement of her intentions. She had been aware last night that the accidental pairing of herself and Lord Pelham coming back inside behind the others had aroused a sense of disquiet in the older woman on her daughter's behalf, however unreasonable it might seem to a disinterested observer. Knowing, as Mrs. Hingham did not, that she planned to leave today, she had not allowed this to trouble her—*then*. Would that she had possessed the requisite nobility of character to ignore the woman's jealous attempt to embarrass her this morning. The unpalatable truth was, of course, that however blameless her behavior toward Lord Pelham, she did harbor forbidden feelings in her heart for a man who belonged to another woman. Her quick proclamation just now of plans to leave Beechwood had actually been a guilty denial of any personal interest in her host.

Claudia heaved an inward sigh. Regrets would butter no parsnips; the deed was done. She had been playing the coward these past two days, avoiding any mention of leaving in the children's presence. Since it was obvious that her departure would be delayed until the morrow, she might as well have the necessary scene with the children at once and get it behind her. As for Mrs. Hingham, she reflected, sending a veiled glance across the table at the woman now reading Julian a lecture on the merits of well-scripted sermons as desirable literature, although some allowance must be made for the natural instinct of a parent to advance an offspring's interests, this woman had showed herself to be small-spirited by her frequent digs at the children. Claudia had no intention of allowing such a person any valid ammunition to fire in her direction.

Julian's eyes were sending her a desperate appeal for intervention as he remained pinned down by a barrage of sanctimonious platitudes. His plight brought her out of her sober reverie. She nipped in with a polite request for clarification on some point, thus drawing the matron's fire and permitting Julian to withdraw with a graceful excuse a moment later. Claudia maintained a show of interest until Mrs. Hingham had exhausted the topic and begun to speculate on Lady Powerby's possible plans for the morning when she eventually put in an appearance downstairs, whereupon Claudia made her escape.

Before heading to the children's room, Claudia stopped by Lady Powerby's quarters to give her reluctant hostess a nudge toward the small saloon, where the Hingham ladies had retreated. Her body felt unusually heavy, in consort with her spirit, despite her best efforts to appear normal. Why must Lord Pelham choose this of all days to preside over a farm emergency, she wondered grimly as she steeled herself for a tearful session with the youngest Brewster children.

As he rode through the farm gate, Lord Pelham tossed a coin to the youngest Nickelby child, who had cheerfully kept his horse Challenger company while the baron was inside the house arranging to get some temporary assistance for the ailing farmer. They were a good family; the house had been neat, spotless, and redolent of Mrs. Nickelby's cinnamon bread, which the bustling little woman had urged on him to the detriment of his waistline but the benefit of his soul. He'd passed a pleasant half hour with the farmer and his wife and been brought up to date on the current situation with the man's health, which was at last improving.

A glance at the watch he pulled out of its pocket confirmed that it was barely midmorning. Challenger was indicating that he'd welcome a good run after being cooped up in the farmyard, but Miles kept him on a tight rein while he pondered his next destination. He could be at the boys' school before noon. Perhaps George would not have left for Piggy's by then, and

he really ought to see the Head in person to smooth over the
incident of Julian's leaving without permission.

His decision taken, Miles let the big chestnut have his head
as they made for the road. With the next few hours accounted
for, he no longer needed to keep his thoughts on a tight rein either. There was ample time in which to review his bizarre behavior at breakfast this morning.

It had not been his intention on arising to desert his guests
and disappear from his house for the better part of the day.
He'd gotten up in much the same state of frustration and indecision in which he'd retired last night, but with an added com-
pulsion to do *something* ticking inside his head like an
unexploded bomb. He'd spent the last two days acting the concerned host, catering to his guests and arranging entertainment
and society for their pleasure. This was what he'd expected
when he'd issued the invitation to Martha and her parent.
What he had not expected was that he would be playing his
role of host unwillingly, with a bad grace that shamed him in
his clear-headed moments, and which he devoutly hoped he'd
been able to conceal from everyone.

And what he could never have anticipated in his worst
nightmare was the simultaneous presence in his house of a female who invoked in him all the physical desire he patently
did not feel for the woman he'd asked to become his wife.

It had been bad enough in the beginning when he could remember his last sight of Claudia Herbert sauntering off on the
arm of a dissipated roué in a Parisian gaming house. At least
then he could simply condemn his own lust as a phenomenon
of the base masculine nature the church would say we are put
on the earth to overcome. After two days of observing her ten-
derness with the children, her patience with his difficult aunt,
and her ability to manage his complicated household, however, he could no longer summon up a picture of a promiscu-
ous, worldly, and selfish female whom a man would be
ashamed to love, no matter her physical attractions. He was
forced to admit that Claudia was an infinitely desirable creature whom honor had placed beyond his grasp. That being the
case, he must lose no time in bundling her off to Kent with the
grateful thanks of all his family so he could concentrate on

wooing his prospective bride. No other course was consistent with a gentleman's honor.

Esther's first appearance downstairs had prompted the decision that had lifted a weight from his conscience. Unhappily, he had then relaxed his former prohibition against singling Claudia out for attention, although he could say with truth that this had not been deliberate. He had not realized how often his eyes had strayed to the lovely young woman with the beautiful sad eyes during the dinner party until a censorious Mrs. Hingham had waited outside the door when the guests had left as if to prevent a suspected tryst. At least that was how her action had struck him at the time.

His own weakness thus forcibly recalled to him, Miles had done his best to smooth the situation before the party separated for the night. His sleep had not been restful, but he had arisen with every intention of readying his carriage and horses to serve Miss Herbert at her earliest convenience, which he had every reason to suspect would be today. He had dressed as usual in riding togs and gone down to breakfast in a mood of dutiful resolution.

So much was quite clear to him. It was not until he had nearly finished his solitary meal, grateful to be spared conversation before he'd had his coffee, when he'd evidently taken leave of his senses. Martha and her mother had come in and had no sooner sat down when the woman launched into one of her everlasting lectures. He could not for the life of him recall the subject a few hours later, but at the time his whole being had rebelled, making escape his primary urge. He'd invented an emergency that would remove him for a large portion of the day and swept out on a spate of insincere apologies.

And here he was, riding off to see a boy who had most likely left school hours ago and an official he need not see at all. Bizarre was the only word for his behavior.

When Winchester came into view some time later, Miles had had sufficient solitude, despite the traffic clogging the road, to examine his recent conduct with ruthless honesty. His conclusions, though not complimentary to his character, destroyed the defensive myth that he'd acted irrationally this morning.

In trying to explain his actions, he'd gone back over the events of the dinner party and resurrected observations noted and dismissed at the time as irrelevant, such as the look on Martha Hingham's face when she recognized Lord Frame, and Mrs. Hingham's annoyance at the meeting, as well as her subsequent supervision of her daughter as though to prevent any interaction between the pair. Though he had not consciously considered this in reference to his own relationship with Martha at the time, he was now convinced that he must have glimpsed a remote possibility of escape on some deeper level. If one accepted this theory, then it followed that any action that would delay Claudia's departure would allow time for the present situation to change in his favor. Obviously, Claudia could not travel without her host's knowledge and assistance, so his absence today guaranteed her remaining at Beechwood until tomorrow at least. It was a desperate chance perhaps, but he had seized it this morning when he bolted from the breakfast room on a seeming impulse. If time might resolve the imbroglio and leave his honor intact, then he must delay the moment of Claudia's removal.

Miles was pondering ways to render his carriages unusable for a spell when he ran George to earth in Piggy Nettles' quarters, where the two boys were attempting to cram a crumpled and possibly mildewed pile of what might originally have been clothing into an already overflowing valise. As Miles watched this exercise in futility from the doorway, George was seized by an inspiration that entailed spreading a shirt on the bed, piling the doubtless aromatic surplus onto it, and enclosing the contents into a bundle by tying the arms of the shirt around it.

Flushed with success, George looked up while his comrade tied knots, spotting the spectator in the doorway. He gave a whoop of delight.

"Uncle Miles!"

As they shook hands, Miles estimated that his nephew had grown more than an inch in the two months he'd been at school. He was going to be taller than Julian one day, and broader, too, like his father. The lad had his mother's blue eyes and something of her cast of countenance, but it was Esther who most resembled his sister.

"I needed to see the Head today," Miles lied cheerfully, "so I thought I'd pop in and see you before you left for Piggy's. I presume this is Piggy?"

"Yes, of course. Piggy, this is my uncle, Lord Pelham."

"How d'you do, sir. I am very pleased to meet you," Master Nettles replied with a bow that did his parents credit, before resuming his knot tying. That shirt would never be the same again, Miles mused before returning his attention to his nephew, who was asking about Esther's injured leg.

"She is doing fine now. I gather Julian has written to you?"

"Yes, and Roberta, too. Who is this Claudia person who saved the situation at Beechwood?"

"Miss Herbert is a lady who met Julian on the road and gave him a ride home after he had wrenched his knee. She stayed on to help Esther."

"Gudgeon," George said in amiable reference to his brother before adding, "Julian wrote that this Claudia is a real trump, and Roberta says she is the most beautiful woman in the world after Mama."

"Miss Herbert is indeed a beautiful young woman whose kindness has earned her the affection of your brother and sisters."

"Will I meet her?"

Miles hesitated, then said, "Some time, I trust," before changing the subject to George's visit to his friend's home. He remained with the boys, chatting about school happenings and vacation plans, until the Nettles' carriage arrived about twenty minutes later, whereupon he slipped both boys some money and waved them off.

The baron's interview with the school head was equally successful. After indulging himself with a hearty lunch in one of the city's better inns, he set out on the solitary ride home with a seething combination of morose doubts and cautious hopes for company.

The sight of a strange carriage in his stable yard when Miles reached home produced a line between his brows that smoothed out as he recollected his invitation to Alicia Marshall to bring her daughter to visit his nieces.

As Miles swung a leg over the chestnut to dismount, Calloway, his head coachman, came hurrying up to take the animal.

"The roads are like a dustbin after this dry spell, sir. You must have done a deal of riding today—you and Challenger are nearly the same color."

Miles looked down at his dusty leathers and boots with a grimace and wiped a handkerchief across his hot face, admitting, "It was worse than I expected. Cool him down, Calloway, but don't let him drink too much at first."

"I'll take good care o' the boy like always, don't ye fash yesel', sir."

"I take it that is Mrs. Marshall's carriage?" Miles asked, angling his head in the vehicle's direction. "When did she arrive?"

"About an hour ago. Her driver is having a pint wi' t' lads. Anything else, sir?"

"No—wait! There is something I wish you to do for me," Miles said and proceeded to give a detailed order that caused the burly coachman's jaw to drop, though he forbore to question his employer, merely signifying his comprehension with a grunted syllable.

"And keep your mouth shut about this, Calloway, understand?"

"Now why would I want to have everyone know ye've run mad or had a touch o' the sun?" retorted the coachman, leading Challenger away and shaking his head.

Miles shook his own head at this piece of insubordination, but there was never any use trying to curb the coachman's tongue. Calloway had put him up on his first pony at the tender age of three and later taught him to drive. In all these years the faithful servant had never scrupled to speak his mind to someone he'd known from the cradle, though he saw to it that none of the grooms or stable hands dared to follow his example.

Not being fit to be seen in all his dirt, Miles hurried up the back stairs to his room and rang for his valet, his thoughts on the gathering downstairs. The Marshalls were good neighbors and lively company. Alicia was doing him a service by her

visit today and might be persuaded to increase her benevo-
lence if he went about it the right way.

A half hour later, Miles strolled into the garden room, the
epitome of the well-dressed country gentleman in his unwrin-
kled coat of Bath suiting and pale gray inexpressibles. One
swift glance around assured him that the feminine portion of
his household was all present and accounted for. Esther,
Roberta, and their visitor were grouped around the small dining table in the corner, playing a game, while the others were
scattered around the sofa where his aunt, nestled in her shawls,
presided over the teapot.

Every face with one exception had brightened at his entrance, a sure sign that all was not smooth sailing and an infu-
sion of new blood was most welcome. The exception was
Claudia Herbert, who briefly raised a pair or reproachful hazel
eyes to his before resuming her study of her teacup.

"Good afternoon, ladies. What a refreshing picture you all
make for a man who has spent the day in the saddle on dusty
roads—and what a welcome sight is that teapot. My throat is
parched."

A twitter of simultaneous greetings rose into the air like
birdsong, and he was urged to sit down and partake of some
refreshments by a chorus of eager voices.

"Where did you go today, Uncle?" Susannah asked as Miles
headed over to greet the children before taking a seat among
the women.

"I had business in Winches—"

"Oh, Uncle Miles, did you see George?" Roberta put in eagerly.

"Yes, sweetheart," he replied, bending to kiss Esther and
Roberta and greet the sweet-faced Lucy Marshall. "He is
bursting with rude health as usual and sends his love to all."

In another minute Miles had accepted a cup from his aunt
and joined her at one end of the sofa near Mrs. Marshall, looking cool and crisp in a lavender cotton gown that lent a hint of
that shade to her gray eyes.

"I am in your debt, my dear Alicia, for taking pity on my
guests after my abominable desertion of them today. I am persuaded your delightful company was greatly appreciated."

"I have been made royally welcome," Mrs. Marshall said above a polite chorus of agreement from the other ladies, "and stuffed with your cook's delectable fruitcake, for which, you are aware, I cherish a strong partiality. Indeed, I am persuaded there would be no voice raised in argument were I to declare this the supreme example of the art form."

Miles's lips twitched at the dancing devils in his neighbor's eyes as she produced this hyperbole. He was unsurprised to hear Mrs. Hingham enter a mild caveat to the effect that the cake, though assuredly excellent, might benefit by the addition of a little lemon peel for a touch of piquancy.

"Now that is a most intriguing suggestion, ma'am," Mrs. Marshall replied, turning a rapt face to the older woman before addressing her hostess. "Do you think lemon peel would improve the mixture, Lady Powerby?"

Alicia was doing it up too brown, Miles thought, noting that Claudia's lips trembled slightly while she gazed into her cup with a peculiar intensity. Susannah and Martha Hingham cultivated expressions of polite interest.

"All fruitcake is anathema to my digestive system," Lady Powerby said flatly.

"Have you ladies been exchanging ideas on nutrition this afternoon?" Miles asked lightly, fixing his mischievous neighbor with a warning look.

"Actually, Mrs. Hingham and I had discovered a mutual affinity for whist just before you arrived," Mrs. Marshall replied, her expression guileless in the extreme, "and I was about to propose an evening of cards at Marshland tomorrow, that is if you have no other plans?"

"I can think of nothing more delightful," Miles said with unfeigned pleasure as his neighbor did what he had hoped, unprompted. "I trust I speak for all," he added with a smiling glance around the circle.

"Thank you, but I fear you must hold me excused, Mrs. Marshall," Lady Powerby said. "I find that late nights do not agree with me at my time of life, nor does the night air."

"Naturally, I am disappointed to lose your company, ma'am, but I assure you I do understand, and I would never be able to forgive myself if I were responsible for putting your health in jeopardy."

Lady Powerby found nothing excessive in this sentiment and nodded graciously to her guest.

"I hope we can count on you, ma'am?" Mrs. Marshall continued, turning to Mrs. Hingham, who expressed her pleasure, "and you, Miss Herbert?"

"I would be delighted, of course, ma'am," Claudia began hesitantly, "but I had rather expected to leave Beechwood today. I have not yet had an opportunity to speak with Lord Pelham about leaving tomorrow, but . . ." She paused and looked expectantly at her host.

"I am sorry to be the bearer of bad tidings, Miss Herbert, but my head coachman informed me this afternoon that both of my traveling carriages are incapacitated at the moment. I fear it will not be possible for you to leave tomorrow. In fact," he added, turning to smile at a fascinated Mrs. Marshall, "it occurs to me that, except for my curricle, we are all at a loss for transportation tomorrow evening."

"I fear I cannot solve your transportation problem, Miss Herbert," Mrs. Marshall said, "but I can certainly send my carriage for the Beechwood ladies tomorrow, Miles, and leave you and Julian to drive over in the curricle."

"Thank you, Alicia, that is most generous of you. I shall be pleased to accept on behalf of the ladies. By the way, how large a gathering do you plan to have?"

"Oh, not large at all," she replied with an airy gesture of one hand, "just an informal occasion to indulge in an activity we all enjoy. Miss Hingham has informed me that she does not play, nor does Susannah. What about Julian?"

"Yes, Julian enjoys cards," Miles replied, wondering if she was going to play his hand for him.

She was. "Well then, there are four of you who play, plus John and me. Duncan does not care for whist either." She appeared to consider, then said on a sudden inspiration, "I know. I'll ask the Mountjoys to join us. Sir William and Lady Mountjoy are avid players, and we'll let the young people amuse themselves however they please, shall we? Round games or charades or music—will that do?" she finished, sending a

bright smile to Susannah and Miss Hingham, who said all that
was civil in return.

Neither the baron nor Mrs. Marshall appeared to notice the
sudden disappearance of Mrs. Hingham's complacent expression as Mrs. Marshall said with satisfaction, "That is settled
then. And now, ladies, I really must pry Lucy away from the
girls, for it is later than I thought."

The next few minutes were devoted to leave-taking. Mrs.
Marshall's carriage was sent for, the children made happy
plans to meet soon again, and the adults recited all the time-
honored formulas suited to the occasion.

Miles walked outside with his neighbor and her daughter to
see them into their carriage. They talked the merest nothings
until, having assisted Lucy into the carriage, he offered his
hand to her mother, who assumed a look of exaggerated concern.

"By the way, Miles, I must tell you how excessively
shocked I was at your announcement earlier."

Though naturally wary, Miles did his duty. "And what announcement was that, Alicia?"

She shook her head mournfully. "I never thought I would
see the day when any piece of rolling equipment at Beechwood was out of commission, but *two* vehicles at the same
time? What a singular misfortune! John will not credit it when
I tell him."

"And you intend to tell him, of course?"

Her eyes rounded in surprise. "Of course. I tell my husband
everything."

"I'll go bail you don't," Miles retorted, pinching her gloved
fingers as he handed her up into the carriage.

Mrs. Marshall smiled, but returned no answer save a gay
valedictory wave.

Miles stared after the departing carriage for a few seconds, a
rueful little smile tugging at his lips. Alicia Marshall's ready
tongue was not famed for discretion. If he did not proceed
with caution, he could find himself a figure of fun in the
neighborhood.

Chapter Twelve

Claudia fled the garden room before the baron returned from escorting Mrs. Marshall and Lucy to their carriage. His bland announcement that both his traveling carriages were broken down had canceled all her former impatience to speak privately with him. Indeed, she thought with unwonted ferocity, were she to speak to him now, she could not trust herself to remember the restraint required of a lady. Not for a moment did she believe that the Beechwood carriages were both out of commission—or, if they were, the damage had been done at Lord Pelham's express command!

Why had he done it? she demanded of herself as she closed her bedchamber door behind her with more vehemence than was strictly necessary. She freely absolved him from any intent to hurt her; he had no knowledge of the French criminal who was seeking her in the area. His actions in preventing her removal might have made sense in a twisted fashion if he'd been intent on seducing her for his own pleasure, but he had made no attempt to lay a hand on her since the impulsive embrace that first night. Her imagination was unequal to the task of inventing a situation in which her presence could be other than an obstacle to a man in the middle of a courtship—unless—she paused and examined the possibility that he hoped a presentable female might incite jealousy in his chosen bride and move her to accept his offer if she was undecided. It seemed a pretty weak theory in view of his failure to pay her the sorts of little attentions that might trigger possessiveness in Miss Hingham.

With her name came a picture of Martha Hingham into Claudia's mind, cool and attractive, affable and even-tempered, her manners always perfect. She also possessed a discreet tact that sought to mitigate the effect of her mother's more abrasive personality on the inhabitants of Beechwood. Being scrupulously fair, Claudia could state unequivocally that there was nothing in Miss Hingham's character or behavior that could excite censure in any person of nice sensibility.

Having rendered unto Miss Hingham her due, Claudia felt herself entitled to hold the opinion that the young woman was not in love with Lord Pelham with no fear that her judgment was clouded by her own illicit feelings for him. A girl in love must have been betrayed by *some* involuntary sign, however poised and controlled her demeanor—a special light in her eyes or a softening in her expression when looking at him, a nuance in her tones when speaking to or of the beloved— something that was not present in ordinary social intercourse.

Intent observation on her part had discovered nothing of this nature in Martha Hingham's demeanor. Having proceeded this far in her reasoning, Claudia unaccountably failed to note the corollary—that *she* had been at great pains to disguise her own tender feelings for the baron during this same period. Of course she might have come to see this had not a knock on the door distracted her at that point in her deliberations.

It was Roberta reporting that her uncle had just carried Esther back to her room.

"Is . . . is your uncle with Esther now?"

"No," Roberta replied, "he went back downstairs. Do you wish to talk to him? I'll run down and tell him."

"No, thank you, sweetheart," Claudia said hastily, smiling at the sweet-natured child who had grown so dear to her in little more than a sennight. Lucy Marshall's visit had done wonders for both girls, who had been chastened and teary-eyed this morning at the imminent loss of their companion. Roberta was looking much more cheerful now. Claudia accepted without rancor that the children would forget her before she forgot them. All sorts of new adventures and acquaintances would come their way in the future, while nothing remotely satisfying awaited her at her aunt's home in Kent. Accompanying the child into Esther's bedchamber, Claudia slammed the door on that negative line of thinking. Sufficient unto the day, and so forth. Now it was time to get Esther settled for the evening before changing for dinner.

Claudia entered the saloon with even less enthusiasm that night and a renewed determination to remain in the background.

Even Susannah's and Julian's high spirits were insufficient to maintain the relatively harmonious tenor that had characterized the previous evenings during the Hingham ladies' visit. Lord Pelham continued to epitomize the ideal host, diligent in his concern for the comfort and ease of his guests, but tonight his efforts met with limited success. Miss Hingham, though unfailingly polite, appeared somewhat abstracted, even losing track of the conversation from time to time. Her pretty apologies and renewed attention were accepted benevolently by her host, but less so by her parent. Mrs. Hingham was generous with her compliments and dissertations as usual, but her comments took on an edge and her fixed smile became more blatantly insincere as the evening dragged on. For her part, Claudia remained quiet unless directly addressed, when she replied with a gentle courtesy that did nothing to prolong any topic. She forced herself to project some faint warmth when speaking to the Hingham ladies and Lady Powerby. No effort was needed for Susannah and Julian; none was made for Lord Pelham. Nor were any of her smiles expended on her host that evening.

During the tea-drinking ritual prior to the ladies' retiring, the two matrons indulged in another of their barbed exchanges. Lord Pelham sent Claudia a look of agonized appeal that she steeled herself to ignore, although she felt like a worm for being so uncooperative. Happily, Susannah interjected a comment that sent her great-aunt off on a tangent before the discussion could become too heated. Claudia affected not to see the reproachful look Lord Pelham cast her before he wafted a delicate suggestion in his aunt's direction that she was valiantly concealing fatigue. Never loath to admit debility, Lady Powerby summoned a wavering voice and agreed that it was more than time for her to seek her bed. She accepted her nephew's arm, bade the assembled company a feeble good night, and tottered to the door.

Miss Hingham was not far behind her hostess, treading purposefully in her wake after delivering a soft general farewell that took her mother by surprise. Mrs. Hingham, intent on catching up with her daughter, was forced to relinquish her recent surveillance of Claudia's movements as they might pertain to Lord Pelham, though she did cast a parting glance brimful of suspicion at the young woman on her way out of the room.

Thus it was that Lord Pelham, after assisting his aunt up the staircase, returned to the saloon to find Claudia in the act of bidding the twins good night.

"Not you, too, Miss Herbert? It seems that everyone is suffering from a case of exhaustion this evening, or perhaps boredom would be a more accurate description?"

"Not at all, sir," Claudia said coolly. "Everyone stayed up later than usual last night, so it is merely sensible to retire a little early tonight." She continued to walk toward the staircase, very conscious of his dogged presence at her side and intent on reaching the sanctuary of her room.

"Have I offended you in some way, Miss Herbert?" he asked, matching his step to hers.

"Why, how should you have offended me, Lord Pelham?" Claudia replied with studied innocence.

"That is what I have been asking myself during this interminable evening. I have examined my conscience to no avail, and yet I sense a slight hint of reserve in your manner that is quite troubling."

Suspicious of his judicious tone and the absence of any trace of anxiety in his appearance to support his claim to be troubled, Claudia suppressed the instincts of her better self to offer the reassurance he so unfairly sought. He was making sport of her, and she would not allow him his little victory. "Surely, a man with a clear conscience has no cause to suspect slights, sir," she returned with a cool smile.

"That should comfort me, of course, but alas, I still sense a chill in your manner."

"A pity, but I cannot be expected to assume responsibility for your absurd fancies, my lord. Thank you," she added as he handed her a bedtime candle at the foot of the stairs. "Good night."

Claudia proceeded up the stairs at a measured pace, refusing to give in to the impulse to race away from the electric blue eyes boring a hole in her back.

Actually the eyes of the man at the foot of the stairs held a gleam of rueful amusement as he pondered the discovery that a delicate, dimpled chin could look remarkably stubborn, given the right circumstances.

Coming back into the saloon, the baron happened upon a rare instance of the twins embroiled in a disagreement. Julian was putting up a feeble defense. "I did not say you were *wrong*, Su, I merely said that *I* did not notice anything amiss."

"Squabbling, children?"

"Then all I can say is that the masculine sex must be excessively unobservant," Susannah sniffed, turning to address her uncle next. "I suppose it also escaped your notice that Claudia was . . . oh, not out of sorts precisely, but certainly not her usual self this evening."

"Your supposition is incorrect," the baron replied promptly. "Not only was I aware of Miss Herbert's seething discontent, but I did not find the cause obscure either."

Two pairs of fine gray eyes questioned him mutely, reminding Miles that he had perhaps gone past the stage of prudence with his boastful claim. Too late to draw back now. "She is annoyed with me because she believes I have delayed her departure deliberately," he replied in careless tones.

Julian's eyes widened and Susannah's narrowed at this casual explanation. "Did you?" Susannah asked bluntly.

"Now why should I wish to annoy Miss Herbert after all her kind assistance to this family?"

Put like that, it certainly seemed unlikely—at least to Julian. Susannah forbore to question her uncle's answer, but her expression when she bade him good night a moment later was a study in feminine speculation.

On the day of the Marshalls' card party Claudia arose with a fresh resolution that did not include continuing the undeclared warfare with her host that had made the previous evening a

trial of grim endurance. For the length of time it took to reach
her bedchamber last night, she had relished a petty satisfaction
at getting some of her own back after Lord Pelham's arbitrary
decision to delay her departure by sabotaging his carriages.
Within a few minutes of reliving the evening in her memory,
however, her own behavior began to take on an aspect of
childish retaliation that caused her to blush with shame in ret-
rospect. The course she had pursued last night could achieve
nothing positive and would result in the discomfort of all those
around her if she proceeded to make her resentment any more
obvious. This conclusion did not lessen Lord Pelham's culpa-
bility one whit, but carrying a grudge was heavy work. For the
short time that remained of her stay at Beechwood, she would
do better to keep to the high road. There would be regrets
aplenty when she returned to Kent; let them not include shame
for a lack of charity on her part.

This high-minded resolve did not include any intention of
putting herself in Lord Pelham's path any more frequently
than necessary, however. She elected to share Esther's breakfast, thus removing herself from the planning stage of any proposed activities for the entertainment of the baron's real
guests.

When Roberta came into her sister's room after breakfast,
she informed Claudia that her uncle, Susannah, and the Hingham ladies intended to walk into the village shortly; and that
her uncle had commissioned her to present his compliments to
Claudia and extend an invitation to her to join the walking
party.

"That is very kind of your uncle, Roberta. Would you please
convey my appreciation to him and explain that I had planned
to refresh the flower arrangements this morning. The gardener
will have left buckets of cut flowers ready for me."

The obliging Roberta promised to perform this errand, saying as she opened the door, "I'll help you with the flowers if
you like, Claudia."

"Thank you, sweetheart, I'd enjoy your company, but I
would not like Esther to feel herself abandoned up here while
we putter with the flowers . . ." She allowed her voice to trail

off and beamed a smile at Roberta when the child volunteered to keep her sister company instead.

An hour later, Claudia was working on the last of the flower arrangements in the ground-floor room the late Lady Pelham had had fitted out for this task when Susannah stuck her head in the doorway.

"I thought you might be here, Claudia," she said, strolling into the room. "Oh, that is quite exquisite with the graceful willow branches among the cut flowers."

"Thank you, Susannah. I was under the impression that you were going to the village with the others this morning."

"I begged off in order to write a letter to my parents. So much has happened at Beechwood lately that I wished to write it all down while it was fresh in my mind."

"I hope you stressed the fact that the doctor is certain that Esther's leg is healing just as it should."

"Yes, I told them there was no cause for any concern."

Susannah wandered about the small room, bending to smell the roses in one finished arrangement and finger the petals of a pink dahlia in another. Coming back to the worktable, she picked up a pair of shears and idly snipped at the air a few times before putting them down again and resuming her walking.

Claudia, half her attention diverted from her task by Susannah's aimless movements, picked up the discarded shears and paused for a second, studying the lovely girl in her crisp gown of polished blue cotton set off by a white collar and sash. There was a tiny line between her brows, and her underlip was thrust forward a bit. Whatever thoughts were occupying Susannah's mind must be of a troublesome nature, Claudia concluded, snipping a couple of inches from a stalk of delphinium before inserting it into the blue-and-white Chinese vase.

"Is something troubling you, Susannah?"

"Oh, no," the girl denied quickly. "I was just thinking, that's all."

"Thinking about what?"

"About Uncle Miles actually."

Grateful for the warning, Claudia composed her features and reached into the bucket for another stem of delphinium.

After a second or two when nothing further was forthcoming, she glanced across the worktable to find the girl staring at her. "Yes? You were thinking about your uncle?" she invited, and returned her eyes to the fingers placing the flowers into the half-completed arrangement.

"Claudia, does it seem to you that Uncle Miles and Miss Hingham are in love with each other?"

Claudia's hands stilled, and she returned Susannah's glance briefly. "My dear girl, I would never presume to judge of anything so personal, especially about persons with whom I hold but a slight acquaintance," she replied with what she devoutly hoped was sufficient firmness to discourage the girl from pursuing the subject.

She should have known better; Susannah was made of sterner stuff. "Does that evasion signify that you do not believe they are in love?"

"Susannah," Claudia protested on an exasperated laugh. "It means just what I said—I don't know their feelings any more than you do."

"Well, I do not believe they are in love," Susannah declared, undissuaded and defiant. "At least not with each other."

"What do you mean by that cryptic remark?" Claudia demanded sharply, staring in her turn, her fingers making no pretense of work now.

Susannah's eyes slid away, and she hesitated. "Only that there is absolutely no sign that either one regards the other with any sentiment warmer than . . . than disinterested approval," she finished lamely.

"Susannah," Claudia began, choosing her words with care, "believe me, my dear, it is not for others to estimate the warmth or lack of it between two people who are contemplating matrimony. Obviously I cannot command you not to indulge surmise, since you are doing just that, but I feel I ought to caution you that your uncle will not welcome any interference in his private affairs from you or anyone."

Susannah's beautiful face had taken on a mulish cast at the beginning of this speech, but eventually her friend's earnestness made an impression, for she gave a shrug and said with a creditable assumption of nonchalance, "Oh, I have no intention of saying anything to either at present, but I shall certainly continue to observe them closely. They will be back before lunch, I gather. I'd best go upstairs and try to get my great-aunt out of her rooms before then."

At the door Susannah turned to the woman watching her exit and added casually, "You know, Claudia, for someone who claims only a slight acquaintance with my uncle, you seem terribly certain of his reactions."

On this Parthian arrow, Susannah took herself off, leaving Claudia a prey to uncomfortable surmises of her own as she resumed her interrupted task with automatic skill.

Having been no farther than the orchards since her arrival at Beechwood, Claudia was very interested in the countryside they rode through on the drive to the Marshall house that evening, finding it attractively homely, though slightly parched after the recent dry spell. She would have feigned an interest even had the scenery been supremely dull in order to avoid the necessity of affecting blindness to the constraint that had sprung up between the Hingham mother and daughter. She had noticed, of course, and so had Susannah, whose bright eyes traveled between the two as she kept up a running stream of commentary on the locality through which they. She pointed out the high brick wall and wrought iron gates defining the Rockingham property and drew their attention to an arched stone bridge that could be glimpsed spanning a stream on another estate.

Claudia, mindful of the lecture she had read Susannah that morning, tried to suppress her own speculations to no avail. She had avoided the saloon today. Julian had carried Esther out into the garden after lunch, and she had spent most of the afternoon there with the two younger girls. All had seemed normal at lunch, but she had noted the strained atmosphere between the Hingham ladies at dinner. Though wild horses could not have dragged an admission from Claudia in front of Susannah, her mind had flown instantly to the enigmatic person of Lord Frame in speculating on the cause of the rift. Mrs. Hingham's original enthusiasm for the card party had vanished from the moment Mrs. Marshall had stated her intention of in-

cluding the Mountjoy household in her invitation. Having witnessed the meeting of Lord Frame and Martha Hingham at the
dinner party and divined their tingling awareness of each
other, despite the lack of opportunity for subsequent conversation, Claudia did not hesitate to ascribe Mrs. Hingham's reaction to fear that Lord Frame's presence in the area might
jeopardize her objective of achieving Martha's betrothal to
Lord Pelham. She did not believe that Susannah had been in a
position to take note of these occurrences. Her conclusion that
her uncle and Martha Hingham were not in love was based entirely on a lack of loverlike behavior from either over the
course of Martha's stay at Beechwood. Her suspicions were
aroused now, however, and she would be alert to any nuances
in the air this evening. Susannah adored her uncle, and her nature was the opposite of retiring, a combination that did not
bode well for discretionary behavior on her part.

Glancing at Susannah's animated countenance as she prat-
tled informatively to the nearly silent Hingham women, Claudia gave herself a figurative shake. She had cautioned
Susannah as strongly as possible. She could do no more to
avert a confrontation between uncle and niece that might damage the loving relationship they had forged so quickly. Her
own enthusiasm for the card party at this moment was about
on a par with Mrs. Hingham's, she reflected as the carriage
swept between stone gateposts onto a tree-lined drive.

The Marshalls were relaxed and genial hosts. The elder
Marshalls and the son of the house were chatting with the
Mountjoys and Lord Frame when the Beechwood party was
shown into a long room that must have been the great hall in
the building's original incarnation. The inner wall held two
fireplaces, and the long wall opposite was studded with magnificent mullioned windows. It looked to Claudia as if there
was a minstrel's gallery at the far end. Noting the several
small tables set out beyond the seating area in front of the
nearer fireplace, she had hopes of getting a closer look at this
intriguing survival from olden days.

The present mistress of Marshland came toward her guests,
the picture of modern perfection in a simple gown of yellow
silk that shimmered with her movements. Claudia was struck

anew by the woman's vibrancy and charm as she made everyone welcome individually.

As Martha Hingham removed the white shawl she had worn
in the carriage, Mrs. Marshall said with spontaneous admiration, "How lovely you look, Miss Hingham! That lavender-
blue gown deepens the color of your eyes and lends them a
special sparkle tonight."

Miss Hingham blushed with pleasure at the sincere compliment, and confusion robbed her of some of her customary
composure when she thanked her hostess shyly.

Claudia could not help thinking that Mrs. Hingham did not
appear as gratified to hear her chick praised as might have
been expected. The matron inserted a hasty comment to the effect that all the Beechwood young ladies had done their hostess proud this evening, a sentiment with which no one was
likely to dissent. Claudia, tucking a wayward curl back into
the heavy knot at the back of her head, disciplined a smile as
she reflected on her own growing distaste for the two black
gowns she had been wearing alternately since her arrival in
Hampshire. At least Susannah, adorable in leaf green sprigged
muslin, upheld the Beechwood honor as she pouted and dimpled at a teasing remark from Mr. Marshall.

An efficient hostess, Alicia Marshall had no intention of
permitting her guests to get too comfortable or to dawdle over
private conversations. While her husband, assisted by the butler, handed drinks around, she pointed out the two tables that
had been set up for the whist players and announced the first
pairings for play. She then indicated the large table near the pianoforte at the end of the room near the gallery. Her smile included all those not playing whist. "Duncan and I gathered up
all the games we could find, everything from nursery games
like spillikins to cards for cassino, silver loo, and speculation.
If you would rather play charades or make music, the room is
large enough that you will not disturb the whist players. Before we separate though, I should ask if you would prefer to
play whist, Lord Frame? If so, I am persuaded that Julian
would be more than happy to give up his place to you."

Lord Frame hastened to assure his hostess that he was quite
content to remain in such delightful company and, moreover,

would be equally happy to play games or listen to music as his fellow outcasts decided. This remark was uttered with a solemnity belied by a twinkle in his eye and elicited a ripple of surprised laughter and smiles from the assembled company with one notable exception. Mrs. Hingham transformed her affronted expression into one of stiff dignity when she saw that she was a minority of one, and she led the parade of whist players to take their places at the tables. Unhappily for her ability to observe the "outcasts," Mrs. Hingham was steered by Mrs. Marshall to the table at the greater distance from the gallery end of the room, where suggestions and countersuggestions were already being debated amid much laughter.

Claudia, paired with Mr. Marshall at the other table against the team of Lady Mountjoy and Lord Pelham, closed her mind to possible undercurrents and abandoned herself to the enjoyment she derived from pitting her skill against others' in a card match.

An hour later, as she and her host accepted the congratulations of their vanquished opponents, she smilingly protested that their success had been more a question of luck than skill tonight.

"I cannot remember an evening when the cards have run so consistently in favor of one partnership," she replied when Lord Pelham complimented her play at the end of the session.

"It was rather one-sided, to be sure," Lady Mountjoy agreed, "but you played your cards skillfully, Miss Herbert; I feel thoroughly trounced. Now, if you will all excuse me, I think I shall look over my husband's shoulder to see if his luck has been any better than mine." She rose from her chair with a smile and a swish of skirts.

As the gentlemen rose politely, Mr. Marshall declared his intention of seeing that all the glasses were replenished before the next round of play. "Thank you, partner," he added with a grin and a bow to Claudia. "It was indeed a pleasure, and one I shall hope to repeat in the near future."

Lord Pelham sank back onto his chair when their host ambled off, giving Claudia a smile that caused her pulse to accelerate alarmingly. "I daresay you will accuse me of flummery if I assert that it was a pleasure to be beaten by such an able player, Miss Herbert, but you may believe me when I say that this past hour has been more enjoyable than any in recent memory."

The deep timbre of his quiet voice increased the physical sensations assaulting Claudia, and as the sense of the words sank in, shock waves vibrated along her nerves. "Are you trying to flirt with me, Lord Pelham?" she demanded.

The harsh words were no sooner uttered than regretted—or not the words so much as the accusatory tone. Surely, she was experienced enough to return a light answer in this type of situation. She clamped her teeth together to prevent her too-ready tongue from making bad worse, and hid her shaky hands beneath the tabletop. She looked everywhere but at the man beside her until compelled by the thrumming silence to meet his burning regard for an instant before her glance skittered away again. It had been long enough to see the taut control he'd exerted over his features, apart from his eyes.

"I would not so demean you," he replied evenly, then adding in an impersonal tone, "May I take it that your father taught you to play cards?"

"No," she replied quickly, determined to do her part to restore a cordial atmosphere. "Actually, it was the aunt who raised me after my mother died. I do not believe it would be overstating the case to assert that Aunt Portia is addicted to card playing—to the point that she will not tolerate the briefest of social exchanges during a contest." She was proud of the light laugh she achieved as she raised her glance to his again.

"And is Aunt Portia responsible for your impressive knowledge of herbal remedies also?"

Large hazel eyes widened in astonishment. "Why . . . yes . . . indirectly at least. She was ten years older than my mother, who was her favorite sibling. It was my mother who taught me to recognize and use herbs when I was a young child. Later, Aunt Portia added greatly to my knowledge."

"And now there is only Aunt Portia?"

"Yes," Claudia replied, glancing down at her clenched hands to conceal the pain of this reality from his probing eyes.

The unlikely intimacy that had sprung up between Claudia and Lord Pelham was shattered at that point by the finish of

the contest taking place at the second whist table and the resul-
tant stirring around as the play resumed with new combina-
tions of partners. Although she held up her end well enough
that her play required no apology, Claudia did not again
achieve in the later rounds the level of concentration that had
sparked her early play.

Chapter Thirteen

Susannah was lying in wait outside Esther's room the next morning when Claudia headed down for breakfast. Her surprise was only momentary as she recollected her strong impression at the end of the evening at Marshland that Susannah was big with news. In spite of a recurrent tendency to drift off into foolish contemplation of the meaning, if any, to be attached to the short conversation with Miles Pelham at the whist table, she'd been nervously aware of the significant looks Susannah was sending her when the games broke up. There had been no opportunity for private conversation while the Marshalls' guests consumed delicious refreshments before taking their leave. Obviously, something had occurred during the course of the round games engaged in by the five non-whist players that had made a strong impression on Susannah, but Claudia had been unable to discern any clues from their outward appearances. Lord Frame chatted with Mr. Marshall and Lord Pelham at the end of the evening, while Miss Mountjoy and Miss Hingham, both seeming rather subdued—or perhaps merely tired—sat close to their respective mothers, who had embarked on a desultory conversation. Naturally, any conversation of a private nature was impossible in the carriage on the way home, and the party had broken up upon reaching Beechwood. The women had gone up to their rooms at once, but, Claudia recalled, Lord Pelham had asked his niece to remain behind as there was something he wished to ask her.

All of this flashed through Claudia's mind as she smiled at the girl in the hall. "Good morning, Susannah. I sensed last night that there was something you wished to tell me."

"Yes, but Uncle Miles wanted to ask me about my letter to my parents, and by the time he and Julian and I went up to bed, it was too late to disturb you. Claudia," the young girl went on eagerly, "I discovered something vital last night."

"Yes?" Claudia invited.

"It turns out that Martha Hingham and Lord Frame did not meet at our dinner party the other night. They knew each other years ago in London."

The effect of this announcement was a disappointment to Susannah as Claudia merely nodded. "Yes, I know."

"You *know!* How?"

"I was standing beside Martha when Sir William brought Lord Frame up to be presented."

"Why did you not mention this when I was talking to you yesterday?" Susannah demanded indignantly.

"Why should I have mentioned it to you? What does Lord Frame and Martha Hingham being acquainted have to say to anything?"

Susannah's thunderstruck reaction to the mild rejoinder spoke volumes about her lowered estimation of her friend's intelligence. Claudia withstood a suspicious examination of her innocent expression by probing gray eyes and hid her amusement at the assumption of exaggerated patience in the girl's voice as she said, "If you had watched Melissa Mountjoy's pitiful efforts to imply that she and Lord Frame are as good as betrothed last night, you would not say that. She is wildly jealous of Martha. She suspects that there is something between her and Lord Frame. Does that surprise you?"

"No," Claudia admitted. "That was the impression I, too, received from Miss Mountjoy's behavior at the dinner party." She looked Susannah straight in the eye and said bluntly, "It would be more to the point, however, to ask yourself if there is anything in Lord Frame's behavior or Miss Hingham's to suggest that Miss Mountjoy's suspicions have merit."

Susannah's eyes shifted away, and she conceded reluctantly, "Not really, except that they *did* speak privately together for a moment when Melissa was helping Duncan to set out the cards for a game of speculation."

"And was there ever a moment in the course of the evening

when *you* might have spoken privately with a gentleman of your acquaintance—Duncan Marshall, perhaps?"

"I suppose so."

Susannah's grudging admission brought them to the bottom of the staircase. Claudia, reading the frustration in the young girl's face, felt a surge of affection for her, knowing concern for her uncle's future happiness lay behind her actions. As they approached the breakfast room, Susannah turned to her friend and whispered fiercely, "No matter what you say, Claudia, I know Martha Hingham does not love my uncle. I said I would not interfere, but if she is in love with another man, I'll see to it that Uncle Miles is not kept in the dark."

"Short of asking her straight out, how would you know if she was?" Claudia inquired with honest curiosity.

Susannah sent her friend a darkling look, but took advantage of the proximity of their destination to avoid an answer.

To their surprise the breakfast room was deserted except for Julian, peacefully consuming the contents of a plate heaped high with ham slices, eggs, and toast.

"Where is everyone?"

Julian stopped munching and greeted Claudia politely before addressing his sister's question. "A groom came with a message for Uncle Miles a few minutes ago, and he headed to the stables without his coffee. Roberta sneaked out to pick some roses for Esther before Wilbanks gets around to the rose garden and catches her stealing his children." The boy grinned at his own pleasantry and returned his attention to his plate.

"Roberta knows the duties and life story of every servant on the estate," Susannah explained for Claudia's benefit. "She winds most of them around her little finger; in fact, most of them spoil her excessively, but Wilbanks prefers plants to people. She will feel the rough edge of his tongue if she runs afoul of his cutting schedule."

"Wilbanks has been more than generous with the flowers he has sent to the house since I've been here," Claudia replied. "I have found him most accommodating and tremendously knowledgeable."

Julian looked up from his plate again and swallowed a gargantuan mouthful. "He told me the other day, Claudia, that you put him strongly in mind of his late mistress."

"Your grandmother?"

Julian nodded. "He said you both respect the plants."

Claudia beamed a smile at him. "I could not imagine a nicer compliment."

"From Wilbanks that is the equivalent of a love letter," Susannah agreed. "I always feel he is poised to pounce each time I bend down to smell a flower."

"I wonder what is keeping Mrs. and Miss Hingham this morning," Claudia said, glancing at the untouched places set for these ladies before accepting a cup of coffee from Jimson, who had just come back into the room with another plate of maple syrup muffins.

"I have not heard anything, Miss Herbert," the butler replied before departing once more.

This small mystery was cleared up in the next five minutes as Mrs. Hingham sailed into the room on a wave of apologies and explanations. It seemed that Martha was prostrated this morning with one of her—happily rare—migraines. "When she gets an attack of migraine, there is nothing for it except to take to her bed, keep the room darkened to subdue the accompanying nausea, and wait until it goes away."

The occupants of the breakfast room said all that was sympathetic and proper to the occasion and pressed the cook's offerings on Mrs. Hingham, who seemed rather distraught for someone who generally gave the appearance of masterly competence in all domestic areas.

"Is there anything we can order from the kitchen for Miss Hingham, ma'am, perhaps a tisane or some soothing herbal remedy?" Susannah offered, casting a look of appeal to Claudia as she spoke.

Mrs. Hingham thanked her profusely and explained at some length that no traditional medications had ever had the least efficacy in her daughter's case. "The only thing she ever desires during such periods is to be left completely undisturbed until she can bear to contemplate food or drink once more. I have had her water jug filled and have taken the liberty, through my abigail, of instructing the housemaid who does up our rooms to leave Martha's room alone today. I hope you will not consider me presumptuous in acting thusly, but—"

"Of course not, ma'am," Susannah assured her. "It was the sensible thing to do. Have you tried these muffins? They are one of cook's specialities."

Mrs. Hingham shook her head at the plate proffered by the daughter of the house, reminding her that she never took anything save a boiled egg and some dry toast in the morning. "Martha's indisposition comes at a rather awkward time," she went on after accepting the toast rack and making her selection. "Lady Mountjoy invited us to inspect the Norman baptismal font in the church with her and Miss Mountjoy this morning and then to go back to Middle Park for lunch. She plans to send her carriage for us at eleven."

"Well, if you feel you must decline, my uncle will be happy to send a message to Middle Park for you, but since Miss Hingham requires only solitude and sleep, may I suggest that you keep your appointment with Lady Mountjoy and Melissa? An outing will help prevent you from dwelling on a situation that maternal devotion is powerless to alleviate. I believe the baptismal font is one of the oldest remaining in the country and in excellent condition, too."

Claudia mentally applauded the ease and graciousness with which Susannah was dealing with the verbose matron and her maternal concerns and conscience this morning. The girl seemed to have matured noticeably in the past sennight, rising admirably to meet the increased demands on her.

Mrs. Hingham's protests died down gradually, the last being a halfhearted statement of her reluctance to seem to undervalue her hosts' many efforts to entertain her by jauntering off with another party.

Again Susannah proved equal to the task of overcoming the lady's qualms, mentioning that she had hoped to show the village to Claudia some time today as her friend had not been able to take advantage of the previous day's walk. Naturally, she would not dream of deserting their other guests, but as poor Miss Hingham was indisposed and Mrs. Hingham had been bidden to view the church, then today would present the perfect opportunity to carry out her own plan.

Claudia, lost in admiration for Susannah's performance, watched Mrs. Hingham balance the possible consequences and resign her resistance to doing what she had wished to do all along. Both parties to the negotiations being satisfied that all the forms of civilized intercourse that pertained had been observed, breakfast proceeded to its end in harmony. Julian finished first and left on business of his own, followed shortly thereafter by Claudia, who went back upstairs to sit with Esther.

Claudia had taken Susannah's talk of conducting her to the village as part of the girl's diplomatic handling of Mrs. Hingham's reticence and promptly dismissed it from her mind. She was therefore surprised when Susannah came into Esther's room about midmorning, asking if she was ready for their outing.

Somewhat flustered, Claudia looked up from the embroidery frame she was holding while she demonstrated stitches for Esther to copy. "Oh, Susannah, I beg your pardon. It was my impression that you were talking for Mrs. Hingham's benefit at breakfast earlier. Naturally, I would enjoy seeing the village before I leave Hampshire, but I do not think I should leave Esther alone." She cast a dubious glance at the small girl, who was indeed readying herself for a protest, but Susannah nipped this in the bud, employing the firm tone that Esther generally accepted as final from her eldest sister.

"Roberta is coming up to stay with you, my pet, while Claudia gets a little breath of fresh air. I have brought my best watercolor paints here for you, and Roberta is getting some fruit from the kitchen to arrange in this Chinese bowl so you may both try your hands at painting while we are gone."

The novelty of the proposed activity in conjunction with the rare privilege of using her sister's treasured paints and brushes produced the calculated effect. Esther's protest died aborning. When Roberta arrived a few minutes later with a basket of fruit and a small potted plant, she found a table all cleared and her sister installed in a chaise with a lapboard to work on. A stand holding the paints and brushes was placed between hers and another chair for Roberta. While Susannah arranged the subject matter on the large table near the window, Claudia filled small containers with water and tore pages from Susannah's large sketch pad.

When the older girls left the room, the budding artists were already deeply engrossed in their preliminary sketches amid much chatter. Susannah smiled at Claudia as she closed the door softly behind them. "They won't even miss you," she predicted with a trace of smugness.

"I am discovering that you have hidden depths, Susannah," Claudia said admiringly.

"Heavens, do not, I beg of you, reveal this opinion to a single soul," Susannah protested with mock alarm. "It would complicate my life excessively."

"I would not dream of queering your pitch," Claudia promised solemnly, drawing a giggle from her mischievous friend.

It was cooler today with long wisps of cloud scurrying across the sky. The air was redolent of earthy smells as the young women walked down a dusty lane at a fairly brisk pace. The hedgerow was alive with the rustling of the bird and animal life that called it home.

"This will bring us to one end of the village," Susannah explained. "We can go back to the house through the orchard, which is a more direct route."

"I am just relishing the breeze in my hair and the ground under my feet," Claudia confessed, lifting her face to the sun as it came out from behind a fast-moving cloud.

"Poor Claudia, you have been so confined and your generous nature continually imposed upon by all of us ever since your arrival at Beechwood like a gift from heaven."

"That was not a complaint, Susannah," Claudia cried hastily. "Pray believe that I do not feel in the least imposed upon. Everything I have done I did quite voluntarily. I was happy to be of use, and I have loved being at Beechwood with all of you. I shall miss you all when I am back in Kent." She fell silent and averted her eyes from Susannah's intent gaze, more than a little embarrassed by the fervor she heard in her own voice.

"I wish you did not have to leave. Are you quite certain you cannot stay with us?"

"Air dreaming and wishful thinking are dangerous pastimes, Susannah," Claudia said gently, keeping her eyes on a wren that hopped out of the hedge ahead of them, then, sensing danger, streaked back to safety. She was grateful when Susannah drew her attention to a particularly thick clump of mayblossom.

A companionable silence obtained between the pair until they entered the village, which Claudia declared one of the prettiest she'd ever seen. All the cottages seemed to be in good repair, and most sported window boxes burgeoning with colorful blooms.

"Mrs. Lumley is inordinately proud of her hollyhocks," Susannah said, indicating a fence overwhelmed with tall stalks of red, white, and pink blossoms.

"And well she should be. They are enormous—taller than I am!" Claudia tore her eyes from the gigantic flowers to follow the movements of a trio of children who were playing with a ball and a dog. Farther ahead an apron-clad woman came out of a house and hurried down the street to knock on another door and disappear within.

"That was Josie's mother," Susannah said.

"Josie? Do you mean the helpful little maid at Beechwood?"

"Yes. Most of the servants come from the village. You can see why everything that happens in the big houses in the area is soon known in the village. I'd like you to meet someone."

"Of course. Who?"

"Nanny Griswald in the next house," Susannah said, opening the gate leading to a small cottage with a freshly painted door. "She was my grandmother's nurse originally and came to Beechwood when Grandmother married. She became first my mother's nurse, and then my uncle's."

"She must be very old."

"Nearly eighty, according to Uncle Miles, but she has scarcely a wrinkle on her face and is very bright and alert. She still tends her garden, despite painful arthritis in her feet and legs."

"Lovingly, I should say." Claudia gazed at the riot of roses and pinks lining the short walk, and stopped to admire the violas with their little faces dancing in the breeze.

"She is a bit hard of hearing, so speak clearly," Susannah warned as she knocked on the door.

A round dumpling of a woman with apple cheeks in an unlined face beneath a snowy mobcap opened the door to them and smiled at the young girl. "Why, Miss Susannah, come in, come in, dearie. Now isn't this nice?"

They followed their hostess into the dim interior of the cottage. Susannah held out the basket she'd been carrying over her arm. "Cook sent you some of her spice muffins, Nanny Griswald, and some honey and butter."

"Well now, isn't this a treat. There's nothing goes better with a cup of tea than Cook's spice muffins, I always say. Will you stay for a cup of tea, Miss Susannah?"

"Not today, I'm afraid, Nanny. We have left the children painting in Esther's room and should get back for luncheon, but I thought you would like to meet our friend Claudia Herbert."

"Who's this, do you say, Miss Susannah?" The little old lady peered up at Claudia with shrewd dark eyes.

"This is Claudia Herbert, Nanny. I told you about her last week. She took care of Esther when she broke her leg."

"How do you do, Nanny Griswald."

The old nurse's face broke into a huge smile as she captured Claudia's outstretched hand in both of hers. "I'm that pleased to meet the good soul who tended my Miss Celeste's baby, miss. Roberta has told me all about how good you've been to them. I was that worried when I first heard about little Esther's accident with only Lady Powerby at the house, who would never lift a finger to help a living soul in all the time I've known her. I'd have gone up there myself, creaky legs and all, if Roberta had not come the next day and told me how you had arrived out of the blue as it were to take over the sickroom and run the house while Mr. Miles was away. God will bless you, dearie, for your kindness, be sure He will."

"Please, Nanny Griswald, I did nothing except what a good neighbor would do. I must tell you how much I admire your garden, especially your roses," Claudia added, nodding to a table where a blue bowl spilling over with pink roses scented the room.

"Aye, they are my children these days, my roses." The old woman's bright dark eyes raked Claudia's face, and she said suddenly, "So you are going to wed Mr. Miles! I wish you joy, dearie. He was always a—"

"*No*, no, Nanny Griswald, I am afraid you've misunderstood," Claudia blurted out, looking to Susannah for assistance.

"It is Miss Hingham, the young lady you met yesterday, who might marry my uncle, Nanny," Susannah said loudly, "although nothing is settled yet. No announcement has been made, so you won't speak of it to anyone yet, Nanny?"

"I was never one to carry gossipy tales, Miss Susannah, but you may tell your uncle for me that he'd do much better to wed this young lady than the other one—this one has a good heart *and* a pretty face. Do you have a mother?" the old woman asked a red-faced Claudia.

"N . . . No, ma'am, my mother has been dead these twelve years."

"Well, I feel for your loss, miss, don't think I do not, but that is better for Mr. Miles than to wed that other one and take on a mother-in-law like that creature who was here yesterday. She's the sort that has to give the good Lord a helping hand with all His works. She'd be forever interfering, but there, it's none of my business, as Mr. Miles would surely tell me. He'll do exactly as he pleases, no matter what anyone says—he always did. Men can't see farther than their noses anyway," the old woman finished on a disdainful sniff.

Claudia was rendered speechless, and Susannah was fighting to preserve her countenance in the face of this tirade. She soothed the old lady with platitudes and promised to deliver her message, a remark that earned her a fulminating look from her friend, and at last managed to engineer their escape before any additional embarrassment could be inflicted on the hapless Claudia.

At first when they left Nanny Griswald's house, Claudia was so busy trying to recapture her composure that she was nearly oblivious of her surroundings, except that somewhere in the back of her mind she was aware that Susannah was humming a little tune as they walked.

"That was a rather odd man."

"I beg your pardon, Susannah. What did you say?"

"Only that a man near the wheelwright's acted rather strangely just now, staring after us as we passed. When I looked more closely at him, he jumped back inside."

"Oh." Claudia went back to musing over the embarrassing scene with the baron's former nurse. She eyed her companion obliquely, wondering if there was any hope of convincing her not to mention the conversation to her uncle.

They left the village street and began to walk through a grassy field that started a gentle ascent. Though reluctant to bring up the subject in the faint hope that Susannah had dismissed it from her mind as trivial, Claudia could not prevent herself from saying, "Nanny Griswald looks marvelously well-preserved, but I gather she becomes a bit confused at times, which is understandable at her age."

"Oh no, her mind is remarkably acute," Susannah replied.

"But you saw just now how she confused me with Miss Hingham."

"Only for an instant, if that," Susannah rebutted cheerfully. "It is my guess that she simply wished to make known her views on the subject of my uncle's marriage after meeting you both."

She should have known she'd regret broaching the subject, Claudia thought, unreasonably irritated at Susannah's insouciance, but, having gone so far, she must press on if she could prevent the baron from hearing an account of his old nurse's views on his choice of bride.

"It is naturally flattering to have Nanny Griswald's approbation," she began, "but you can see she is biased in my favor because I helped the child of her former nurseling. It is equally obvious that she has transferred an impulsive dislike of Mrs. Hingham to her blameless daughter. There is no need to distress your uncle by repeating such uninformed opinions."

"I do not believe Uncle Miles would be distressed to hear Nanny Griswald's opinions," Susannah said blandly, "nor would I call then uninformed since I share them. I think you would be the perfect wife for my uncle, Claudia."

Claudia stumbled over a stone and came to a halt halfway up the incline. "Susannah, please, you are old enough to know that your opinion does not matter, nor does Nanny Griswald's. In the case of marriage, the two parties involved must consult only their own preferences; after all, it is they alone who must fulfill the contract."

"That sounds very philosophical, Claudia, but the simple truth is that I have seen the way Uncle Miles looks at Martha Hingham and"— she held up her hand when Claudia would have spoken—"I have seen the way he looks at you when he thinks himself unobserved."

The words hung there in the space between them like a palpable presence. Claudia's eyes dilated, and she could not look away from Susannah's challenging gaze for a long moment. "No!" she cried at last. "You do not know what you are saying, my dear. Promise me you will say nothing of this to your uncle. You must not interfere in his private life."

"Don't be upset, Claudia. I will not do anything rash. This I will promise gladly, but if a little plain speaking can prevent a horrible mistake, then I shall not hold back."

Claudia was shaking her head despairingly, but she felt that no argument would sway Susannah and that she had already said too much. She plowed ahead, dimly aware that they were approaching an orchard. In another moment they were surrounded by the mature trees in full bloom. The ground was more level, and the walking became easier.

Suddenly, Susannah seized Claudia's arm and dragged her to a stop behind the trunk of a large tree.

"What—?"

"Shhh!" hissed the younger girl. "Look over there by the stone wall. What do you see?"

Claudia followed Susannah's pointing arm. "Someone standing among the trees as we are doing."

"Do you see *who* it is?"

Obeying the command in Susannah's voice, Claudia peered around the tree trunk again. "It looks like Martha Hingham," she said in surprise.

"Martha Hingham, who is supposed to be in her bedchamber suffering from the migraine."

"Perhaps she thought the fresh air might help."

Susannah looked at her friend pityingly. "Do you really believe that? Is it not obvious that she fabricated a headache in order to meet someone in secret?"

Claudia glanced around the whole area within their compass. "Who? In any case the orchard is not all that private. We can see her from here, and anyone walking up from the gardens would see her after a certain point."

"What better place could she go unless she knew the estate very well and could direct someone to a more secluded spot? She knew her mother would be away this forenoon, and it is my guess that it is Mrs. Hingham she most desires to deceive. And as for whom she is meeting—look!"

Claudia shifted her eyes from Susannah's triumphant face to the place where Martha Hingham stood no longer. She was hurrying toward a man approaching from the direction of the village as they had done earlier. Susannah pulled her around to the other side of the tree for better concealment.

"Just as I thought—Lord Frame!"

"How can you tell from this distance? I cannot identify him with any confidence."

"My eyesight is very acute," Susannah returned stubbornly. "Aha. You asked once how I'd know if Martha was in love with another man. There is your answer."

Claudia's eyes, too, were glued to the tableau taking place within their line of vision. Her heart lurched in her breast as Martha Hingham was drawn unprotestingly into the man's embrace. Claudia said shakily, "I feel like the lowest form of keyhole peeper!"

"A keyhole peeper would be able to hear what was being said, but it does not really matter. With our own eyes we have

seen clear evidence that Martha Hingham is in love with another man." There was a note of defiance in Susannah's voice
as she looked Claudia in the eye. "I do not intend that she shall
deceive my uncle any longer. I am going to tell him what we
have seen this morning."

"Wait, Susannah." It was now Claudia who detained her
friend when she would have marched straight back to the
house, presumably in search of her uncle, although they did
start off in that direction to lessen the chance of being spotted by the trysting lovers. She stopped the girl with a hand on
her arm and said urgently, "Do not speak to your uncle just
yet. I am persuaded that Miss Hingham's principles are
of the highest. Putting two and two together, it seems reasonable to postulate that sometime in the past she met and fell
in love with Lord Frame, but for some reason—parental opposition perhaps—they did not marry. It was quite clear the
other evening at the dinner party that they had not been in
contact with each other since that period. Mrs. Hingham has
obviously been promoting a marriage with your uncle, but I
do not believe Martha has given him an answer as yet or
there would have been an announcement upon their return.
Now that she and Lord Frame have agreed that their feelings
have not changed, I promise you she will tell your uncle the
truth."

Susannah listened intently, but her silence did not indicate
conversion. After a long moment while Claudia watched her
mental struggle with understanding eyes, the girl surrendered
to her friend's reasoned argument. "Very well, Claudia, I
shall do nothing, for the moment at least." Her face cleared,
and she smiled. "It is not that I dislike Miss Hingham, you
know; it is merely that she is not the right wife for Uncle
Miles. You are."

"*Please*, Susannah!"

"I'll say no more on that head—for the moment." This time
there was a hint of devilry in the beautiful brunette's smile.
"Shall we go back now? It must be nearly lunchtime."

Having carried her point, Claudia relaxed, but her expression did not mirror her friend's unclouded joy. "Do you mind
if I do not go in just yet, Susannah? I am not hungry, and I

think I'd like to walk by myself for a bit. What is that wooded area off there to the left?"

"The copse? It is all on the estate so you should not get lost, though part of it is thickly overgrown and rocky. I will see you later then." With a wave of her hand, Susannah headed back toward the house.

Chapter Fourteen

Claudia was reeling mentally under the disclosures of the past hour and desperate to regain her balance. If her judgment of Martha Hingham's character was correct, it was now highly unlikely that this young woman would become Lord Pelham's wife. She and Lord Frame appeared to be in love, based on recent observations. Unless there were other reasons beyond the pecuniary that had prevented a marriage years ago, the barrier to their union had been removed with Lord Frame's ascension to his uncle's honors and fortune. Martha was of age, so there was no need for parental permission, and it would seem from today's clandestine meeting that the habit of filial obedience had been broken decisively.

Claudia's steps were driven by the energy of her thoughts, but she was even less aware of her surroundings as she plunged into a densely wooded area than when she had kept pace mechanically with Susannah coming away from the village. There was even more to think of now with the promise of a radical change in the situation at Beechwood. Her own agitation alarmed her and covered her with shame. If, as she had told herself upon the baron's arrival with a prospective bride, that circumstance had absolutely no relevance to her own role at Beechwood, then the converse must be equally true now. The absence of a potential wife should have no bearing on her position, which remained exactly what it had always been, temporary and accidental. She had no right to be experiencing flutters of anticipation or hope. The irony was that she had warned Susannah about the dangers of indulging in wishful thinking not an hour since.

She was not so naive as to be blind to the fact that Miles Pelham regarded her in a mildly lustful fashion. This was not a novel experience. No, the novelty—and the shame—lay in her response to his desire. Knowing he thought her little better than a lightskirt should affront her pride, and it *did*, but it could not entirely erase a wanton yearning to follow where he led. With this shocking admission the elixir that had been bubbling in her veins since Martha Hingham had walked into Lord Frame's arms went flat. If this is what she had come to under an occasional burningly tender look from electric blue eyes, then it was time to take herself away from temptation. She had nothing left but her self-respect; she could not afford to lose that.

Suddenly, Claudia tripped on the spreading root of a tree, saving herself from a fall by catching at the rough trunk of another with painful results. Shaken and annoyed at her carelessness, she grimaced as she surveyed the damage to her hands, two broken fingernails and an assortment of abrasions. Bending to brush some dirt from her skirt, she discovered the hard way that there was also a splinter of wood in the base of her right thumb. She considered waiting until she got back to Beechwood, where she could soak it before pulling it out, but each step she took seemed to increase the throbbing.

Glancing around to get her bearings, Claudia found she had lost all sense of direction. The undergrowth was thicker here than where she'd entered the copse; she could no longer see a definite path. All the trees looked alike, and the sky seemed much less blue than earlier. She frowned and peered in all directions before heading where the growth looked thinnest.

A few minutes' walk brought her to a small clearing surrounding a grass-topped ledge. Thankfully, she eased down onto a fairly smooth boulder at the base of the outcrop and inspected the splinter, seeking a piece above the skin that she could grip. It took a little painful probing, but eventually she raised a corner enough to seize in her teeth. A second later the splinter was out.

Heartened by this small success, Claudia jumped up and entered the woods again where the path seemed most defined. She had only the haziest notion that these woods might extend to the small lake she could see from Esther's and her own bedchambers, but since she could not even guess at the direction she had come from, this theory was of no practical use in deciding which way to head. Well, she decided with fatalistic calm, Susannah had said the copse was all on Beechwood property. Sooner or later she would strike something familiar.

Claudia was hungry, her hands were sore and stinging, and the walking was difficult enough to demand her attention. She was also annoyed with herself for the stupidity that had allowed her to stray from the perimeter of the woods in her self-absorption. As she doggedly followed a rough path, all these feelings swirled around in her head. Premonition and fear were not among them, however. She had no inkling that she was not alone in the copse until she negotiated a slight curve in the path and saw a man facing her from a distance of less than twenty feet.

A fraction of a second sufficed for recognition. Fright and flight followed simultaneously. Thought did not enter into the decision at all. Claudia found herself racing back the way she had come, her skirts held up high with no consideration for modesty. She'd not heard him before, but now his pounding steps sounded above the banging of her heart. This was her worst nightmare come true—her father's murderer had caught up with her. Weeks of running and hiding had all been for nought.

Each breath was like needles in Claudia's throat now, and though she dared not look back, it was clear from the increased sounds that he was gaining on her. The clearing was dead ahead. She could not outrun him; her only chance to escape was to elude him in the densest part of the woods. She entered the clearing and veered to her left instantly, heading back to the trees. She'd taken but two running paces with her pursuer's steps even louder in her ears when she again became the victim of a snaking tree root. This time she sprawled onto her hands and knees, gasping for breath and deafened by the beating of her heart in her ears.

The Frenchman was upon her before she could begin to struggle to her feet. He grabbed her upper arm, jerking her to her feet as she reeled backward into the clearing. Claudia was dimly aware that he was muttering in French, but comprehension was beyond her as she fought to gain control over her shaking limbs.

"At last I have caught up with you! It would have been much sooner had you not stopped using the false name under which you traveled in England. It seems an eternity that I have been in this barbaric country of yours!"

He still spoke in French, but now Claudia understood the sense of his words. It would be inaccurate to say she had conquered her fear, but the sullen resentment in her captor's voice kindled a corresponding anger in her breast. For the first time Claudia stared directly into the face of the man who had killed her father and hunted her like an animal, and fear gave way before a burning fuse of hatred. It was a loathsome face up close, just as she would have expected, she decided dispassionately, her eyes raking over shiny, sallow skin, unshaven and pitted with pox scars. His eyes, dark, small, and lashless, were set close to a large, humped nose over a thin slash of a mouth. When he spoke, his few discolored teeth added to the unprepossessing picture he presented.

"You have something that belongs to my employer, and I have come to retrieve it."

The man took a step forward as he spoke, and Claudia inched away, then stopped, furious with herself for not standing her ground under his intimidating stance. "I have nothing that belongs to your employer," she said distinctly in English.

His lips thinned even further as he snarled, "Your father took that necklace, and now you have it. Do not bother to deny it."

"I don't deny it," she replied with forced calm. "Killing my father did not get you the diamonds, and neither will killing me."

"You are mistaken, mademoiselle. My employer does not desire your death, nor do I, but I *will* have that necklace."

"How do you propose to get it?"

"You may be willing to die for a piece of jewelry," he said with a sneer, "but I think your friends will be happy to exchange it for your life. I have found a place where I can keep you hidden until your friends deliver the necklace to me."

"No one else knows where it is," she replied flatly.

"I promise you, mademoiselle, that it will not take very long to persuade you to write a note to Lord Pelham with that information." The look of anticipation on the man's brutish face sent a frisson of sheer terror down Claudia's spine, but only hardened her resolution to deny him any satisfaction.

"You will have to walk to the other end of the village where I left my horse. I had to follow you on foot or risk losing this chance. Come."

"I'll go nowhere with you. You will have to drag me every single step of the way," she warned him, backing away toward the ledge.

"Not if I twist your arm behind your back like so," the Frenchman snarled, leaping at her again. He succeeded in grasping and twisting one arm so tightly that Claudia cried out in pain, but that did not stop her from kicking backward with sudden vicious purpose, her sturdy half boot making sharp contact with bone.

The Frenchman grunted with shocked pain and cursed volubly. His grip on her arm loosened just enough for Claudia to wrench free. She crawled away from him on hands and knees until she could scramble to her feet. He came after her, limping and cursing, but now there were other sounds of running feet in the woods, and Claudia summoned up the breath to scream, "Help me!"

Her attacker, bent on retribution, was heedless of the imminent approach of assistance for his victim. He lunged at her, and she dodged his grasp once again as Lord Pelham burst into the clearing.

"*Claudia*, are you all right? Who is this man?" he called as he raced toward the pair.

"My father's murderer! Take care, Miles, he carries a knife!" she panted, dodging as the enraged Frenchman lunged at her again.

By stopping briefly to respond to the baron, Claudia had given up her advantage, however, and she found herself backed up against the ledge. The man launched himself at her, and this time her attempt to evade him was unsuccessful. She went reeling backward under his weight, crashing into the rock. Pain exploded inside her head, and she knew no more.

In the same instant Miles seized the assailant's shoulders and hurled him away from Claudia's limp body. His hands trembled with fear as he gently felt all over her head. A lump was already rising on the back of her skull, but her neck did not appear to be broken, he saw with prayerful relief.

Miles's concentration on the unconscious girl nearly cost him his life in the next few seconds. As he straightened out Claudia's limbs, he sensed movement behind him. Turning swiftly, he barely averted having a knife plunged into his back. He saw the steel slice into his left shoulder, although he was unaware of pain at the time. His powerful rising motion had knocked the man backward as he struck.

Miles was standing over his attacker before the man could gain his feet. With cold precision he brought the edge of his rigid hand down on the man's neck, putting all his strength behind the blow. The sound of the bones snapping nearly sickened him, and he fought nausea as the would-be assailant crumpled to the ground, his head at an unnatural angle.

Miles's thoughts defied description as he stared grimly at the dead man and the bloodstained knife that had dropped from his hand, but his brain was rapidly assessing information and projecting possible consequences of this incredible incident. The most vital concern was to ensure that no harm would come to Claudia when this became known, as it must in some measure with a corpse to account for. First things first though. He turned back to Claudia, who showed no signs of regaining consciousness. He bent over over, frowning at the weakness of her pulse, knowing he must have help, but agonizing over a decision to leave her alone, lest she awaken to the horror of the scene in the clearing.

The sight of blood, his blood, dripping steadily down on Claudia's gown brought him out of a state of mental paralysis. He tore off his cravat, not without difficulty, and made it into a pad that he stuffed inside his slit coat sleeve, letting out a hissing breath at the pain the action caused. With a last lingering look at the too-still young woman lying on the dusty ground, he clamped his teeth together and hurried out of the clearing, his face a study in furious control.

The next few hours passed in a frenzy of activity.

Miles's arrival at his stable yard produced a sensation that he, not being concerned with the effect of his grisly appearance, quelled with a series of brusque commands. He sent a groom for the doctor and, after demanding paper and pen, scribbled a note for Lord Rockingham who was the local magistrate. This he entrusted to a stable boy in between issuing curt commands to get a litter and blankets ready to carry an injured person out of the clearing in the copse.

Calloway, who had been implementing his employer's orders in his usual efficient fashion, balked when he understood that the baron intended to return straightway to the clearing with the grooms.

"That shoulder must be seen to at once, sir. Ye've lost a lot of blood by the look o'things."

"Later. See that Challenger is saddled at once."

"By the time t'lads have horses saddled, I'll have it bandaged proper," the old coachman insisted, producing clean cloths and liniment. "Sit ye'sel' down afore ye fall down."

Recognizing the truth in his old teacher's words, Miles reined in his seething impatience and submitted to the coachman's ministrations. He was scarcely a cooperative patient as he tried to monitor the various activities he'd set in motion from the stool Calloway had shoved under him.

"Sit still if you don't wish to start this gushing like a fountain again," the coachman ordered. "Who did this piece of work?"

"I don't know, a stranger."

"Who is the injured party—this same stranger?"

"No, Miss Herbert. He attacked her, and she hit her head on the ledge. She's deeply unconscious."

"Where is the man?" asked Calloway, continuing to wrap his cloths around the shoulder wound.

"He's dead."

Calloway grunted, then said, "I'm coming w'ye. Head wounds can be tricky."

"Thank you, Calloway." Miles put his hand on the coachman's shoulder as he got to his feet wearily. "I trust you more than most medical men."

* * *

By the time the litter bearing Claudia's still form arrived at the house, the staff had been alerted and the doctor had arrived. Miles would have carried her in his arms on Challenger had he not respected Calloway's warnings that, with no weather problems to complicate the matter, it was better to play safe and avoid any jolting of the injured girl. He also realized, though he had not admitted it, that his left arm was more useless than not at present.

Beyond asking the baron how long Miss Herbert had been unconscious, Dr. Martin had nothing to say as he followed the litter upstairs to direct the grooms to Claudia's bedchamber.

A frightened Susannah, who had been in the entrance hall with the doctor, seized her uncle's arm, the right one, fortunately, when he, too, would have gone up the stairs. "What happened to Claudia, Uncle Miles? The groom who told Jimson that she was injured did not know how it had happened. Did she fall?"

"She was attacked in the copse by a man—a foreigner. She hit her head on a rock ledge when he tackled her as she tried to escape him." Miles continued up the staircase.

Susannah recoiled from his harsh tones, horror spreading over her pale countenance as she trailed after him. "How terrible! I wonder if it was that man we saw in the village this morning—he certainly was a stranger, though I have no idea whether he was a foreigner or not."

Her uncle stopped in midflight. "What is this? You and Claudia met a foreigner in the village?"

Susannah shook her head. "We did not meet him. There was a man near the wheelwright's who stared after us very rudely as we passed on the other side of the street and then ducked back inside when he saw that I wondered about him. I don't believe Claudia even noticed him."

"What was she doing in the copse?"

"She said she wanted to walk by herself for a while, that she did not want any lunch. Will she be all right, Uncle? She looks so . . . so lifeless." Susannah shuddered, and Miles put his arm around her shoulders.

"We shall do everything possible to help her. Do your sisters know she is hurt?"

"I forbade Josie from telling them. The servants all know, of course, they always do."

"The children will have to know sooner or later, but not before we have better news to tell them. What about Mrs. and Miss Hingham? Where are they?"

"Mrs. Hingham went off to see the church and have lunch with Lady Mountjoy and Melissa. At breakfast she said that Miss Hingham is keeping to her room with a migraine today."

"I see."

Upstairs they found that all hope of keeping the news of Claudia's injury from the children for the present had vanished. Roberta had heard the grooms and the doctor, and discovered the situation. Both girls were weeping and clinging together while they begged Dr. Martin, who had gone into Esther's room, to make their friend wake up. The harassed physician asked Susannah to help him get the patient into bed while her uncle comforted the children.

Miles wisely kept to himself the instinctive protest that *he* should be the one to help Claudia and concentrated instead on dealing with the children's fears. He attempted to project a confidence and optimism about Claudia's condition that he was a long way from feeling in his own heart. When the inevitable question came about how their friend had been injured, Miles opted for a slightly softened version of the truth.

The volatile Esther reacted with instant anger. "I would like to *kill* the man who hurt Claudia!" she declared vehemently, then burst into tears again.

Roberta looked at her uncle with wide shocked eyes. "How could *anyone* wish to hurt Claudia when she is so good?" she asked in simple disbelief.

The children's utter faith in the young woman who had dropped into their lives by the sheerest accident no longer seemed quaint to Miles as he tried to explain the existence of wanton evil in the world without robbing them of their trust and confidence. It struck him that his own acceptance of Claudia's word that the stranger was her father's murderer had been equally simple and complete. How could anyone be around her for any period of time without sensing the essential goodness of which Roberta had spoken?

When the children asked where the bad man was now, Miles had no qualms about deviating from the strict truth. He told them merely that the man had gone away and would not be allowed to hurt anybody else, delivering the half-truth with a conviction that gave them the reassurance they sought on that score.

Unfortunately, the doctor was unable to provide the solid reassurance they all sought that Claudia's recovery would be swift and complete. When he finally emerged from the sickroom, it was to counsel patience while nature set about the work of healing the damage Miss Herbert had suffered.

To the baron in his library later he was more forthcoming but not more encouraging. "I have read about cases in which persons who were deeply unconscious like Miss Herbert have awakened after many days and gone on with their lives as if nothing had happened."

"But you wish me to understand that this is not always the case?" Miles asked, submitting his shoulder to the doctor's attention, but never taking his eyes from the man's face.

"Unhappily, yes. Often the patient . . . wastes away without ever regaining consciousness."

At these words Miles went very still, presenting a countenance devoid of all expression.

After a moment the doctor continued, "Her pulse is slow but regular, which is a good sign. I understand that her father died recently. Does she have any family, someone who might come to her now?"

"There is an aunt in Kent whose direction I do not know. The children might, or perhaps my aunt."

When he'd unwrapped the blood-soaked bandage, Dr. Martin pronounced himself satisfied with Calloway's handiwork as far as it went. "The cut is clear to the bone, however, so I am going to sew it up to prevent more bleeding later." Absent any response from his patient, the physician proceeded to carry out his stated intention in total silence. The occasional tensing of the baron's muscles under his hands was the only indication that the procedure caused him any discomfort. The doctor spoke again as he finished applying a new bandage. "About the person who did this—"

"He is in no need of your services," Miles said shortly.

"I see. As far as Miss Herbert is concerned, I have explained to Miss Brewster that, except for keeping her warm and having someone watch over her at all times, there is really nothing that can be done."

"I understand."

The doctor was putting away his supplies when Jimson announced Lord Rockingham's arrival.

"I advise you to rest that shoulder today, my lord, and keep your arm in a sling when you are up to prevent further bleeding."

"Thank you for your care and advice, doctor," Miles said. "Jimson will show you out."

Having done his duty and mentally disavowed responsibility for patients who refused his professional advice, the doctor bowed and took his leave after promising to return the next day to check on Miss Herbert. He bowed to Lord Rockingham as they met in the doorway and left the room behind the butler.

Despite his consuming anxiety for Claudia's physical recovery, Miles had not lost sight of her concealment of a vital piece of information from everyone at Beechwood, for he'd take his oath that she'd told no one her father had not died a natural death. Whatever her reasons, he intended to guard her secret at all costs, he acknowledged to himself as his old neighbor came hurrying into the room now, red-faced and perspiring.

"Your servant had to chase all over the estate to find me," Lord Rockingham said, pulling a large handkerchief from an inner pocket and wiping his forehead as he pulled off his hat. "I came back with him as soon as I'd sent one of my people up to the house to let them know where I'd gone. This is a damned bad business, what?"

Miles was already holding out a brandy to his lordship, who examined him more closely as he accepted the glass, watching his host's movements as he walked back to the side table bearing a decanter and another filled glass that he took up and drained.

"You look like the wrath of God," Lord Rockingham said frankly.

"I haven't had a chance to wash off the dirt yet." Miles held up the bottle in invitation and, when Lord Rockingham shook his head, poured himself another glass.

"What happened, Pelham? Your note said only that Miss Herbert had been attacked in the copse on your property and there was a man dead."

"That is it in a nutshell." Miles sipped from his glass.

"How is Miss Herbert?"

"Unconscious. Martin avoided the word 'coma,' but he didn't promise she'd come out of it either. All we can do is wait—and pray."

"Amen. It's a damned shame, that's what it is. Thought she was a nice girl. Lady Rockingham was very impressed with her at your dinner party. Said she was a real lady. Who was it attacked her?"

"I don't know; he was a stranger to me, perhaps a foreigner."

"What makes you think that?"

"He was swearing in French," Miles replied, knowing the man had been seen in the area and that it would come out sooner or later.

"Does Miss Herbert know him?"

"No." Miles brought forth the lie in the same terse manner in which he'd responded thus far.

"Know that for a fact, do you?"

He'd best keep in mind the native shrewdness behind Lord Rockingham's bluff joviality. Miles paused briefly as if considering and temporized. "Not really. All she said was, 'Help me,' before he lunged at her again."

"I only ask because I believe Miss Herbert was in France recently, if rumor is correct?"

"That is true. I was also in France recently, and I don't know the man," Miles replied evenly.

"Why don't you just tell me how it all happened—everything you saw, from the beginning."

With the single omission of Claudia's identification of her attacker, Miles recounted the whole incident, starting from the sounds he heard in the copse as he was crossing it on his way home for lunch.

"Well, I shouldn't worry about having to stand your trial," Lord Rockingham said when his friend had finished describing how he'd hit the man. "That shoulder of yours and the bloody knife testify to the Frenchman's murderous intentions. Wonder what he was doing on your property."

"My niece Susannah reported that when she and Miss Herbert were in the village this morning, they passed a man who stared at them, then ran into the wheelwright's when she seemed curious about his interest."

"Did she say whether Miss Herbert recognized the man?"

"Susannah says she doesn't believe Miss Herbert even noticed the fellow, if it was the same man."

"He must have followed them back here. When did Miss Brewster and Miss Herbert separate?"

"According to Susannah, Miss Herbert wasn't hungry and decided to walk by herself for a bit longer."

Lord Rockingham had nothing more to ask in his magisterial capacity for the moment.

Revived by the brandy he'd consumed, Miles insisted on accompanying him to the scene of the attack, where he'd left one of the grooms to see that nothing was disturbed.

By the time Lord Rockingham had made arrangements for the removal of the body, the temporary effect of the spirits had long since worn off. Miles was exhausted mentally and physically when he returned to the house, but rest was out of the question. It was time to change for dinner, a process that, thanks to an accumulation of dirt and his wounded shoulder, took much longer than usual.

Late though he was, Miles stopped by Claudia's room for his first look at her since he'd watched the litter vanish around the landing hours before. The maid who let him in said she had noticed no change since she had taken Miss Susannah's place when the latter had gone to dress for dinner.

Walking over to the tester bed, Miles gazed down at the young woman for whom he had killed a man and lied to the representative of the law today, and a sense of helplessness came over him. The alluring dimples were effaced, and her beautiful hazel eyes were hidden. The dark thicket of lashes that was one of her greatest charms lay still on cheeks without a vestige of color. So corpselike was Claudia's appearance that the baron could not prevent himself from touching the hand nearest him to reassure himself that all warmth had not departed from the body he had once embraced and ever after yearned to possess in every sense of the word. If only he could know that her spirit had not departed, never to return to the warm shell. His jaw set like a rock, he turned and left the room, brushing past the attendant without seeing her.

He had himself under rigid control when he entered the saloon a few minutes later with an apology for his lateness.

Mrs. Hingham rushed forward to express her dismay at the terrible events of the day. "Martha and I feel just dreadful about poor Miss Herbert, do we not, Martha?"

"Of course, Mama."

"I am happy to see you looking recovered at least, Martha. Susannah told me you were indisposed today."

"I am fine now, thank you, Miles."

"Where is Aunt Sophronia?" Miles glanced at the sober twins.

It was Susannah who replied, "The shocking news of Claudia's condition brought on my great-aunt's palpitations, and she felt too unwell to join us tonight."

"The groom said the man who hurt Claudia tried to kill you too, Uncle," Julian said, eyeing his stiff left arm. "Is your arm badly cut?"

"No, it will heal quickly."

"Is it true that that man is dead?" Mrs. Hingham asked.

"Yes, ma'am, but I think we will not distress the young ladies with any details of that, if you please."

Mrs. Hingham subsided, and so did Julian, the woman looking disapprovingly while the boy could scarcely conceal satisfaction.

Dinner limped along with Mrs. Hingham taking on the thankless task of maintaining a civil conversation with minimal cooperation as she described her reaction to the church treasures and the Mountjoys' estate. She and Julian were the only ones who did justice to the repast set before them that night.

The baron elected to accompany the ladies back to the saloon directly after dinner when it came out that Julian had promised to read to his young sisters, who were missing Claudia's comforting presence, and Susannah had arranged to sit with Claudia until midnight.

"I told one of the maids to go to bed right after her meal, Uncle Miles, so she could take over for me then until I return in the morning."

"Thank you, Susannah; that was good thinking," said her uncle with his first natural smile of the evening. "Tomorrow I shall get one of the women from the village, probably the Widow Biggins, to take over some of the nursing duties. Good night, my dear."

Miles resigned himself to a long evening of forced amiability without the twins' bracing presence, but there was still one more unlikely happening in store for him that day.

The three persons remaining had scarcely seated themselves when Martha turned to her host and said with less than her customary assurance, "I had intended to seek a private interview with you tomorrow, Miles, but with all that has happened today, I believe it might be best to tell you and Mama at the same time. I . . . I am sorry, but I have decided not to accept your offer of marriage."

Mrs. Hingham's gasp of dismay covered the surprised relief that Miles owed it to Martha to suppress. Martha turned to her parent and said with more filial feeling that tact, "I am sorry, Mama, I did truly try to convince myself that Miles and I could make a successful marriage, but it is no use. Once I had seen Edwin again—" She broke off and turned to an attentive Miles then before going on earnestly, "Four years ago, Lord Frame, who was just Mr. Carr then, offered for me, but my parents refused permission because his prospects seemed negligible to them. Naturally I accepted their decision, but I could not forget him, and when we met so unexpectedly at your dinner party, I knew I still loved him—"

"Quiet, Martha, you do not know what you are saying. She is still light-headed from the migraine—"

"No, I am not light-headed, Mama," Martha interrupted in turn. "In fact, I did not have a migraine today at all. Last night at the Marshalls, Edwin said he had to see me alone, and we arranged to meet this morning in the orchard. I pretended I had the migraine because I knew you would not let me out of your sight otherwise." Again she turned to Miles, leaving her parent with mouth agape like a landed fish. "To come to the point, Miles, Edwin still wishes to marry me, and I him. I do beg your pardon most humbly—I never intended to deceive you."

"Of course you did not, my dear Martha. Your conduct has always been above reproach in all things. Indeed, no blame attaches to anyone in this affair," Miles said, avoiding Mrs. Hingham's eyes. "You had not contracted a formal engagement, and Lord Frame's new circumstances have certainly made him a desirable *parti*, when all that was ever lacking was the economic security that parents have a duty to seek for their daughters."

For the first time in his experience of her, Mrs. Hingham had no glib theory to propound, no prescription or better method to offer in the situation. Looking deeply chagrined, she admitted, "There is nothing I can say, my lord. My daughter is of an age to make her own decisions."

"And like the good parent you are, ma'am, your greatest wish is for her happiness. I perfectly understand."

Mrs. Hingham smiled faintly and stood up. "Thank you, Lord Pelham, for your understanding and your hospitality. I believe I shall retire now if you have no objection. Tomorrow will be a busy day if we are to leave Beechwood—that is, if one of your carriages can be repaired by then?"

"There is no need to hurry your departure, ma'am," Miles replied, concealing his understanding of this final little dig, "but if it is indeed your wish to leave tomorrow, I shall see to it that a carriage is ready when you are, and an escort also, naturally."

Miss Hingham took advantage of her mother's decision to retire early then to escape the inevitable awkwardness that must prevail in the altered circumstances, saying her good night also with patent relief at the harmonious conclusion of her ordeal.

Miles remained standing at the bottom of the stairs when the ladies had ascended with their candles, his face sober as he reflected on how different this moment would have felt if only it had occurred twenty-four hours earlier.

Chapter Fifteen

Within the hour the baron sent Jimson to bed and trudged up the stairs himself, having discovered that his aching shoulder and the pervasive sense of dread concerning Claudia's condition had rendered him unfit for any task requiring even a minimal ability to concentrate.

Without conscious prompting his legs took him into the dressing room next to Esther's bedchamber, where the sight of the empty cot jolted him back to mental alertness. The events of the day had been so harrowing that he had to battle a sudden irrational panic while he told himself that it was not very late. Roberta might be bidding Susannah good night, or perhaps Esther had been restless, and she had gone in to succor her younger sister. Both were eminently reasonable theories, but he was aware of his own racing heartbeat as he pulled open the door that led to Esther's room and entered without his usual nighttime caution.

As he gazed down at the two children huddled together in a welter of sheets, Miles experienced an unfamiliar burning sensation behind his eyelids. In his own wretchedness he must not forget that he was not the only—or even the prime—sufferer at Beechwood tonight.

He set his candle on a table and gingerly set about pulling the tangled bedcovers from under the sprawl of limbs, reflecting on the quiet miracle of love that had taken place in his home in the last fortnight. It had not been a one-sided outpouring of love by lonely children but a true exchange. He'd seen the affection Claudia bore his young relatives in her face on numerous occasions these past few days and, to his discredit with a prospective bride in residence, had wished on each of those occasions that her feelings included him.

Claudia had always treated him with punctilious civility that verged on aloofness. Far from being discouraged, however, once he'd discovered the warmth and spontaneity of her personality, he had found a crumb of comfort in the studied nature of her response to him. It cost her something to keep him always at arms' length, and once or twice her mask of cool reserve had slipped and he'd basked briefly in the sunshine of her approval until she succeeded in reasserting her unnatural control. He'd treasured those rare moments of true rapport and, God willing, had every intention of amassing similar memories for the rest of their shared lives.

Miles's jaw was set like Gibraltar as he lightly covered his sleeping nieces and took up his candle again. He entered Claudia's room after a soft tap on the door, his eyes going immediately to the still figure on the bed before he sought Susannah's gaze, a question in his own.

"There has been no change," she said softly. "She has not moved a muscle in all the time I've been here. I'm terribly afraid, Uncle Miles."

"So am I," Miles admitted in a moment of weakness. His instant regret faded when he saw that if his admission had failed the child seeking comfort, it had awakened the woman's understanding in Susannah. Her eyes held compassion as she pressed her fingers over his hand on her shoulder.

Quickly, he told her about Martha Hingham's announcement in the saloon tonight that she intended to marry Lord Frame, realizing almost at once that his niece had not reacted with the astonishment he would have expected had he given the matter any prior thought. He halted his explanation and looked searchingly into her face, across which a parade of emotions had passed, including, if he read her correctly, triumph.

"You do not seem surprised by this turn of events," he said in invitation.

"No," Susannah agreed. "I saw Miss Hingham meet with Lord Frame in the orchard this morning."

"But when I asked you where Mrs. Hingham and Martha were today, you told me Martha had kept to her room with a migraine."

"No," Susannah rebutted, "I told you that *Mrs. Hingham* said Martha was in bed with a migraine today. I would have told you at once about the meeting with Lord Frame, except that Claudia urged me not to. She said Miss Hingham would do the right thing, that she was a person of integrity."

"So Claudia also witnessed the lovers' meeting."

"Yes, but Claudia had said all along that you would not welcome interference from anyone in your private affairs."

"I see. Were you and Claudia in the habit of speaking about my private affairs then?"

Susannah eyed her uncle warily, but there was little to be gleaned from his voice or countenance. "Claudia did not encourage the conversation, but I knew that Miss Hingham did not love you, and I was . . . concerned."

"I beg your pardon, my dear. Anyone acting as stupidly as I did in proposing a loveless marriage should not be surprised to find his decision questioned—at least in private," he added smilingly, "by those near to him. I would like to ask you something," he went on briskly. "When you told me about the strange man who stared at you in the village, you said you believed Claudia had not even noticed him. What led you to believe this?"

Susannah blinked at the change of subject and paused to gather her thoughts. "I mentioned him as we were leaving the village and Claudia did not know to whom I referred."

"How could she have failed to see him when you were together?"

"Thinking back over the incident, I believe Claudia was too intent on her own thoughts at the time to notice what was going on around her."

Miles frowned. "Do you have any idea what was occupying her mind to such an extent?"

Susannah hesitated, then shot him a glance from under lowered lids. "Well, I had brought her to meet Nanny Griswald, who made a lot of her taking care of Esther. Then she embarrassed Claudia by mistaking her for your intended bride and congratulating her. When we corrected her, she urged me to tell you that you would do much better to marry Claudia instead—"

"She did, did she?"

"Yes, because she said Claudia had a good heart in addition to being pretty, and she didn't have an interfering mother," Susannah finished blandly.

"That reminds me," Miles said, his eyes going once more to the unconscious young woman, "do you happen to know the name and direction of Claudia's aunt in Kent?"

Recalled to the gravity of the situation, Susannah sent him a stricken look. "I'm afraid not. I do not believe Claudia ever mentioned her name or direction."

"Is there anyone else, do you know, any relation who would come to her now?"

"I don't know; she never mentioned anyone else. How terrible to be so alone in the world," Susannah said in a subdued voice. Then she brightened. "Wait! I believe Jimson handed Josie a letter after lunch today to put in Claudia's room." She jumped up and hurried over to the dresser. "Yes, here it is, Uncle. Will you open it?"

Miles inspected the elegant script. "No name, simply *Sunnymede, Aylesford, Kent*," he murmured, turning the missive over. "Much as I dislike to invade Claudia's privacy, I feel we must grasp at every straw that might offer a hope of helping her."

His decision taken, Miles opened the letter and ran his eyes down the single sheet. "Ah, 'Your devoted aunt, Portia Bannon,' " he read with satisfaction. "I shall write to Mrs. Bannon before I go to bed," he said, turning on his heel. "Be sure to send for me if there is the slightest change, Susannah, and tell the maid who replaces you the same thing. I'll see you in the morning, my dear, and thank you for your kindness and sacrifice."

"I love Claudia, too, Uncle," Susannah said simply.

His normal existence rapidly assumed an aspect of unreality as Miles merely went through the motions of living, dealing with his duties as host, estate owner, and surrogate parent with

an automatic efficiency that involved only a small portion of
his intelligence and almost none of his emotions.

He paid his respects to his aunt before breakfast on the day
of the Hinghams' departure and after his first visit to Claudia's
room had revealed her to be still as deeply unconscious as
ever. After apologizing for the necessity to disturb his relative
at an unusually early hour, he conveyed Martha Hingham's
decision to her in a few sentences, ending with a tactfully
worded request that she bestir herself to bid the departing
guests a gracious adieu later that morning.

Lady Powerby, who had made no secret of her dislike for
the proposed connection from the start, then confounded her
nephew by taking unwarranted umbrage on his behalf at the
dissolution of it. His assurances that he was more relieved than
heartbroken cut no ice with his aunt, who embarked instantly
on a speech verbally excoriating both Hinghams for the kind
of shabby behavior that totally vitiated all pretensions on their
part to any degree of breeding, which was precisely what she
could have told her nephew, had he taken the natural precau-
tion of consulting her intimate knowledge of society before
committing an imprudence that inevitably would have sunk
the Pelham name in the eyes of the world. Since this diatribe
was as convoluted as it was lengthy, Miles ceased trying to
follow the nuances of her argument when it became clear that
injured family pride was the wellspring of her annoyance. He
took a firm grip on his patience and his temper and, when
sheer exhaustion had finally dried up the flow of vitriol, set
about soothing his aunt's ruffled feathers, while at the same
time trying to secure a promise that she would uphold her role
as his hostess when parting from the Hinghams. Appealing to
that same family pride and the obligations it imposed on its
members to set an example for lesser mortals finally won her
reluctant agreement to forgo the pleasure of giving Mrs. Hingham a piece of her mind.

By the time this concession was wrung out of her, Miles
was running short of patience, tact, and temper, but as he prepared to leave his aunt's suite, she disarmed his annoyance by
inquiring about Claudia's condition with a hint of genuine

concern. The smile he gave her on parting was weary but affectionate.

No untoward incidents marred the painstaking goodwill that prevailed at the Hinghams' leave-taking later that day. All the children except Esther accompanied the departing guests to the entrance, where the repaired carriage, freshly washed, its bright blue paintwork gleaming in the sun, awaited the passengers. Lady Powerby unbent sufficiently to felicitate Miss Hingham on her choice of husband, giving it as her opinion that Lord Frame's manners and bearing proclaimed the true gentleman. This elicited a grateful smile from Miss Hingham, and for once her parent forbore to comment; in fact, Mrs. Hingham had been uncharacteristically subdued since her daughter's shattering announcement the night before, barely concealing her eagerness to be gone from Beechwood behind a torrent of compliments and expressions of gratitude and goodwill.

When Miles handed Martha up into the chaise after performing the same service for the abigail and Mrs. Hingham, she thanked him once again and then lowered her voice to say for his ear alone, "I hope and pray with all my heart that Miss Herbert will recover, Miles, for her sake and yours." Light blue eyes met his with more feeling than he had ever seen her display.

Grateful, he raised her gloved hand to his mouth and saluted her fingers. "Thank you, my dear," he said softly before closing the door and stepping back. He gave Michael, the second coachman, a signal, and the carriage set off behind a team of matched grays that were good for two full stages. Riding beside it, armed and spurred, was his own groom, who saluted smartly as he trotted away from the entrance front.

As the members of his family filed back into the house, Miles gave one last look at the carriage disappearing from view. This marked the end of a strange chapter in his life, a brief chapter, by the grace of whatever fortune had sent Lord Frame to this neighborhood at a crucial point in his existence.

Mrs. Biggins, a respectable widow from the village, was installed at Beechwood that afternoon. She was possessed of strong common sense, boundless energy, and neat, capable hands that made light of all household and nursing tasks. A disinclination for idle chatter and a somewhat scathing tongue toward those who indulged in gossip kept her from being universally popular among the village women, but this did not stop them from turning to her first when help was needed in a crisis. In the baron's view this was not the least of the widow's assets, though he'd have willingly made a pact with the devil if that would bring Claudia back to him.

At the widow's own request, a cot was brought into the sickroom for those few hours during the twenty-four that she felt it necessary to sleep. She tolerated Susannah's or the housekeeper's presence then and during the half-hour periods twice daily when Miles insisted that she close the sickroom door behind her and take some air.

Dr. Martin gave Mrs. Biggins his unqualified endorsement when he discovered her in charge of Claudia's care that first afternoon. The doctor checked on his patient each day, reporting to the baron in the library before he left the house. The assessment on the second day of Mrs. Biggins's stay was the same as all those since the incident.

The baron had risen from his chair behind the desk at the doctor's entrance. He received the news impassively as always, but the medical man, noting the little muscle that twitched in his cheek, was not fooled.

"Her color is good, and her pulse is regular, which is a good sign," he repeated. "There is nothing to do but wait, but I realize, of course, that there is nothing more difficult. I'll see you tomorrow." He turned abruptly and left.

Miles continued to stare at the door after the doctor had gone, seeing still the shadow that had appeared in the man's austere gray eyes when he had spoken of waiting being the most difficult thing. He had always regarded Martin, a childless widower, as cold and slightly inhuman, though obviously hardworking and knowledgeable in his field. He had come to Hampshire only five or six years previously, after the death of his wife. He lived alone, except for servants, and shunned society almost completely. The local hostesses who had thrilled at the presence of that most desirable of creatures, an extra man, had finally ceased trying to lure him into their saloons and dining rooms and left him to his solitary habits. The man's eyes had looked almost haunted just now. Suddenly, Miles knew that Martin was familiar with the difficulties of waiting from personal experience, almost certainly a tragic experience. As far as Miles was aware, the doctor's work had become his whole life. He'd permitted himself no human society on a personal level, and his own humanity was drying up. There had been a minute crack in the doctor's usual professional demeanor today though. He had allowed himself to display a flicker of sympathy. Miles saw this as additional evidence of the beauty of Claudia's spirit that attracted people to her.

It was while the diminished family group was finishing dinner that night that Claudia's aunt, Mrs. Bannon, arrived. No sounds of the arrival had penetrated the garden room at the back of the house where the meal was being served. Jimson, accepting a message from one of the footmen, approached the baron and presented him with a card and the news that a lady wished to speak with him.

"William has put her in the library, sir."

Glancing at the visitor's card, Miles rose to his feet, saying eagerly, "Claudia's aunt is here."

"At this hour?" Lady Powerby demanded, but her nephew was halfway to the door and did not deign to reply. He caught up with the footman in the long passageway leading to the main house.

"William, please ask Mrs. Trowbridge to ready the bedchamber next to Miss Herbert's room for our guest," he ordered before outpacing the young man on his way to the library.

Claudia's aunt was not in the chair on the near side of his desk where he would have expected to find a visitor, certainly a female caller, but stood perusing his bookshelves, a volume of Latin poetry in her hands. Miles stared in fascination as she turned to face him. Magnificent was the word that rushed to his mind as he gazed at a woman every bit as old as Lady Powerby but tall and ramrod straight with a wonderful figure and a wealth of pure white hair beneath an attractive straw hat. Her features were strong and clear-cut, her jawline still firm. He amended his first impression that she must have been a

beauty in her youth; there was too much intelligence and character in her face perhaps for conventional beauty, but she was
without doubt a handsome woman now in her sixties.

As he came into the room, Miles saw that his visitor was
studying him with as much interest as he must be displaying.
He bowed and extended his hand. "I am Miles Pelham, Mrs.
Bannon. I am delighted to meet you, but I must confess myself
astounded to see you so soon. You could not have had my letter until today, surely?"

"It was on my breakfast tray this morning. I am an early
riser, Lord Pelham, and my coachman was used to my late
husband's style of traveling, which was to cover as much
ground as quickly as conditions permitted. I set out within the
hour."

Concern chased admiration from Miles's eyes as he exclaimed, "That is over a hundred miles! You must be exhausted. Pray, have a seat, ma'am. May I persuade you to
accept a glass of brandy or a cordial for a restorative?"

"I am a trifle fatigued," Mrs. Bannon allowed, "but I have
been sitting all day—or jouncing, to be more precise. After I
have seen my niece, I shall be glad of a pot, not a cup, of tea."

Mrs. Bannon's well-modulated voice was firm, but there
were violet shadows under direct hazel eyes that put him
forcibly in mind of Claudia's. "You shall have it, ma'am," he
promised. "We'll go up to Claudia's room as soon as I set my
people to taking care of your coachman and carriage." He
opened the door to give his orders to William, who was stationed outside. "Do you have an abigail with you, ma'am?"

Mrs. Bannon shook her head.

"One of the maids will unpack for you then." He offered his
arm, and Mrs. Bannon placed her hand on his sleeve. She did
not lean her weight on his arm, however, as she walked
steadily up the stairs, her back straight and her breathing unde-
tectable to his alerted senses.

Mrs. Bannon questioned him about the circumstances surrounding her niece's injury as they headed down the corridor
to her room. Except for omitting Claudia's identification of
her assailant, Miles told the truth, knowing already that his

love's formidable Aunt Portia was not someone to whom one lied with impunity.

Mrs. Bannon's eyes narrowed at the ugly tale, but she did not comment, nor did she exclaim a moment later when she saw her niece lying so still on the big bed. She walked up to the head of the bed and laid the back of her fingers against Claudia's cheek for a moment before taking her wrist in her fingers. Mrs. Biggins and Lord Pelham remained quiet while this examination took place.

"You are sure there are no broken bones or other injuries?" she asked.

"The doctor says there are no visible injuries except for a lump on the back of her head."

"Then she will recover when the injury heals itself," Mrs. Bannon said with what struck Miles as genuine confidence.

"It seems as though she might wake up any minute, but so far she hasn't," Mrs. Biggins said at that point.

"I beg your pardon, ladies. Mrs. Bannon, this is Mrs. Biggins, who has been caring for Claudia for the last thirty hours or so. Mrs. Bannon is Miss Herbert's aunt," Miles explained, noting with gratitude that the two women looked at each other with mutual respect. He gave them a moment or two to forge an understanding and then said, "Mrs. Biggins, would you be so kind as to ask them in the kitchen to send a pot of tea and refresh—"

"No food, thank you, sir," Mrs. Bannon said. "I dined at the last post inn."

"As you wish, ma'am. Shall you like to drink your tea in your room, which is next door to Claudia's, while you take off your hat? If you feel up to it, you may then meet the rest of my family, but we shall understand if you desire to postpone the introductions until tomorrow after you've had a night's repose."

Mrs. Bannon declared herself able to join the rest of the family after she made herself presentable, and Mrs. Biggins left for the kitchen on her errand of mercy.

Miles's eyes drifted as they invariably did to the unconscious young woman, willing her to return to him. Mrs. Ban-

non's eyes watched him watch Claudia. "You are in love with
my niece," she observed, and it was not a question.

"Yes," he admitted readily, "but that is because I met Claudia first."

There was a charged silence, and Miles cursed himself for
an impulsive fool; then Mrs. Bannon said sternly, "Young
man, if you are trying to inveigle me into a flirtation, I must
tell you that you are twenty years too late."

Miles laughed for the first time in three days, startling himself. "You do yourself a grave injustice, ma'am. Actually, I
think I am in love with the whole family."

The advent of Mrs. Bannon brought about a perceptible
lightening of the anxious atmosphere at Beechwood. The
youngsters' spirits rallied under the sway of her brisk confidence, and the acrid taste of fear in Miles's mouth occurred
with reduced frequency. Even Lady Powerby responded more
favorably to the bracing optimism that Claudia's aunt embod-
ied than could have been hoped, given her earlier antagonism
to Mrs. Hingham's brand of positive thinking. Mrs. Bannon
listened attentively to Lady Powerby's catalogue of symptoms
and vowed her intention of assembling a group of herbal remedies to employ in a massive program to render relief to the sufferer on several fronts. Mrs. Biggins and Mrs. Bannon
established a good working alliance to share the responsibility
for Claudia's care, which also contributed to an easing of tension in the household.

Still the hours passed slowly, leaving Miles with too much
time for unproductive ruminating. An inability to concentrate
on the written word kept him from deriving any consolation
from his favorite authors, and his circular thoughts offered
none either. He battled constantly to keep the door shut against
any consideration of what he'd do with the rest of his life if
Claudia did not recover. This sort of negative thinking led
straight to despair and would render him useless to five children and a feeble old woman who depended on him. Speculation about Claudia's feelings for him and his chances of
winning her heart was equally fruitless and lured him toward a
dangerous optimism that was very likely unfounded. Of com-

pelling interest was the mystery surrounding Claudia's last weeks in Paris and her father's violent death, if her words to him in the clearing were to be taken literally. Was it really possible that a French criminal had murdered her parent and pursued her across the Channel? The formation of theories to account for the possibility did not advance his knowledge by a single fact. He hoped that Louis Frenier might be able to shed some light on the subject, but he'd not yet received a reply from his friend. Patience and waiting—could there be any less attractive options in creation?

Claudia mustered the strength to open her eyes, a task that had been beyond her strength for a long time. She saw an unfamiliar female face looming over her, and her lids closed again. Apparently, the strange dream still wasn't over, but she could swear that she heard her aunt's voice speaking her name.

"Claudia, wake up, child. Try to open your eyes."

Was she home at Sunnymede? Was Paris the dream? Confusion clouded the eyes Claudia opened at her aunt's repeated urging. Her lips trembled into a smile as she saw the woman who had raised her. "Aunt Portia. Was Paris the dream then?"

"No, my love. Paris was real."

Tears of weakness spilled from under her lashes. "Papa is dead," she whispered.

"Yes, Claudia. I am truly sorry, but you are at Beechwood, alive and safe."

"*Beechwood! Miles!* Is M . . . Lord Pelham all right?" Eyes wide in terror, Claudia clutched at her aunt's hands that sought to restrain her upward motion.

"He is fine, my dear. Please, lie back down. Does your head hurt? Any other part of you?"

Claudia stared vacantly at her aunt while memory surged back. Her eyes lighted on a strange woman at the foot of the bed, her bed at Beechwood. She appealed mutely to her aunt.

"This is Mrs. Biggins, who was taking care of you when I arrived here."

"How . . . how long?"

"It has been three days since the . . . the incident."

"Three *days*?"

"Yes, do not tease yourself about that yet, Claudia, but tell me how you feel at this moment."

"Fine . . . a little shaky."

"Does your head ache?"

"I don't think so. It's sore." She explored the back of her head with her fingers and winced.

"Do you remember what happened in the copse when you were injured?"

"Yes." Again tears trembled on her lashes and seeped down her cheeks.

"Have your cry, my dear, if you must, but then turn your thoughts to the present and the future. Everyone at Beechwood will be thrilled to see you restored to yourself. They have all been very anxious about you."

"I must leave Beechwood," Claudia said, avoiding her aunt's eyes as she plucked at the sheet covering her. "I must go home to Sunnymede."

"Of course, whenever you wish, but now you must have something to eat—"

"And a bath," Claudia interrupted, sounding more like herself. "My hair feels so dirty."

"Mrs. Biggins and I shall arrange everything," Aunt Portia promised with a satisfied smile.

Roberta burst into the library, her face alight. "Uncle Miles, Claudia is awake!"

"Thank God!" Miles dropped his pen on the desk blotter, wondering if he looked as joyful at receiving the glad news as Roberta did at the telling of it. "May I see her?"

He half rose, subsiding back into his chair as Roberta said, "Mrs. Bannon says Claudia will be ready to receive you in an hour. Esther and I are going to help dry her hair. The back of her head is still very sore." She danced out the door on the words, but paused when her uncle called after her.

"Does your aunt know?"

"Susannah went to tell her." Roberta disappeared from view, leaving Miles to savor the relief of having his prayers answered.

Over the next hour he looked at the clock on the mantel

scores of times, checking its disobliging slowness against his watch each time. Now that the moment he'd prayed for was nearly upon him, he realized he had no idea what he would say to Claudia, especially when he'd rather dispense with conversation altogether in favor of taking her into his arms and declaring his undying love.

Miles was still dithering over the most seemly opening when his knock was answered by Claudia, bidding him to enter.

She was seated in a chair upholstered in pink brocade. Miles took one step forward and stopped. "You look beautiful," he said involuntarily, even before a swift glance assured him that they were alone in the room.

A little color warmed Claudia's cheeks, and she dropped her eyes to the fingers plucking at a fold in the skirt of her willow green muslin gown. The fingers stilled as she said, "Aunt Portia brought this old dress with her, assuming quite correctly that I would not have any lightweight clothes with me." She looked up at the quiet man devouring her with his eyes and began again hastily, "Lord Pelham—"

"You called me Miles at our last meeting," he reminded her softly.

"M . . . Miles then," she amended before rushing on. "Please tell me what happened to . . . to the man . . ." Her voice trailed away.

"You mean the man who murdered your father?"

"Yes," she whispered, her eyes full of apprehension. Her hands were clasped so tightly together the knuckles showed white.

"He'll never trouble you again."

Shock dilated Claudia's pupils. A shudder shook her body, and he saw her throat move as she swallowed with difficulty. "I . . . see."

Standing a few feet away from her chair, Miles waited, unsure what was going through her mind as her eyes clung to his, still troubled. "I . . . the night . . . it happened I raged and cried and wished myself a man so that I could kill the man who had caused my father's death." He opened his mouth, but she gave a slight negative shake of her head and continued, "Not this man, who was merely hired by—"

"This man," Miles said distinctly, "tried to kill *me* when I bent over your unconscious body. Had I not been faster than he, his knife would have plunged into my back instead of my shoulder."

Claudia's face whitened, and tears began to course down her cheeks before he finished, causing Miles pangs of conscience for adding to her misery. She turned her head away, mumbling an apology as she fumbled for a handkerchief.

Claudia's distress was Miles's undoing. He threw caution and prudence to the winds, swooping down on her weeping form.

"Please don't cry, my darling," he blurted, pulling her upright by the shoulders and wrapping his arms around her trembling but unresistant body. "You've had a terrible time, I know, but it is over now. I won't let any danger come within striking distance of you ever again."

Miles capped this grandiose claim by taking advantage of her weakened state to press a kiss on her parted lips. This action had the desired result of drying up Claudia's tears. If it did not quite stop her trembling, neither party to the long and mutually therapeutic embrace was disposed to cavil. Miles was not completely steady himself when a need for oxygen made him raise his head an inch or two. He stared down into her bemused face and made an effort to contain the exultation that raced through his body. "It is much better when you cooperate, do you not agree, my love?"

Claudia blushed in confusion and hid her face in his coat without replying.

"You *will* marry me, my dearest love, will you not? Look at me," he commanded in sudden terror when he felt her head move in a negative fashion against his chest.

The radiance their shared embrace had brought to her lovely face had faded, leaving her mournful. "Oh, Miles, I cannot . . . you do not know what happened in Paris. There might yet be a scandal . . . your family—"

"Claudia stop and get your breath. In a moment you may tell me all the events that led to your father's death and your departure from France, but before you begin, I would like you to answer one question." He frowned and muttered, "I seem to recall a scene like this once before."

"Yes." Claudia's lips twisted into a little grimace. "But you asked two questions as I recall."

"This time there will be only one," he promised, trying to see into her heart through the beautiful eyes that had struck him all aheap in the dingy atmosphere of a gaming house.

"And that is?"

"Do you love me?"

He saw the answer in the light that flared in her eyes, but he tightened his fingers a little on her shoulders, needing the words. "Tell me, Claudia."

"Yes, oh yes, Miles, from the moment I saw you, I believe, although in the very next moment I told myself the opposite after you looked at me with such cruel disdain."

He took her in his arms again, absorbing the scent and feel of her slender body. "I wanted to cut de Bouchardet's throat," he admitted, rubbing his cheek against her silken hair.

"And mine?"

"No, not that. I just wished to forget I'd ever set eyes on you. It was impossible though. I can see now that jealous disillusionment prompted my idiotic decision to contract a marriage to a woman of unblemished character who had no power to torture me. I have been incredibly fortunate to escape the trap I rashly set for myself."

"I believe Miss Hingham and Lord Frame will be very happy together."

"I hope so. You are still looking fragile, my love. Perhaps we should postpone the story of Paris until you are more rested."

"No, Miles, let me get the telling over. I am so weary of dissembling, but I could see no other course at the time."

"Then let us be comfortable at least," Miles said, scooping up his beloved and settling into the chair with her cradled in his arms.

By the time Claudia ended her story, Miles was thoroughly shaken at the fearsome ordeal his lovely girl had suffered. His grim expression must have alarmed her because she tried to disentangle herself from his grasp, but he tightened his arms convulsively. "Good Lord, Claudia, it's a near miracle you are still alive. By God, I'll see that scoundrel Marple brought to book if it's the last thing I do—no, don't fear that your father's reputation will be besmirched; there is more than one way to skin a cat. But oh, my dearest, why did you not tell Lord Malmsey everything? He'd have helped you and kept you out of danger." Without giving her a chance to mount a defense, he went on, muttering as if to himself, "Such foolish courage, and all for nothing!"

"I saved Lady Selkirk's necklace. I would not call that nothing," Claudia protested, a little hurt by his dismissal of her sacrifice.

"That is because you do not know what is an open secret in English society. Selkirk gambled away the family diamonds years ago. You have risked your neck for a paste replica that he had made at the time."

The words were no sooner uttered than regretted. If only he'd had the wit to bite his tongue off! Miles was prepared for hysterics as he watched disbelief, anger, and acceptance chase across his beloved's revealing countenance.

"I have always disliked both Lord and Lady Selkirk," she said with disgust, "and I can only pray I need never meet them in the future. The post is good enough for the return of their trinket, but oh, poor Papa." Tears sparkled on her lashes again.

"That does not change the fact that your father died protecting the honor of his name, my love. This is what you must remember."

Claudia looked so grateful for this crumb that Miles had no choice but to kiss her again.

They were engaged in this pleasurable activity when a firm knock brought them back to reality. Mrs. Bannon's clear, precise tones easily penetrated the thick door as she issued a warning.

"Claudia, if you and Miles remain alone together in that room much longer, your wedding will have to be by special license if we hope to avert a scandal."